ADAM HALL
QUILLER MERIDIAN

QUILLER MERIDIAN

ADAM HALL

AVON BOOKS ◆ NEW YORK

AVON BOOKS
A division of
The Hearst Corporation
1350 Avenue of the Americas
New York, New York 10019

Copyright © 1993 by Trevor Productions, Inc.
Published by arrangement with the author
Library of Congress Catalog Card Number: 92-21853
ISBN: 0-380-71534-1

Published in hardcover by William Morrow and Company, Inc.; for information address Permissions Department, William Morrow and Company, Inc., 1350 Avenue of the Americas, New York, New York 10019.

First Avon Books Printing: May 1994

AVON TRADEMARK REG. U.S. PAT. OFF. AND IN OTHER COUNTRIES, MARCA REGISTRADA, HECHO EN U.S.A.

Printed in the U.S.A.

RA 10 9 8 7 6 5 4 3 2 1

To

**Master-Sergeant Dave Bagley
(US Marines)**

Contents

Chapter 1

Bucharest

They found me in Rome and the embassy phoned my hotel and I went along there and talked to London, and Signals said something had come unstuck in Bucharest and "Mr. Croder would be grateful" if I could get on a plane and see if I could pull anyone out alive. They hadn't actually put it like that—they'd said "if you could be of assistance in any way"—but when Mr. *Croder* can find it in his rat-infested soul to tell you he'd be grateful for something it can only mean that some kind of hell has got loose and he wants you to get it back in the cage.

That was soon after six and I caught the last night flight out of Rome and got into Bucharest at 9:34 and put my watch forward an hour and found someone waiting for me with a battered-looking Volvo. We exchanged paroles and he asked me if I wanted to drive and I said no because I didn't know this city and there was obviously a rush on and he could take short cuts.

His name was Baker and he was small and wrapped up in a bomber jacket against the cold and smelled of garlic and looked rather pale, but that was possibly his normal winter complexion.

"What happened?" I asked him.

"I don't know. The DIF just sent me to pick you up."

"What's his name?"

"Turner." He got past a meat truck and caught a fender, just slightly, because the streets were iced over in places. He was driving just this side of smashing us up but I didn't say

9

anything because he knew what he was doing.

I hadn't heard of a director in the field called Turner. He must be new. New and inexperienced and at this moment sitting at his base with a dry mouth and a telephone jammed against his head listening to his control in London and trying to tell him it hadn't been his fault, and the best of luck, because when a mission hits the wall it *must* be the fault of the DIF because he's running the executive in the field and it's his job to keep him out of trouble.

"Where are we going?" I asked Baker.

"The railway station. Freight yard."

We lost the back end and he touched the wheel and used the curb to kick us straight and when he'd settled down again I asked him the question I'd been trying not to ask him ever since we'd left the airport.

"Who's the executive?"

He gave me a glance and stared through the windscreen again and tucked his chin in. "Hornby." He said it quietly.

I hadn't heard of Hornby either, and it didn't sound as if I ever would again. He must have been new, too—they were cutting down the training time at Norfolk these days and sending neophytes into the field without a chance of getting them home again if anything awkward happened. I'd told Croder how I felt about it and he'd said he'd pass it on to the proper quarters, but it wouldn't do any good: he felt the same way as I did, and those pontifical bastards in the Bureau hierarchy obviously hadn't listened even to him. Say this much at least for Croder: he's a total professional and one of the three really brilliant controls in London, and he doesn't get any kick out of going into the signals room and listening to those calls coming in from the field—*I don't know if I can make it. They've cut me off and I haven't got long. Can you do anything, send anyone in?*

There'd been a call like that reaching London this evening, sometime before six, and Hornby's control had said yes, he'd find the nearest executive and send him into the field, and that was why I was sitting in this dog-eared Volvo

skating through the streets of Bucharest a little bit too late—
it's nearly always a little bit too late, because things happen
so fast when a mission starts running hot that there just isn't
time to pull people out.

"Was there a rendezvous?"

Baker glanced at me again. "I don't know."

Didn't want to know. All he wanted to do was get me
to the freight yard and drop me off and go home and try
and sleep. They're not all like this, the contacts; most of them
are seasoned and they've learned to get used to things blowing up, but one or two hang on to a shred of sensitivity and
this man was one of them, I could feel the vibrations.

"How long have you been out here?" I asked him.

"In Bucharest?"

"Yes."

"Year, bit more."

"Picking up the language?"

With a nervous laugh—"Trying. It's a bitch."

There was some black ice and we spun full circle across
a waste of tarmac, perhaps a car park, and soon after that
we picked up the colored lights of signals on the skyline and
Baker touched the wheel and hit gravel and sped up and we
started bumping across some half-buried railroad ties, and I
told him to slow down and cut his lights and the engine and
take me as far as the line of trucks below the big black water
tank that stood silhouetted against the sky.

I got out and told him to go home, then I stood there
for ten minutes in the shadow of the end truck and waited
for my eyes to adjust from the glare of the headlights to the
half-darkness. I didn't know if the local supports had got the
area protected, or whether they too lacked experience. Bucharest isn't a major field and you can't expect first-class
people wherever you go.

There was a film of cloud across the city, lit by the streets,
with only a few lights in the freight yard, high up on swan-
neck poles. Smell of coal, steel, soot, sacking, some kind of
produce, potatoes or grain. Very little sound, but I was pick-

ing up low voices over toward the main passenger station.
The air was still, cold against the face. The outline of the
trucks was sharper now and I began moving, keeping my
feet on hard surfaces, tarmac, ties, rails, going slowly, feeling
my way in.

A plane was sloping down to the airport, its strobes
winking against the ocher smudge of the horizon, the high
thin scream of the jets fading across the sky. There was some
kind of bell ringing, up there toward the main station; perhaps a train was due in. I went on moving.

There was something I didn't know. London had called
me in either because I was the nearest shadow executive to
this area or because this was something that needed a lot of
experience to handle. Neither idea seemed to work: there
must be shadows closer to Bucharest than Rome, and the
Bureau couldn't have had a mission running in a minor East
European state that would need a high-echelon executive to
handle the mess when it crashed. I would have to ask London
what the score was, when I got into signals with them.

The air was colder still here, away from the line of trucks;
something of a night breeze was getting up.

"It's all right," I said softly.

I was behind him and my left hand was across his mouth:
I didn't want any noise.

He struggled quite hard until I put a little more pressure
on the throat; then he slackened, and I took if off again.
"Don't worry," I said. "I know Mr. Turner." I released most
of the hold so that he could half-turn and look into my face.
I didn't offer him the parole I'd exchanged with Baker at the
airport: this man could be anyone, not one of ours. I took
the last degree of pressure off his throat and he asked me
who I was, good English, recognizable redbrick U accent. I
didn't tell him, but I asked him for the parole and got it, the
code name for the mission, *Longshot*.

"When you're protecting an area," I said, "try and find
some really deep shadow, and try to stand where there are
no hard surfaces round you . . . look for gravel, or whatever

loose surface there is. If you'd done that, I wouldn't have seen you so easily, and you'd have heard me coming."

"Jesus," he said. He'd already been upset by the Hornby thing.

"Amen." It was routine, especially in minor fields where people hadn't been through full training. We're expected to help them along, and I'd shocked him first to drive the lesson home, because one day it could save his life. "Where is everybody?" I asked him.

"Over there." His breath clouded in the faint light.

"Was it a rendezvous?"

"Yes."

"Hornby and who?"

"A Russian."

Not a Romanian. That could be the answer to the question I had for London.

"What was the Russian's name?"

"I don't know."

"Find some shadow," I said and left him, moving along a rail under the cover of the next line of trucks until I came to three people standing there close together. One of them spun round very fast and had a gun out and I stopped and lifted my hands. *"Longshot,"* I said.

The man lowered the gun but didn't put it away. "Where are you from?"

"Rome."

"Who sent you?"

"Mr. Croder."

He put his gun away and told me his name was Fry. He looked appallingly young.

"What happened?" I asked him. The other two backed off a bit to let me into the group. One of them had been sick somewhere; I could smell it.

"Hornby was to make contact with a Russian here."

"What was his name?"

"Zymyanin."

"Did he turn up?"

"We don't know."

He was a thin man, Fry, with eyes buried deep under his brows so that in this light I couldn't see them, just caught a glint now and then.

"Where's the head?" I asked him.

"On the other side of the rail." I could hear one of the other people shivering, his mouth open, shivering through his teeth, hands stuck into the pockets of his leather coat, his head down, probably the one who'd been sick.

"Well put him into something," I said. "Not you," I told Fry, "we've got to talk."

"We weren't going to move him," Fry said.

That was out of the book, but not everything in this trade's in the book; in fact very little that really matters, none of the deadly vibrations you pick up in a red sector, nothing of what we call mission feel, the unnamed sense that allows a single photon of light to hit the retina and alert the brain, the sound of a sleeve folding in the dark as the knife is raised, the smell of gun oil. We were standing here at the site of a blown rendezvous and the contact on our side had been killed and the contact on the other side was missing and we didn't know how many of the opposition might be standing off in the shadows waiting for the right time to move in, waiting perhaps for the man from Rome to get here.

They were worried about booby traps, that was all, Fry and the other two. It's in Chapter 3 of the *Practical Field Manual* with its red cover: *Never move a dead body without first considering that it might conceal a booby trap or other explosive device.*

"Get a sack," I told Fry's people, and went across to the body and turned it over to show them it was safe. In terms of security the opposition had been unusually sensitive: when you blow a rendezvous by killing the opposite number you don't normally take the trouble to disguise things, but the people who'd blown this one had staged an accident or a suicide for the local police and left Hornby's body on one side of the rail and his head on the other, so they wouldn't have triggered them with explosives as well—it would have spoiled the picture.

"Where from?" one of the men was asking.

I looked up. "What?"

"Where do we get a sack?"

"Oh for Christ's sake," I said, and went across to the flatbed freight truck and got out my penknife and ripped open one of the sacks and poured out the grain and came back and got Hornby's body into it and picked up the head, my hands more tender now because this husk, this coconut, this Yorick-thing with its matted hair and its staring eyes and its gaping mouth had recently been the vessel of all this man's experience, and now it was here between my hands, a bony urn containing the traces of a human life, etched among the infinitely complex network of nerve synapses and cerebral electronics until only a little while ago they had burned out like a firework show and left a shell of ashes for the world to grieve on.

I took off his watch and put it into my pocket. Wives and mothers sometimes ask for them as keepsakes.

"Come on," I said. "I need some help." Hornby's arms and legs were difficult because rigor mortis had set in. "How long have you been here?" I asked Fry when we'd finished.

He checked his watch. "Nearly two hours."

In the faint hope that Zymyanin had got clear before the pounce and would come back here to do business as arranged. It sometimes happens.

"If he doesn't show up," I said, "have we lost him?"

"Not if he's still alive. He's been keeping in contact with our DIF. Are you taking over as the executive?"

"I don't know," I said. "I'm here to clean up the mess, for the moment." I didn't mean Hornby, I meant the whole mission: there was going to be a lot to do, and the first thing was to trace the Russian contact, Zymyanin, if we could. If, yes, he were still alive. "But you'd better tell me all you can, because there might not be a DIF for this mission anymore." That sometimes happens too, even though the director in the field is required to stay out of the action in his ivory tower throughout the duration. He's not always safe there: it depends on how bright he is. They'd got Hornby and they might have got Turner too, by now. "When did you last signal him?" I asked Fry.

"Soon after we got here. There's a public phone up there at the station."

"How long did Turner tell you to wait here? For Zymyanin?"

"My discretion." He didn't sound complaining. He should have. The director in the field isn't meant to leave anything to the discretion of the support groups or anyone else except the executive; he's meant to *direct* them.

"Who's the control in London for *Longshot*?" I asked him.

"Mr. Pritchard."

That wasn't surprising: Pritchard was halfway over the hill and had done his bit for the Bureau, due for his pension, give him a minor job in Bucharest to end his career with. But Zymyanin was a Russian, and the Russians still weren't playing a minor role in international intelligence. If London wanted me to take over *Longshot* and get the wheels back on I'd need a new control, someone like Croder.

The bell sounded again from up there at the station, and a whistle blew. It was rather comforting on this stark and deathly night to know that someone was playing at trains.

"How many people have you got," I asked Fry, "protecting the area?"

"Four."

That was a lot of people, seven in all, for the support group of a minor mission. Turner must feel there was safety in numbers.

"You can pull them out," I said. "Zymyanin won't be coming back."

"How do you know?"

His tone was challenging and I said, "Because I've been in this trade for seventeen years and the number of missions

I've seen blown by totally incompetent directors in the field would make your hair stand on end, and since we're on the subject there's one of your people up there with shit in his pants because I came up on him from behind while he was watching the pretty blue and green signal lights, so find someone who can *train* him before you put him into the field again, you want to get him killed?" That was how the poor devil lying down there in his sack had got killed: he hadn't checked out the area or surveilled local traffic before he'd moved in for the rendezvous, he couldn't have, and he was meant to be an *executive*. I turned to the man standing next to Fry, not the one who was shivering. "Go and phone the embassy and ask for their DI6 man and tell him you're Bureau and give the parole and the code name for the mission and ask him to get a car sent here to pick up the body and send it back to England."

He took his hands out of his pockets. "He'll want to know what—"

"He'll want to know where the body is and that is *all* you'll tell him, you understand? There's no scrambler on that phone up there. All right, get going."

"Yes, sir."

He swung away and I looked at Fry again. "How many cars have you got here?"

"Three."

"Where are they?"

"In the station yard."

"Which is the newest one?" This was Bucharest.

"The Honda."

I asked him for the number and the keys and he gave them to me, taking his time, resentful, a very resentful man, understandably.

"All right, pull your people out as soon as the body's been picked up." I got Hornby's watch out of my pocket. "Give this to the embassy people and ask them to put it into the diplomatic pouch addressed to the Bureau, property of

Hornby's estate. Where do I find your DIF?"

Fry put the watch into his pocket. "I'm afraid I can't tell you."

Not afraid at all, he was delighted, had read the book. The location of the director in the field is sacrosanct, never to be disclosed if there's the slightest doubt as to the bona fides of the inquirer. This man didn't have any doubts: he'd been told by his DIF to expect someone sent in from Rome by Mr. Croder and I'd satisfied him on that and I'd also known the code name for the mission. He was just getting a bit of his own back, that was all.

"I respect your reticence," I told him. There was still nothing more than the glint of reflected light in the shadow of his brows. "But it'd save me having to call London."

"Sorry," he said.

"That's all right." I went over to the shape in the sack and put my hand on it, a shoulder, I think, and held it for a moment, *requiescat in pace*, so forth, there but for the grace of God. Then I came away and asked Fry, "How many missions have you been with?"

"Four."

"This the first crash?"

"Second."

"Oh, Jesus, two out of four, what stinking luck." I touched his arm. "Hang in there, it gets better as we go along." I moved away along the line of trucks toward the passenger station and heard his voice behind me.

"Hotel Constanta."

I turned and nodded and walked on again.

Chapter 2

Moscow

*H*e opened the door but not much, just his tense gray eyes in the gap, and I went through the introductions and he let me in and said he was on the line to London, so I shut the door behind me and slipped the lock and waited, watching him, an angular man with thinning hair and a straight uncompromising back and expressive hands, using one of them now, cupping the air with his fingers to hold out his explanations until they were ready to accept them, London, Pritchard I suppose, because he was the control for *Longshot*, or perhaps Croder had taken over and was perched there under the bright lights of the console in the signals room with his metal claw scratching at his knee, the only evidence that he was in a towering rage because there'd be nothing in his voice except the cutting edge of his careful articulation as he skinned this poor bastard alive.

"No, sir. There was no question of that. I just told the support group to wait thirty minutes, and if the executive hadn't reported that the rendezvous was established then they should go in with the utmost caution and find out what had happened."

Holding his own, not flustered, even with the angel of death at the other end of the line, copybook phraseology, "rendezvous was established," "utmost caution," so forth, drive you mad in the ordinary way but he just wanted to show he was still in control, I rather liked him, you give a man like this a *jodan-zuki* and you wouldn't get feathers out, you'd break your wrist.

"Yes, sir, I understand that." He'd dropped his right hand, spilled his explanations all over the floor, Croder wouldn't buy them, he should have known that, Croder wouldn't buy a box of matches from you even if you were starving. "Yes, he's just come in." He looked across at me and held out the telephone—"COS."

Chief of Signals: Croder.

I took the phone. "Good evening."

There was silence on the line for a couple of seconds, while Croder wrenched his mood round and put his towering rage onto the back burner for a while—this was my impression. When Croder and I made contact with each other we both had to keep our cool: we shared what some people called a flint-and-tinder complex.

"I'm most grateful to you," he said at last, "for giving up your holiday in Rome at such short notice."

"I wish I could say it was worth it. There's nothing I can do here."

"We thought there might be time."

"Yes, I understand that. Are you keeping the mission running?"

The green LED was glowing on the scrambler to show that it was in sync with the unit on the Government Communications HQ signals mast at Cheltenham, and the red LED was unlit: we weren't being bugged. But it always worries me to trust a telephone with ultrasensitive information.

"No," Croder said. "I'm taking it off the board."

So we'd lost the Russian contact, Zymyanin. And for the record book under *Longshot: Mission unaccomplished, executive deceased.*

"Then blame COT Norfolk," I told Croder. "No one else."

I didn't say that for the sake of the man standing over there watching the street from the window: I'd been wrong—this crash hadn't been Turner's fault even though he'd been the DIF running the mission locally. Hornby had just gone and got himself killed because he hadn't secured his approach to the rendezvous, couldn't have done.

"Please explain that," Croder said on the line. No edge to his tone—he just wanted to get things clear, and so did I. I'd been in a towering rage myself ever since I'd picked up that man's head from the dirt in the freight yard, because you could still see the youth in its face, the clear skin, the smoothness around the eyes.

"In my opinion," I told Croder, "the Chief of Training at Norfolk is sending people into the field too young and too soon." I looked across at Turner. "How old was Hornby, d'you know?"

He turned from the window. "Oh, early twenties."

"They're sending out kids," I told Croder, "and they're getting them killed." The chief of support down there in the freight yard had looked even younger, could have been nineteen.

In a moment Croder said, "Your comments are noted." All I'd get, and I let it go. "In the meantime you should know that the Soviet, Zymyanin, has signaled us and given his whereabouts."

"Oh really."

"He arrived in Moscow twenty minutes ago."

"Intact?" There could have been some shooting down there at the rendezvous point.

"Yes. He's quite experienced."

An older man, well trained. *Bloody* Norfolk.

I waited. A tram went moaning through the street below. Turner watched it, not actually seeing it, I knew that. He was trying desperately to pick up what information he could from my end of the conversation with Croder: he'd been the DIF for the mission but I already knew more than he did about the crash. I cupped the mouthpiece and told him, "Zymyanin's alive and well." It'd help him to know that his executive hadn't compromised the contact and got him killed, too.

He shot me a look of relief and I lifted the phone again.

"We would like you to meet him there," Croder was saying.

Meet Zymyanin in Moscow.

Bloody nerve. Someone else could do that.

"We could see *Carmen* tonight," she'd said at lunch today at Gaspari's, "if you would like that. I have a permanent loge at the opera house." Valeria Lagorio, her huge dark eyes glowing, two locks of black hair dampened and curled into perfect circles against her shadowed alabaster cheekbones, you don't go to Rome, do you, my good friend, to wade through the ice-cream wrappers in the Coliseum. As things were, I'd had to break my date with Valeria when the embassy had phoned my hotel, and that was going to take a dozen very expensive gardenias and a champagne supper at the Palazzo di Firenze just to get things back on track again.

"You've got plenty of people in Moscow," I told Croder, "who can look after Zymyanin."

It was only three weeks since they'd pulled me out of the Atlantic with a helicopter, and not in terribly good condition. I'd got another week to go before they could put me in a briefing room again, officially, and we can always ask for more time if we don't feel we've got our nerve back: go into a new mission with your scalp still tight and you'll crash, somewhere along the line. I felt fit enough, but I wanted my final week, it was in my contract and I'd already done my bit—instead of sitting in a plush and gilded box at the opera tonight with the totally breathtaking Valeria Lagorio I'd been grubbing around in a freezing freight yard stuffing a body in a sack, not quite my idea of a holiday.

"Zymyanin," Croder was saying, "is an important man, and we think he's carrying an important message—was carrying it to the executive in Bucharest and may still be able to give it to us if we show willing."

I didn't say anything, so he knew he'd got to go on, give me the whole thing. "It's not, you see, just a case of someone—anyone—'looking after' this important Soviet contact in Moscow. Since the rendezvous with the executive in Bucharest was set up, a great deal of raw intelligence has been coming in for analysis, and I should tell you that if we'd known as much as we do now about Zymyanin, we wouldn't have left it to a minor cell to find out what information he has for us. We would have asked him to make the contact in Moscow, not Bucharest, and we would have sent in someone of very high caliber to meet him." One of the windows vibrated as a truck rumbled past the hotel, and I watched its brake lights come on at the intersection. "We would like," Croder said, "to do that now."

I said, "I hope it all goes well."

They'll use you, those bloody people in London, they'll use you like a pawn on a chessboard if you let them. This man was pussyfooting me into going out again, putting his cold steel claw into a velvet glove and stroking me with it.

"Our intention," he said carefully, "is to put a new mission on the board and bring a high-echelon team together. I would undertake to control the new operation personally, and I have asked Ferris to direct for me in the field." A beat. "He has agreed."

The lights went green and the truck pulled away through the intersection, a big round cabbage dropping onto the street and rolling into the gutter. It looked sickeningly like a head.

"I'm still on leave," I told Croder. We always played this game and he always won, but I still put up a bit of protest because there was usually something I could get out of him in exchange. This time I had something important.

"I am aware of that," he said, "and of course I apologize."

You don't take an apology lightly from Chief of Signals. It's like God apologizing for the Flood.

I watched the woman at the opera house, Valeria Lagorio, one pale ivorine arm resting on the crimson plush of the loge, her huge eyes intent on the stage. Then the picture faded as I said, "I'll do a trade with you."

"I'd consider anything you suggest, of course."

"I want you to bring the Chief of Training, Norfolk, onto the carpet at the Bureau and I want you and the whole of the administration—including senior executives and directors in the field—to confront him with the present situation, namely that there are people being sent into the field without a hope in hell of completing their missions before they're killed."

Turner had come away from the window and was leaning with his back against the wall, head lifted, watching me through narrowed eyes. I listened to the static on the line. There was a gale blowing across southern England and the north of France, I'd heard at the airport in Rome, and the communications mast in Cheltenham would be swaying in the dark.

"I will give you my guarantee," I heard Croder saying, "that your demands are met."

It had been a lot to ask, and his answer told me something about the size of the new mission he was mounting.

"Within a week from today," I said.

In a moment—"One can't always command the immediate attention of the administration, but I shall—"

"Within a week," I said.

He could get those pontifical bastards out of hibernation sooner than that if he turned on the heat.

"Within a week," he said, "very well. As it happens, I share your concern in this matter, but that's not to say I shall find it easy to persuade them. I'm sure you—"

"Give them the facts. Show them the records for the past five years, tell them to count the increasing number of times we've seen 'Executive deceased' on the bottom line."

"I can only promise you to do my utmost."

"That's all I ask," I said. Croder's utmost could push a building down. "Where do I report for clearance and briefing?"

I think it surprised him: it was a couple of seconds before he answered. "I'm very pleased," he said. "I'm really very pleased. Let me switch you through to Holmes."

It took half a minute, and while I was waiting Turner came away from the wall and dropped into a chair and just sat there with his hands on his knees, staring at nothing.

I blocked the mouthpiece. "Don't feel you're to blame for Hornby," I told him. "He was in the field, not you, and he made a mistake, that was all." He turned his head slowly to watch me, didn't say anything. "I've tried that death-on-my-hands bullshit, and it doesn't work, drives you up the wall."

Holmes came on the line and I looked around for a scratch pad and found a bit of paper with *Suzana, 6PM* on it in the drawer of the phone table and turned it over and found a bright green plastic ballpoint.

"Sorry to keep you waiting," Holmes said. "Got a bit of a flap on here, doesn't surprise me they've roped you in, only the best for our Mr. C. The thing is, we've got to find you a plane right away."

"How are you?" I asked him.

"Oh, absolutely ripping, old fruit. You?"

"God knows."

"Don't worry, it'll be all right. You've got Ferris, no less, and Mr. C. is extremely pleased you've agreed to take this one on. It's in the 'M' group, by the way—*Meridian*."

Code name for the mission.

He got things worked out within fifteen minutes, sometimes using another phone to get information while I stayed on the line. By the time I reached the airport here in Bucharest there'd be a reservation for me on Aeroflot Flight 291 in the name of Viktor S. Shokin. From the moment I checked in I would use that as my cover name and adopt the identity of a Soviet citizen and would if necessary claim only a rudimentary knowledge of English.

I would be met at Sheremetyevo Airport in Moscow and taken immediately to the British embassy for clearance and briefing.

I put a few questions and got the answers and shut down the signal and left the scrambler on. Turner was sunk into himself and I couldn't think of anything to say that wouldn't sound like a trumped-up sop to his misery, so I just told him I was using the Honda and his people could pick it up at the airport, keys in the usual place. Then I shut the door quietly.

By 1:30 in the morning I was in Moscow.

There was a girl in a navy blue windcheater and fur gloves and zippered ski boots in the transport area and I went through one of the doors and walked with a slight limp as far as the corner of the terminal building and she caught up with me there and gave me *Meridian* in a soft clear voice and said her name was Mitchell.

"Viktor Shokin," I said, and we got into a dirty brown Trabant and drove through the deserted streets under light flurries of snow.

"There's been a change of plan," the girl said, taking a fur glove off the wheel and wiping her nose on it. "They decided they didn't want you seen going into the embassy." She had a small pale face with intent and intelligent blue eyes; sometimes I thought her teeth were chattering—there was no heating in the Trabant and the snowflakes weren't melting on the windscreen, just clogging the wiper blades. She stopped twice on our way through the city and I got out and unstuck them and scraped the glass a bit clearer with the edge of a notebook she had in the glove pocket.

She drove me to a decrepit three-story building in Basilovskaja ulica and parked the car on a patch of waste-ground, burying its nose under a hedge and bringing a small snowstorm down from the leaves—"It helps keep the engine warm." She took me into the building and up two flights of rickety stairs under the light of a naked bulb hanging from the ceiling. The reek of cooked cabbage was sharp enough to clear the sinuses. "They wanted to put me into one of those ghastly rectangular brown-brick workers' complexes a bit nearer the embassy, but I said no, I'd prefer a bit of old-world charm, thank you, even if it was falling apart at the seams."

"Nearer the embassy?" I said.

She swung a quick look at me in the gloom as we stopped outside a yellow-painted door. "I'm actually Bureau, agent-in-place, but I work at the embassy in the cipher room. Don't worry, nobody in this building understands English, I made sure of that on my first day here—stood on the landing and shouted *'Fire!,'* but nobody came out. This is my place." She led me into a sitting room with a Put-U-Up couch and a kitchenette in the corner and a door leading off it. "Make yourself at home. Can I call you Viktor? Me Jane. Would you like a drink or some coffee? Or are you hungry? Did you manage to get any dinner last night?"

I said I was fine.

She unzipped her ski boots and pulled them off and padded about in her thick red woolen socks, going across to a table in the corner and checking for messages. The telephone and the answering machine were linked up with a desk-model scrambler and the green light was on.

"I'm going to make some coffee anyway," she said as she came away from the phone, "got to keep my wits about me, haven't I?"

"Have you had any sleep tonight?" It was now gone half-past two.

"Oh, a couple of hours before London came through, I'm compos mentis, don't worry." A sleepy-looking girl in a thick dressing gown appeared in the doorway by the kitchenette. "It's all right, go back to bed," Jane said.

"Who's this?" the girl wanted to know.

"An old friend. Sleep tight—you've got to be up early."

The girl gave me a lingering look of curiosity and then went back into the bedroom and shut the door.

"Don't worry," Jane said quietly, "she's totally witless and never talks to anyone—she wouldn't know what to say. She's at the embassy too, makes the tea. You want to report in, or shall I do it?"

"Do you go through an operator?"

"God, no, we can dial direct now, through the new exchange."

She went into the kitchenette and I got on the phone and told Signals I was in Moscow. I didn't know who was on the board at this time of night but it sounded like Hagen.

"I'll tell Mr. Croder," he said. "Meanwhile we're waiting for Zymyanin to contact us again and tell us where he wants the rendezvous, and when."

"He's still in Moscow?"

"As far as we know. You'll hear from us as soon as we've got anything for you. Everything all right there?"

I said yes, and shut down the signal. I hadn't caught anything in Hagen's tone but he was probably worried, and so was I. Zymyanin had got here soon after eleven o'clock last night—"He arrived in Moscow twenty minutes ago," Croder had told me when I was at the Hotel Constanţa in Bucharest—and he should have given us his ideas for a rendezvous before now. One of the reasons why he hadn't done that could be because he'd been frightened off by what had happened to Hornby, and he might even think twice about contacting us again. There were other possible reasons, and one in particular that I didn't want to think about.

"Would you like a cup, now I've made it?"

Jane had put a tray on the long carved stool; one of its legs had been mended with glue and string. "It's not Chippendale," she said, "but it's better than the plastic table I found here when I came." She'd taken off her windcheater and was suddenly thin, boyish, in a ballet top under a black cardigan.

I said I didn't want any coffee: there might be a chance of some sleep.

"They gave me instructions," she said, "to clear you for Russia, since it looks as if they'll be running the mission here. You're completely fluent and can pass for a Muscovite, is that right?"

"Yes."

She fetched a couple of faded blue cushions and dropped them onto the floor, one on each side of the stool. "Or do you want to sit at the table?"

"No."

"Okay"—She lugged a weathered black briefcase from under the stool and flipped the buckles open—"this will be yours to keep, as well as the stuff inside." She pulled out a thin typed file and a map and turned them to face me. "Light cover—you probably won't have enough time to study anything deeper, will you? The map's only a few months old. When were you in Moscow last?"

"Before Yeltsin."

"Been a few changes."

"Yes." I hadn't seen any KGB when I'd come through the airport, and there'd been no "concierge" on the ground floor when we'd come into the building.

"They're surface changes," Jane said, "at the moment. The KGB are meant to be calling themselves the MPS—Ministry of Public Security—but of course most of them are still very much KGB under the skin—think of the *power* they had!—and a lot of them are just going through the motions of being nice to the proletariat while they wait for another coup. And there—"

"You think they'll get one?"

"Coups and rumors of coups . . . someone sounds the alarm about once a week, for obvious reasons—unless the Russians and the satellites can get through the winter with enough food and the basics they're liable to storm the government offices and *demand* a coup just to get Yeltsin out. This is mainly embassy gossip, but everyone knows there are something like three million die-hard *apparatchiks* holed up across the country with a hammer and sickle behind the curtains. We can't let our guard down yet, that's all." With a shrug—"But I expect you know all this, from the stuff going through the London signals room."

"It's a help to have it confirmed in the field."

A quick smile "Thank you. Shall I get you cleared?"

She didn't have any printed forms here so I gave it to her verbatim and she made notes—no medical problems, date of last vaccination, no request for a codicil, bequests unchanged. Then she made some notes of her own and I signed them: active-service waiver in the event of death, responsibility for expenses incurred, the undertaking to protect secrecy—most of the forms they had for this kind of thing at the Bureau were from the Foreign Office and totally out of date, and every time we ask them to do something about it, guess what happens. I made the final signature and Jane asked me:

"Do you want a capsule?"

Her eyes widened a little as she watched me.

"Ask them to send one out with my DIF. I shouldn't need one before then."

She looked down. "Or at all, I hope." She made a note and shut the notepad. "They probably told you that as far as we know you'll be operating in the USSR, so there's a good little secondhand clothing shop for men I can take you to first thing in the morning—they've got shoes as well." She finished her coffee and said, "Okay, I'll get you some blankets and we'll pull out the couch, bathroom's through there, you won't disturb Amy." She levered her legs out of the half-lotus and took the pad over to the phone table and put it into the drawer and locked it and came back.

"You do ballet?" I asked her.

"Shows in my walk?"

"Yes."

A wry smile—"Always tell a beginner, can't you? We overdo it, hoping people are going to notice, not many things in Moscow that'll give you status unless you're in the *nomenklatura* and then you'd be in a Zil. Prance along with your feet out and your ponytail dancing and you've got it made." She went over to the Put-U-Up and I helped her. "Stinks of mothballs, but I suppose there are worse things." She brought a white patched sheet and some blankets. "If you feel like some food, just help yourself from the pantry; the fridge is empty, doesn't work. It's only local fare but the bread's terrific, of course. You'll take the call, right?"

"Yes."

She watched me for a moment, her young and intent blues eyes showing the concern of a mother. "You'll be all right? There are more blankets if you need them, but the stove keeps in all night."

"Get some sleep, Jane."

She gave a little nod and went across to the other room, her feet turned out and her ponytail swinging.

I went over the map and opened the thin typed file and gave my cover a first reading: Viktor S. Shokin, 42, married to Natalia Yelina, née Maslennikova, two children, boy and girl, Yuri and Masha, six and seven. Brief history of schooling, university, first job as a stringer for a local newspaper, then a stint as copyboy in the *Pravda* overseas office before joining the Tass agency.

A lump of coke fell inside the big cast-iron stove and sparks lit the mica window. I thought I heard Jane and Amy talking, or it could have been some people in another flat.

Favorite sport, football, no hobbies, slight knowledge of English, Russian Orthodox.

It was just gone 3:15 when I dropped the file onto the floor and switched off the lamp and heard a spring twang as I lay down and started memorizing my cover, giving it another ten minutes. The voices had stopped, and through the small high window the snow drifted in silhouette, black against the haze of the city lights, and the last thing I saw was the steady green glow of the LED on the scrambler over there, and the last thought I had was about the other reason that might have delayed Zymyanin's getting into contact with us again: he could have set up the kill himself at the rendezvous in Bucharest and could be busy setting up another one, for me.

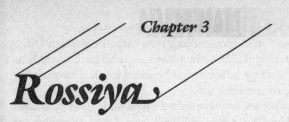

Chapter 3

Rossiya

"I broke K-15," she said, and tilted the frying pan so as to get the butter to run over the eggs.

"Oh Jesus," I said, "and you were trying to impress me by walking like a duck."

"Thought I'd kind of steal up on you."

K-15 was a hands-on but much-used Soviet code that the people in Codes and Ciphers at the Bureau had been trying to break for three years. I knew it had been done but I'd thought it was in London.

"Another egg?" Jane asked.

"If you can spare one."

"No problem," she said. "Black market."

I didn't know when I was going to eat again. There'd been two signals from Control earlier this morning but Zym-yanin still hadn't made contact. It was just gone eight, and the clothing shop wouldn't open until nine. "Even if then," Jane had said. "We might have to bash at the back door."

"You worked on it at the embassy here?" I asked her. On K-15.

"Yes. I'd be an infant prodigy in maths, if I were an infant. When I was six I used to finish Dad's crossword puzzles for him when he was at the office, made him furious. And *they* were in *The Times*."

At the scrubbed pinewood table she said, "Ketchup? I also created *Mystère*." She watched me for my reaction.

"Did you, now."

Mystère was also a hands-on code, noncomputerized,

and C and C had brought in a man from the Foreign Office to try breaking it. He hadn't managed it so far but when he did we'd destroy it, because if he could break it so could the Russians, or someone else.

"I got it from my typewriter," Jane said. "Or that started me off. I use a Canon AP810-III, and I was changing the ribbon when I noticed the characters on the old one. It's a wide ribbon and they're not in a single row, it prints three characters vertically, shifts—wait a minute"—she reached for her pad and got a pencil—"it prints three characters vertically downward, then shifts one space to the right and prints upward again, three"—she glanced up at me—"am I being an infant prodigy all over you?"

"I've worked on codes," I said. "I'm interested."

"All right. Three down, then shift, three up, shift, three down again, like this. And if you read it like that, it makes sense, but we always read in a single line from left to right, and *that* looked like gibberish, and it suddenly struck me— I was looking at a code." She put the pencil down and bit on some toast and munched it. "But if we—say—typed the words, oh, I dunno, 'if you like,' the 'y' comes at the bottom of the first vertical and the 'o' comes at the bottom of the next one, and there aren't too many ordinary words beginning with 'yo' except for 'you'—and you start getting the drift. So at the top and bottom of every vertical I inserted a blind character to break the rhythm, and that was much nicer." She sat back and looked at me. "Had enough?"

"No."

"Glutton for punishment. So I'm reading three horizontal lines of code and I'm not picking up clues from the verticals because of the blinds. At that stage it would have taken a bright teenager maybe half an hour to break, so I threw in a reverse-direction readout and put it on the standard grid and went for three-character alphabetical substitutes and froze it. *Mystère!*" She shook her ponytail. "God, don't tell the man in London." Her eyes were suddenly deep, their color darkening. "Or anyone."

"I'm offended," I said.

"Sorry." She drew in a breath, let it out. "I want that one to run forever."

"It probably will."

"I shouldn't think so. I mean, basically it's terribly simple. But it touched my funny bone to think of all those typists out there—it's probably the same with any typewriter, not just a Canon—using the basis for *Mystère* when they're ordering another consignment of diapers or whatever. More toast?"

"No, I've finished. Are you working on anything new, at the—" Then the phone rang and I went over to it while Jane cleared the table.

"We've found Zymyanin." It wasn't Hagen's voice; this was the man on the day shift, and I recognized him because he'd been on the board for *Solitaire*, name was Carey. "He's still in Moscow."

"He made contact?"

"No. We had him traced—he went to his base in Lenin Prospekt."

"He's worked with us before?"

In a moment, "He's Bureau, but rather a lone wolf." He didn't query the fact that I hadn't been briefed on Zymyanin, didn't want to tread on any toes. "We've got a watch on him, and when he moves, we'll let you know. We think he's frightened, you see."

"Yes." It was possible that Jane didn't know Zymyanin, and couldn't have briefed me. Croder would have assumed I could trust him to know that the Russian was reliable. But it made me uneasy: I didn't much care for lone wolves in a sensitive field like Moscow.

"But he should come round, in good time. If he doesn't, ask for a rendezvous; you'll have to make your own way. We'll keep you posted as to his movements. Don't leave the phone."

I told him I'd got to go and find some clothes.

"Okay, but there's an answering machine, right?"

"Yes."

"Keep as close as you can, though, in case he suddenly takes off somewhere."

I said I'd do that.

"Any questions?" Carey asked me.

"No, but you can look after a couple of things for me. Was Hornby married?"

"Yes."

"Send some flowers, will you?"

"How much for?"

"Oh, twenty pounds."

"Name on the card?"

"Put anything. She doesn't know me."

"Will do."

"And tell Accounts we owe the Soviet Ministry of Agriculture for a sack of Grade A rye grain, one hundred and fifty pounds."

There'd be a squeal from that acidic old bitch in the countinghouse because she's always touchy about passing anonymous funds into Moscow without any explanation, but the rule is that if we damage any property we've got to report it and it's got to be paid for, and in any case this was nothing; the last thing I'd stuck Accounts for was a smashed Mercedes.

"Anything else?" Carey asked me.

I said no and we shut down.

This was at 8:44.

It was midafternoon when London came through with instructions.

Hagen was back at the board.

"Zymyanin has booked out on the *Rossiya* to Vladivostok. Please stand by for Chief of Signals."

Jane had been typing a report for the embassy, and stopped, leaving the room quiet. The sky in the high narrow window was already darkening toward nightfall even at this hour. The snow had eased off soon after we'd got back from the clothing shop.

I heard Croder's voice on the line.

"Your instructions are to board the train and try to make contact with him."

With Zymyanin. I asked Croder: "He signaled you?"

"No. We had his movements monitored. We think he finally decided against making a second rendezvous. Zymyanin is not normally a nervous man, but it seems he was frightened off by the Bucharest debacle."

It didn't surprise me. You don't need to be nervous to get clear from a blown rendezvous with no intention of trying your luck again: it's simply a logical precaution. This trade's chancy enough without begging for an early grave. But what I didn't like was the idea of forcing Zymyanin into a rendezvous he hadn't asked for, because there were a lot of risks and some of them could be lethal, and if it had been anyone but Croder giving me these instructions I would have turned them down. I've taken lethal risks all my life with the Bureau—it's built into the business—but I always need to know in each particular case whether it's worth it.

"What's the situation?" I asked him.

"The situation is that we still think Zymyanin has something of major importance to give us, if we can persuade him. I don't need to tell you, of course, that he may be very difficult to handle by now."

Yes indeed. It *looked* as if the Russian had got clear of the Bucharest thing and was simply unwilling to take any more risks, but that was an assumption, and assumptions are always dangerous.

"You mean," I said, "he might not have got away clean."

"Quite so. He may have been tracked from Bucharest to Moscow."

Tracked by the people who'd killed Hornby.

"He could in effect be still on the run."

"That is possible."

I watched the sky darkening in the window. "He could have been caught," I said, "caught and turned and given new instructions. Is that what you mean by 'difficult to handle'?"

"Something along those lines."

He's got a dry, thin voice, Croder. It's more like the sound of a paper shredder, and if you listen very carefully— as you should, if you are talking to the Chief of Signals— you can almost hear those little bright blades in there cutting the words out for you, the sibilants sharp and clear.

Something along those lines. I wasn't going to let him get away with that. I wanted him to know I was quite aware of what he was asking me to do. "He could," I said—Zymyanin—"have been told to stay out of contact with London and try and draw me into a trap."

In a moment, "That is also possible."

There was a sharp ringing sound in the room; I think Jane had gone into the little kitchenette and had dropped a spoon or something. I didn't like the way it touched my nerves. Vladivostok was on the Sea of Japan, nine or ten thousand kilometers from Moscow, and it would take seven or eight days to get there, straight through the heart of Siberia. In terms of security a moving train comes right at the bottom of the scale: call it a supertrap.

Croder was waiting. "The thing is," I asked him, "is it worth the risk?"

Zymyanin was said to be Bureau, but at most he was an agent-in-place or a roving watchdog; he wouldn't know much about London and if the opposition had in fact caught him and put him under the light and burned everything out of him they wouldn't have finished up with anything major. If they did the same thing with a senior shadow executive he'd blow Big Ben into the Thames if he couldn't get to the capsule fast enough.

It's a built-in risk factor and well recognized at the Bureau: the longer an executive runs and the more he knows, the more valuable he is to the opposition. Nobody likes this but there's nothing we can do about it except take out insurance, and the only insurance you can take out is not to send him into the field again.

Croder's voice came. "I was expecting your question." Whether it was worth the risk, this time around. "Yes, we believe it's worth it."

I didn't ask why. Croder gives no easy answers: he thinks them out, and he must have been thinking this one out ever since *Longshot* had crashed all over the signals board in London and sent people running for cover. He had also been getting input from Bureau agents-in-place in Moscow on the general intelligence background there, and he had finally put Zymyanin into the overall picture and come up with his findings: that it was worth risking the life of a senior shadow and worth risking that shadow's getting seized and interrogated and thrown onto the trash heap with nothing left in his skull but the burned-out circuits of his brain.

So it was a risk, but a calculated risk, and those I will accept. Without them, no executive can function.

"All right," I told Croder, and he asked me to stay on the line for briefing.

I looked round for Jane. "I'm taking the *Rossiya* to Vladivostok."

She came back into the room. "What time?"

"I don't know."

A voice on the line said, "Are you there?"

"Yes." It wasn't Hagen this time.

"Have you been on that train before?"

I said I hadn't.

"All right, the one the subject is on will be leaving Yaroslavl station in Moscow at about 18:00 hours, local time." The effect of the long distance plus the scrambler units made him sound like a robot. "I can't be more accurate than that, because those trains are usually late and this one ran into a snowstorm soon after it left Saint Petersburg. If it in fact leaves at 18:00 hours we'll be running things rather tight, so we're calling on the embassy for help."

We don't normally do that. Any of our overseas missions can end up messy in the extreme, with bodies lying around and the host-country police and secret services asking a lot of questions, and the embassy regards the Bureau under-standably as a stinking fish. But they've got to give us as-sistance if we ask for it, because we answer directly to the prime minister.

I blocked the mouthpiece and told Jane—"18:00 hours."

She nodded and got her notepad and sat on the floor cross-legged by the long carved stool.

"We're going to fax you," the man in Briefing said, "three mug shots of Vladimir Zymyanin to the embassy right away. We're going to ask them to send a courier to Yaroslavl station and get you a ticket for Vladivostok, hopefully soft class if there's one available. That's a two-berther. If we—"

"I want you to make certain," I told him, "that I go soft class. Understood?"

"We'll do our very best."

"No," I said, "I want you to make *certain*, for security reasons."

"Very well."

They could do it if they tried. If the train was full and there wasn't a berth available they'd have to buy someone off and a soft-class passenger would ask for more cash, but they'd have to pay it. It wasn't a question of comfort—al-though eight days on a train would be a sight more bearable with only one companion—it was a question of routine mis-sion security: I'd be operating under light cover and three passengers would be less easy to convince than one.

"There's an embassy car on its way to you now," the man on the line said, "with the complete travel package: visa, maps, vouchers, cash. Questions?"

"Where do I find my director, for debriefing?"

"We're putting him into Novosibirsk, where the train makes a stop. Look for him near the main booking office. You're mutually recognizable, I understand."

"Yes."

"Further questions?"

"No. Just put me back with Signals."

Hagen picked up the line and I asked for Croder.

In a moment: "COS."

"No support," I told him, "unless I ask for it."

"I've ordered none. I know you prefer that."

"Thank you."

We shut down. He was being distinctly cooperative, Croder. I usually have to fight Control and the DIF over the deployment of support groups, because they think the shadow's safer with a whole bloody platoon in the field, but it doesn't work that way—it works the *other* way.

Jane got off the floor as I came away from the telephone.

"There's a list of do's and don'ts," she said, "on the pad here for you to read. I've been on that train." She fetched her windcheater and shrugged her small thin body into it. "I'm going down to warm up the car and bring it round. We need to pick up some other things but we can do that at the station—food, toilet paper, rubber ball, stuff like that." She found her black fur gloves. "Stay here and get your gear together and be ready to leave." At the door she turned with a swing of her ponytail, her eyes dark and intent. "They're running it bloody close, but we'll manage."

Snow had drifted among the streets but there was no more coming down. The sky was oppressive, bruise-blue and swollen among the spires and minarets and rectangular termite nests of the housing complexes. Jane was watching the mirrors—from habit, I thought—as we turned along Kirov ulica past the Ministry of Works. She'd had field training, wasn't just a Codes and Ciphers specialist at the embassy. I felt safe in her hands, don't always, with strangers.

There was a traffic jam outside the enormous red-brick station and when we left the car we were immediately among a crowd of milling people, most of them staggering under the load of a week's supply of food and blankets and clothing. A man in a Royal Navy duffle coat broke from the crowd and brush-passed a package to Jane and melted again. He'd be from the embassy.

"I'll see you at the end of the platform," Jane said, and gave me the package. "The train's in—it's that one, the second along. But we've got a bit of time because they're still loading stuff into the dining galleys. I'll go and do the shopping."

I made my way through the huge cavernous hall to the nearest lavatory, edging among Caucasians, Indians, Mongols, a lot of Chinese—the *Rossiya* was going to end its run in Beijing—their faces jaundiced in the sulfurous light of the massive chandeliers that hung below the roof in the sooty haze. There was an unoccupied stall and I stood with my back to the door—the lock was broken—and studied the three mug shots of Vladimir Zymyanin, turning them to catch the light from the flickering tubes in the ceiling and learning the bony, compact face with its tight mouth and its blank uncompromising eyes, the jaw thrust forward a little and suggesting belligerence, the face of a man not to be found off his guard, not to hesitate for a second if in the course of his business he deemed it necessary to kill—necessary or expedient, to save time or to save trouble, even a little time, a little trouble. I knew his kind, as well I should: he was one of us, and of this I would have to beware.

I don't need to tell you, of course, that he may be very difficult to handle by now.

Croder, shredding his words carefully into the telephone.

I put the photographs away and went back through the crowded hall, not missing a face as I made for the end of the platform.

Jane was already there. "You'll have to make room for this. The food on the train's not uneatable, providing you feel like boiled chicken twice a day for eight days."

She stuffed the bulging plastic bag into the zippered case we'd bought this morning. I thought I saw him, Zymyanin,

turning away from the ticket gate and going down the platform, but wasn't certain.

*He could have been caught and turned and given new instruc-
tions. Is that what you mean by "difficult to handle"?*

Something along those lines.

Whistles had begun shrilling faintly from the front end
of the train, and others sounded, getting nearer. Women
with coats over their white aprons were still heaving crates
and containers into the dining galleys, and gusts of steam
came clouding from some of the windows.

"They've got the samovars up to scratch," Jane said.
"It'd be a good idea if you went aboard now. You've got
everything and you won't be lonely—six hundred people,
this one's full." She stood looking up at me, her black fur
gloves held together in front of her like a muff, her small
face white and pinched in the cold.

"First class," I said.

"What?"

"You did a first-class job."

"Oh. Thank you." She looked down, then up again, her
eyes going dark. "Good luck and everything."

She turned and walked as far as the end of the platform
and didn't look back. I picked up my bags and went along
to Car Number 7.

Six hundred people, and one of them Zymyanin.

*He could have been told to stay out of contact with London
and try and draw me into a trap.*

That is also possible.

The *provodnik* clipped my ticket and I slung my bags
aboard and climbed into the train.

Chapter 4

Night Music

"**S**lavsky, Boris."

He put out a pale bony hand.

"Shokin, Viktor," I said.

He was tall, hungry-looking, his dry hair thinning, the dark-framed glasses too big for his face, his body curving in an academic stoop. "Have you done this trip before?"

"No."

He reached up to the shelf over the doorway and pulled down a paper bundle and slit it open and dumped it into my arms, bed linen, heavily woven, the real thing, none of your fancy nylon. He got his own bundle down and opened it and shook out the sheets. "I do this trip three times a year," he said, and looked toward the open door of the compartment, lowering his voice. "So let me tell you something. We have to be nice to our *provodnik*. A little tip here, a little tip there, you understand?" He had the tone of a lecturer, was waiting for me to say I understood. I said I did. "I know most of them," he went on, nodding his domed head, "but not this one. She must be new. You've seen her, of course. Bit of a battle-ax, wouldn't you say?"

She was the woman, I supposed, who'd checked my ticket when I'd come aboard—large, heavy-boned, lavishly lipsticked, and with hair the color of a copper samovar, the shoulders of her blue uniform unnecessarily padded, the brass winged-wheel emblem glinting on her forage cap, her small bright eyes taking me in as I'd squeezed past her with my bags.

45

"She didn't look easy to tame," I told Slavsky.

"Ha! Well put. But it has to be done. It has to be done." He started making up his bunk, thumping the massive pillow.

Our berths were on each side of the narrow gangway, with a folding table under the window and a jar with some rather pretty blue-flowered weeds in it, the most one could ask for, probably, in the depths of a Russian winter. There was more than enough space for our bags—we could have brought a truckload—and the compartment in general looked habitable, even for eight days at a stretch. The only critical problem was the lack of security: once anyone saw you going into the compartment or coming out of it they had your address, and there was no back door.

"Don't be upset," Slavsky said as he peeled off his jacket, "about the heat in here. The windows are all sealed to keep the dirt out, and nothing can be done about it."

People were moving along the corridor, heaving bags and packages, among them an English couple with their voices raised on the understanding that since the natives couldn't speak their language they couldn't be heard.

"But George, you'll have to look at things the way Clarence does. He says this is World Adventure Number One— that's *exactly* how he put it last night—World Adventure Number *One*. The Trans-Siberian *Express*."

"Clarence is out of his bloody mind about bloody trains."

A group of Chinese struggled past with little red-and-white flags sticking out of their knapsacks; then there were a few passengers on their own, and these I noted. One of them looked in and gave me an expressionless stare and lumbered on with his body angled under the weight of a black canvas bag. This is why I'd asked Croder not to put any support people on this train: if anyone took an interest in me I'd know they weren't Bureau.

"Did you bring some food?" Slavsky asked me.

"Yes."

"And toilet paper? Rubber ball?"

"Yes."

"Then you booked through a good travel agent."

"Yes."

"The main thing to remember," he said, and then broke off and staggered suddenly as the floor jerked under our feet and the heavy steel couplings out there took up the slack and rang like a peal of bells under the huge roof of the station and the crowds lining the platform started calling and waving and holding children up and the passengers filling the corridors waved back, and I never came to know what the main thing to remember was, but I thought Slavsky would tell me sooner or later.

Through the windows of the corridor the hazy glow of the station gave way to a string of lights lining the track, and when the acceleration had evened out I told Slavsky I was going to stretch my legs, but he was buried in a book under the reading lamp and didn't look up.

People were going back into their compartments and leaving the corridors clear, but some girls in gray overalls with the state insignia on them were washing down the walls, and others were trundling vacuum cleaners in and out of the compartments nearer the dining car.

"How many carriages are there?" I asked an apple-faced woman with a mop.

"On this train? Twenty-two."

"A lot of carriages."

"A lot of work!"

I stepped over her gray galvanized bucket and went through the rubber-walled booth into the next carriage, taking my time, noting every face, looking into the compartments when the curtains were open, scanning the faces of the men who stood in the vestibules at the ends of the carriages coughing in the cloud of smoke from their cigarettes. Twenty-two carriages, six hundred people, and I might have to walk the entire length of the train a dozen times, fifty times before I found him, Zymyanin. A lot of work, yes indeed, you were right, little mother.

He would know, Zymyanin, that the Bureau would have wanted to bring him to a second rendezvous with a second contact, because the information he'd got for us was still shut in his head. He would know that when he'd failed to signal London to set up a new rendezvous, Control would make it his business to put a watch on his movements and have the new contact standing by to force him into a meeting if he could. He would know that I was on this train.

"I'm sorry, *Babushka*," I said as I got in the way of her mop.

"I shouldn't be working as late as this!" A stainless-steel tooth flashed in the bluish light. "It was the snow, after Saint Petersburg, that held everything up!"

He wouldn't recognize me, Zymyanin, had never seen me before and would not have been given the photograph of a high-echelon shadow executive; but he would come to know me, come to know who I was, who I must be, when he noticed I was searching the train for someone. And once he'd got a fix on me I'd move immediately into a red sector, if that man had in fact set up a kill for Hornby in the freight yard in Bucharest and had now set one up for me.

That would be all right in the streets of a city or in open countryside where there was adequate cover: the risk would be calculated, the kind we thrive on if we play them right. But here in this long thin tube stretching through the wilderness there were risks dependent on sheer chance, and at any given time Zymyanin could catch sight of me from the far end of a corridor before I saw him. Then he'd bring me under his surveillance, and I might not have enough time to realize it before he made his move.

The thing is, I'd asked Croder, *is it worth the risk?*

I was expecting your question. Yes, we believe it's worth it.

It was the only excuse I'd got for taking it, the only *justification*. Croder's word.

When I came back to the compartment the night sky through the windows of the corridor was sable-black and jeweled with stars as the *Rossiya* ran through open country and the dark.

Slavsky was asleep, I think; he didn't say anything when I changed into the tracksuit we'd bought at the used-clothing shop this morning in Moscow, and stretched out on my bunk. The heating had been turned off not long before midnight and now the air was cold, and tainted with the constant smell of disinfectant from the lavatories. I'd strip-washed half an hour ago, using the big iron bucket in the nearest toilet, the water rust-colored and near freezing; but that hadn't been the main problem, which was to keep things from dropping through the big uncovered drainpipe onto Russian soil, artifacts for posterity. But the little black rubber ball had worked well enough in the handbasin, a stand-in for the missing plug.

I hadn't seen Zymyanin.

In the last five hours I had covered the whole length of the train three times, waiting in line for a late supper in the nearest dining car and surveilling for more than an hour and then moving on, using other passengers—Caucasian, and in groups when I could find them—as mobile cover, wandering with them along the rocking corridors and meeting with bands of Gypsies, some Americans with the Stars and Stripes sewn proudly onto their jeans, a French army colonel in full uniform, a gang of Russian hooligans shouting the odds about the coming revolution, gaggles of winsome little ballet students on their way to the State School of Choreography in Novosibirsk, a Scottish Highlander in a Campbell clan kilt and a party of singing drunks.

I had also met our senior *provodnik* again, Galina, the muscled redhead, and chatted with her for a while before she signed off her shift, putting reasonably direct questions to her about working conditions on the train and especially the rate of pay, and expressing mild shock at its inadequacy considering the daunting responsibilities of her job. There was no excuse for crossing her palm with silver at this stage, but expectations were carefully stirred.

It wasn't that I felt the need for extra comforts of any sort, but for a recruitable agent-in-place with an unbreakable cover who could ferret out information for me that might indirectly further my progress in the mission or even protect my life—because there was a second possible scenario in my mind: Zymyanin might be perfectly reliable, a good agent understandably scared off by the Bucharest thing and unwilling to risk another rendezvous, in which case he was no danger to me. But if the opposition had tried to kill him off along with Hornby in that freight yard, they might have followed him onto the train, to try again.

Zymyanin's own life could be in hazard as the *Rossiya* plunged headlong through the night, and if I made contact with him it could be lethal. A thousand rubles in Galina's bank account to buy her secret services could prove a profitable investment, and to hell with that carping old crone in the countinghouse. We play our little games, we, the brave and diligent ferrets in the field, with wit and sinew as our weapons when we can, but if base money can provide the means of our salvation as we burrow through the dark and treacherous labyrinths then we will use it. We're not proud, my good friend, we are not proud: we find we live longer if we are practical.

On my way through the corridors tonight I stopped to talk to any of the staff who had the time, though not many did: one of them, a weary-eyed girl with calloused hands and stained overalls with the seam torn at the shoulder, told me that the coach attendants, security guards, waiters, cooks, and cleaners worked for nine days at a stretch on the run from Moscow to Beijing, then took a week off in Moscow or Vladivostok, in turn.

"But the pay is good," she said, pulling a lock of damp hair away from her eyes. "I earn a hundred and fifty rubles a month, with free keep."

"That's quite good," I said. It was terrible. "But so you should."

She dragged chips of wood from the rocking floor of the

galley and pushed them into the furnace below the huge copper samovar. "Yes, and then one day I shall be a *provodnik*, in a uniform."

I spent more than an hour in the dining car, because of the three men there, and watched the waiters tussling with a pack of beatniks who were trying to hog a table for a game of cards, swigging their beer from the bottle and making up a dirty song about the revolution—I'd seen them before, along the corridors.

The three men were in their fifties, their faces sharp-boned and weathered, their dark woolen suits well cut and their shoes polished. Four other men, younger and quiet-faced, observant, seemed to be in the same party, although they were sitting at different tables, two of them on each side of the table where the older men were. One of them, the quietest, with the totally expressionless eyes of a wolf, got out of his seat and moved slowly along the dining car and spoke to the party of youths. One of them talked back and there was a hoot of laughter, which died away as the man showed them something. Talk at the other tables had also broken off, and the whole dining car had gone quiet, so that I heard him saying, "Now get out, and stay out."

One of the beatniks began talking back again but his pals told him to shut up and hauled him with them down the aisle and through the glass-panneled door at the end. The man went back to his table and sat down.

I finished my boiled chicken and *pirozhki* and ordered some borscht to fill in the time here; I wanted to see more of the three well-dressed men and their bodyguards, and also of the man who was sitting alone at the far end of the car, and of the young woman in the silver-gray fur hat, also alone, who was sitting nearer my own table.

I stayed in the dining car until almost eleven o'clock, and was one of the last to leave. Then I did some work and decided to turn in, but met the copper-haired Galina and talked to her for a while, not about the people I'd seen in the dining car. There was no hurry for anything on this trip:

the *Rossiya* was now heading into the limitless wastes of Siberia and the winter snows, and there would be time for everything.

Across the gangway in our compartment, Slavsky had begun snoring a little in his bunk. The tumbler covering the massive water beaker on the little folding table was vibrating, sending out a thin and intermittent ringing in the night. There were no longer any voices along the corridor, but a dark figure moved across the narrow gaps in the curtains outside the compartment and stopped, and I watched its outline in the dimmed bluish light out there. I couldn't see whether its back was turned—some insomniac watching the night sky through the outside window—or whether it was facing in this direction.

An eye, applied to a gap in the curtains, would probably catch enough back light from the glass on the window to show itself, glinting. I couldn't see anything like that, but couldn't be sure I wasn't being watched. This was why the interior of a night train comes at the bottom of the list of secure environments: you even have to sleep, virtually, in public. I could have rigged a makeshift screen out of spare sheets across the windows looking onto the corridor, but it would have attracted attention from the train crews outside and Slavsky would have needed an explanation, and I hadn't got one that would have sounded plausible. I was traveling under light cover, and had to blend in as a typical passenger.

The figure was still there, and I watched its outline, knowing that if someone was watching me he would pick up the glint from my own eyes quite clearly, since the only light source was in the corridor. He would know I was watching him back.

I didn't know—nobody knew, except Zymyanin—what they'd done to Hornby before they took off his head. We don't always use stealth when we make a hit; silence isn't necessary on all occasions. And we don't always need to go close or make contact: I choose not to bear arms, but that's unusual in this trade, you could say unheard of. It was night and most people were asleep, and the sound of the train was a constant background; the man out there would only need to fit a silencer and press it to the glass of the window and fire the gun and walk away. If Zymyanin had brought me into a trap, that was all he would have to do to spring it.

The glass on the beaker rang from the vibration of the train, making its thin night music. Slavsky had stopped snoring, and turned in his bunk, and the rustle of the stiff linen sheet made a sound like the hiss of a drawn breath, and touched my nerves.

He could have been told to stay out of contact with London and try and draw me into a trap.

That is also possible.

Even though I had narrowed my eyes, he would catch the light on their conjunctivae, the man out there. The range was short and he could see the target: the point between my eyes, and behind it the brain. He would need only one shot, and couldn't miss.

I watched the outline through the gap in the curtains, waiting for it to move, for only a part of it to move: the gunhand.

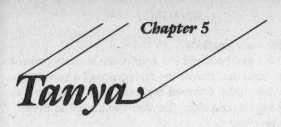

Chapter 5

Tanya

The man was standing near the lavatory at the end of the second carriage along, waiting to go in, I suppose, watching the first light of the morning on the snows. One of the cleaners passed us, lugging a box of rags, and then I went up to the man and stood behind him.

"*Longshot*," I said close to his ear.

He wouldn't know *Meridian*, hadn't contacted London. But he'd known *Longshot*, had seen it crash.

He didn't turn his head. He was the man I'd been watching last night in the dining car, the one who'd been sitting alone. He was Zymyanin. I saw the reflection of his face in the window, sharp-boned, the mouth tight, as in his photographs.

"I need more," he said in a moment, still not turning, watching my own reflection.

"Bureau."

"More," he said softly.

"Zymyanin."

He turned his head now, and looked at me. His eyes were wary, but not afraid, even though he knew I'd caught up with him. I would think these eyes had never been afraid, only alert, wary like this, watching for a way out if he thought he needed one, wherever he was. I knew that look, had felt it in my own eyes. Here was a brother ferret.

"Are you replacing him?" he asked me. Hornby.

"No," I said. "They've taken that one off the books. I'm just here to talk to you, that's all."

He didn't say anything.

A bolt banged back and the door of the lavatory opened and a man came out, one of the bodyguards I'd seen in the dining car last night. I turned my head away until he was halfway along the corridor. "Do you want to go in there?" I asked Zymyanin.

"What? No. It can wait." The smell of urine and disinfectant came drifting across.

I touched his arm and we moved farther away, past the two cleaning women, who were bent over a stain on the carpet, rubbing at it with a block of dark yellow soap.

"I've got nothing to tell you," Zymyanin said, and I heard anger in his voice, though he kept it very soft. "You people have got a *mole* sniffing around, surely you know that. I—"

"Russian," I said. He'd switched to English, was fluent, but it didn't tally with my cover. "There's no mole." They don't exist in the Bureau, can't exist, the security checks are like X rays in that place, they've got to be, we're not the Foreign Office. "It was just incompetence." And inexperience, Hornby's. He'd let a word drop somewhere, full of excitement, it's happened before. I'd picked up the vibes from Turner, his DIF in Bucharest, when I'd been with him in the Hotel Constanta. He'd been holding himself back, sick about Hornby's death but wanting to blame him for what had happened, had stopped himself. I'd admired him for that.

The train rocked across points, and buildings swung past the windows, blocks of darkness lumped together on the snow, some with lights showing, pale in the dawn.

"Incompetence," Zymyanin was saying, "all right, it was incompetence, he got to the rdv early, you understand that? *Early*." I understood, yes, it's one of the cardinal errors, a potentially lethal mistake. "And what guarantee have I got that I can trust *you*?" he wanted to know. "How do I know how competent *you* are? How do I know you haven't brought half a dozen opposition hit men onto this *fucking* train because of *your* incompetence?"

Had a bad scare, he'd had a bad scare, this man, in Bucharest, no fright in his eyes but it was still down there in the gut, I quite understood. I'd been thinking he was a potential danger to me, and he'd been thinking I would be a danger to him if we forced him into a rendezvous, and now we'd done that. It couldn't have been him, last night, standing outside my compartment: if he'd known I was in there he would have run to the far end of the train.

"I know exactly what you mean," I said. It was no good telling him I was a senior executive; one or two senior executives had been found in some foreign clime with their brains raked out of their skulls and the capsules still in their pockets. I had to remember it was only two nights ago when this man came close to getting blown into Christendom like Hornby.

"This isn't a rendezvous," Zymyanin said, watching me, his eyes bright with nerves. "I didn't ask for one and I don't want one, is that understood? I don't want you to come anywhere near me again. I want you to keep out of my way, *right* out of my way."

Someone else went into the lav down there and slammed the door, hit the bolt.

"It must be wine!" one of the cleaners was saying, her voice shrill with vexation, a pink knee showing through the hole in her black stocking as she knelt on the floor with her bar of soap. "It must be red wine again, look, it's not coming out!"

"Some *drunk*," the other woman said, "a *drunk* did this!"

I'd have to talk him round somehow, Zymyanin, get his confidence back. But I didn't trust him at the moment, and he didn't trust me. Now that he'd seen my face he'd remember seeing me last night in the dining car, then a stranger. He would be wondering why I hadn't followed him out of there when he left, and revealed myself then instead of waiting until now. He'd know I'd realized what he'd been doing in the dining car.

"Who are they?" I asked him.

He'd been keeping observation on the three men.

My question didn't surprise him. He would have been expecting it, sooner or later: I was here to get the information he had for us, and it obviously concerned the men he'd been watching, would be watching again.

In a moment he said, "They are former General Kovalenko and General Vilechko of the Army High Command and Special Purpose Militia Detachments respectively, and former General Chudin of the KGB."

However well a spook is trained and however experienced, he sometimes finds it irresistible to tell what he knows to someone he's at least expected to trust, if what he knows is of great importance.

"And they're now in the *Podpolia*?" I asked him. The underground.

"Of course," he said impatiently.

He was impatient with himself, not with me. He'd revealed his flaw, and knew it. I didn't say anything, waited for him to tell me other things now that he'd started.

"This is so *dangerous*," he said, and looked along the corridor again.

"I agree. Who's in your compartment with you?"

"Three Ukrainians, metalworkers, they never leave there, they've brought enough food for the whole trip, play cards all the time."

"I've only got one in with me," I told him. "I'll find out when he's going to stretch his legs, and let you know. We can talk in there." It was a risk: I hadn't wanted him to know my compartment; but he could find out if he wanted to, and in any case he seemed ready to talk now and I had to catch him while he was in the mood.

"Listen," he said on an impulse, "you must have recognized me last night in the dining car—you must have been given a photograph—so why didn't you follow me out of there when I left?"

I thought of lying, but if I lied he'd know it and I'd lose what trust he'd got in me, if he had any at all.

"I had my reasons," I said.

He let his eyes stay on me, not showing anything but his nerves, trying to see what was in mine, seeing nothing. I think it angered him. "Listen, if you want a rendezvous it'll have to be somewhere off the train when we stop for a break."

There are two breaks a day, Jane had put in her notes for me, *when you can stretch your legs and breathe some air, unless the train's running so late that they can't manage it*.

There wasn't any point in trying to rush Zymyanin; it'd have to be drawn out.

"When did you first pick them up?" I asked him.

He might be in more danger than I knew, than he was ready to tell me. I'd have to get what I could, as soon as I could.

"I can't tell you that. At least not yet. We—"

"You were going to tell our contact in Bucharest."

"No."

"Then what were you going to tell him?"

He swung his narrow head up to look at me, a sprig of his dark unwashed hair bobbing as he turned. "I was going to tell him only that those people would be on this train. I—"

"You didn't need a physical rendezvous for that," I said. "You could have just signaled London."

He looked away again, staring through the window, picking at his short ragged nails. A factory of some sort swung by, its chimneys pouring a long dark cloud across the snow-covered roofs of the buildings. "Listen," he said, "this is all I can tell you for now. The Bureau should do every-thing—*everything*—to keep those people under surveillance. That's why I'm here, of course, but I'm also here because there's a cell in Moscow"—his head swung up again to look at me—"a completely unacknowledged, unofficial cell whose purpose is to seek, find, and expose the active members of the *Podpolia* wherever they may be. Many are known, of course, and the KGB is watching them closely. But some are not known, and those we are looking for. That is also why I am here."

There were voices behind me but I didn't turn round, just watched Zymyanin's face, his eyes, as he looked along the corridor. They were men's voices, speaking in Russian, growing louder as they came past. Zymyanin showed nothing, turned his head to stare through the window again.

"... And last week he moved into a new apartment. Shall I tell you about it?"

"No. It'll make me sick."

"Of course it'll make you sick! In his new apartment he has to share one bathtub with thirty other people, and his kitchen is an electric hot plate that never gets hot enough to boil water! I thought Yeltsin was going to make a few little changes here and there, didn't you, for God's sake?"

Snow had begun whirling past the windows; we were running into another storm.

"That is all I can tell you," Zymyanin said, "for the moment." He turned away and took a few steps, turned back, his nerves still bright in his eyes. "When I've got something more, I'll contact you. In the meantime, keep your distance."

He turned and walked on and in a moment the door of the lavatory banged and the bolt went home.

Later in the morning I got out the briefing Jane had given me and went through it and reinforced the mnemonics and folded the three sheets and took them along to the first *provodnik*'s station I could find unattended and pushed them deep under the trash in the waste bin and heard someone coming and got a cup from the shelf and filled it from the samovar.

"That is for *me* to do"—the *provodnik*'s tone shrill and indignant—"I can't leave this place for half a minute without someone coming in here and meddling!"

I told her she made the finest tea in all Russia and said I would tell my grandchildren about it in the years to come, so forth, and she took a pinch of it as a compliment and told me to be off with my wily charm, I should be peddling butter in the black market.

Most of the stuff Jane had given me was standard tourist information, and I spread out the maps in my compartment and looked them over; they showed the route and schedules of the *Rossiya* and vignettes of Tyumen, Novosibirsk, Irkutsk, Khabarovsk and Vladivostok, with the major streets named.

A group of youths trooped past the open door and I went out and stopped them, picking two of the brightest looking and giving them twenty rubles to split and telling them what I wanted. Then I looked for Galina and found her blasting a pallid and red-eyed girl in a torn smock—the bulkheads in Car Number 5 were *filthy* and this was the *third* time the passengers had complained and who would take the *blame* when the reports were sent in? She, Galina Ludmila Makovetskaya, would take the blame, who else, since she was the supervisor for Car Numbers 5, 6, and 7?

When the girl had gone I looked into the small bright still-enraged black eyes of Galina Ludmila Makovetskaya and asked her how everything else was and did she think the snowstorm would cause any problems, and learned that this was a bad day for her because her ingrown toenail was beginning to give trouble just like the doctor had told her it would, but it would mean an operation, only a minor one but the thought of it terrified her. Then I offered her a hundred rubles and explained that since I was a journalist, as she knew, my whole livelihood depended on sniffing out stories, and perhaps she could help me in this.

"The three men," I said, "for instance, who were in the dining car last night. They looked important."

She braced her large body against the bulkhead as the train rocked, and took out a packet of cigarettes. "You smoke?"

"I'm trying to quit."

She lit one with a match from a monogrammed book with the winged wheel on it and blew out smoke and looked at me with her eyes no longer enraged but sharp now, bright with conspiracy. "They used to be somebody. Now they are nobody. They used to fly everywhere. Now they take the train." She gave me their names and former ranks, and they tallied with what Zymyanin had told me. "It's rumored that two of them—the army officers—were arrested and tried for supporting the coup, but were acquitted." A shrug of the big padded shoulders. "Who knows? Who knows who is who, these days, or who they were or what they were doing? Half the army and the KGB have gone underground, as you know, even though they're still marching about for all to see." She dropped ash circumspectly into a tin tray with the ubiquitous emblem on it, and opened a steam valve on the samovar. The heating system for this coach had broken down soon after breakfast this morning, and the warmth was welcome in here. "You wish me to make discreet inquiries about those men?"

The faintest of smiles touched her heavily lipsticked mouth, softening her looks, even though she would smile like this as she buried the knife deep between my shoulder blades if she saw in me an enemy, or even thought she saw. This was my impression.

"Very discreet," I said. "Very discreet inquiries, yes."

I asked her other things, and when people came past us or asked for some tea we talked about the snowstorm and the shocking price of everything now that *demokratizatsiya* was rife in the land.

Before I left her she said, "Of course, I shall have to satisfy others, you must understand." Her eyes glittered in the folds of flesh, squinting at me through the smoke from her cigarette.

"No others," I said. "No others, Galina Ludmila. This is very strictly between you and me. Is that clear?"

A shrug. "Very well."

I pulled out another hundred, which was what she was after anyway.

"No others," she said.

There was no one of interest at lunch in the dining car when I passed through it and later came back. The generals weren't there, or Zymyanin.

In the afternoon the *Rossiya* drew its great and massive length into a village station, and most of the passengers dropped from it and stood in the flurries of snow that came blowing under the red-painted wooden canopy that hung over the platform. It wasn't a scheduled stop, I was told: we were being given a break, the first and last of the day because we were running late. I saw Slavsky doing his knee bends— he'd been trying them on the train but couldn't keep his balance—and a party of Chinese went jogging through the snow outside the station, their little flags jerking on top of their rucksacks while the *petits rats* on their way to the State School of Choreography in Novosibirsk went prancing off in the other direction with their ponytails flying and their laughter echoing under the canopy like the cries of birds. A drunk was throwing up at the end of the platform and I turned and walked the other way, keeping up what pace I could among the crowd and trying to find some fresh air to breathe, not easy, because most people were smoking with fierce concentration to make the best of the break.

I saw nothing of Zymyanin or the generals, but the young woman in the silver-gray fur hat was walking alone through the snow, her fur-lined boots crunching along the cinder pathway.

It was evening when I next saw her. Slavsky liked the compartment door to be open when we weren't sleeping or changing our clothes, and I didn't argue because I wasn't there for most of the time. One of the youths showed himself in the doorway and jerked his head and I followed him along the corridors to the dining car. The other youth was standing in the line behind the young woman, and gave me his place.

There was only one table for two, at the far end, and I joined her there, even though there were other places and she seemed to want to be alone. We sat opposite each other: she was facing the bulkhead, while I could see down the aisle beyond her. It was a small table, and it would have been difficult for us to sit in silence during the meal, but even so, I think she would have preferred that.

"Tanya Rusakova, I believe." I leaned toward her a little as I said it. "I hope I'm not wrong."

Then her eyes were on me for the first time, a shimmering and iridescent green, widening in surprise.

"Yes."

"Shokin," I said, "Viktor Shokin. You won't remember me, but I think we live on the same street . . . Grafskij Prospekt? I've seen you there sometimes. And I passed through your office the other day. You're at the Ministry of Transport, Motor Division?"

"Yes. I'm sorry, but I—"

"You were busy at your desk. I came in for a new driving license, that was all."

"I see." She wished I hadn't recognized her, wished I weren't here.

When the waitress came we tried to get her to bring us anything except boiled chicken, but it didn't work: it was all they'd been given, she said wearily, when the caterers had loaded the galleys in Moscow.

"You're going right through to Beijing?" I asked Tanya while we were waiting.

"No." She hadn't smiled yet, even as a social gesture, perhaps found it difficult, even impossible, because of her state of nerves and the overwhelming hatred she felt for General Vilechko.

"Vladivostok, then," I said, making it an amusing guessing game. She didn't answer, looked everywhere but at me. "I'm a journalist, you see, and we're always asking questions, aren't we? I'm afraid the media haven't got a terribly good reputation for the preservation of privacy. I'm going to Beijing. Have you been there?"

"No." She was studying the menu, using it as a refuge.

"General Vilechko is going there," I said, and she swung her head up and stared at me, more than surprised, shocked. That was my impression.

"I don't know him."

She'd said it too fast, with her mouth too tight, and those fine sensual nostrils had flared and the light in her eyes was still burning, the hot light of the hatred I'd seen when she'd been looking at him, at General Vilechko, here in the dining car last night, her eyes looking down most of the time but on occasion drawn to him where he sat five tables down the aisle.

He'd been the only one of the three facing her; the other two had been sitting side by side with their backs to her. That was why I could be quite sure they'd been for Vilechko, no one else, those sudden looks she'd given him, precipitate, spontaneous, and so very dangerous, though she'd been unaware of that. I would have felt afraid for her if I hadn't also seen, last night, that she could dissemble, Tanya Rusakova, when she wanted to—had given the good general the faintest of smiles as she'd left her table and walked past him along the aisle, what you would call the suggestion of a come-on.

She wasn't a tart. There were a few of them on the train but she wasn't one of them. She wasn't an actress, even though that smile for the general, however tenuous, had taken talent to produce, considering what she really felt for him. She was, as Galina had found out for me, a government clerk in the Motor Division of the Ministry of Transport, living alone on Grafskij Prospekt, thirty-two, unmarried. Her destination was Novosibirsk, not Beijing or Vladivostok, as I'd known. Her brother, an army captain, was stationed there.

General Vilechko was also going to Novosibirsk, and I'd

known that too, and that was why I'd thought it very interesting, that look of shock in the flashing green eyes when
I'd said just now, *General Vilechko is going there too.* I'd been
looking for a reaction and I'd got it, and it had been more
extreme than expected. Most of it was because I'd suddenly
spoken the very name of the man who inspired so much
hatred in her, but it must have been partly because of the
deliberate dropping of disinformation. I'd been prepared for
her to say, no, he's not going to Beijing, something like that,
but it hadn't happened. She didn't want to talk about that
man, not a word, had been tempted, surely, to get up and
find another table if she could, or leave the dining car and
this damned journalist with his damned questions.

Was she worried that I might be right, that she'd been
mistaken, that General Vilechko wasn't in fact going to leave
the train long before Beijing, at Novosibirsk? *How important
was it to her?*

Plates, suddenly, dumped onto the table in front of us,
and the unappetizing smell of boiled chicken, none too fresh.
Thank you, we said. She'd been quick, the waitress, even
though the car was almost full and the other girls were flying
around with trays and dishes and jugs of beer, the fat uniformed supervisor watching them, hands on her hips. I
wished our food had taken longer; I wanted as much time
with Tanya Rusakova as I could get.

Zymyanin had wanted to know why I hadn't followed
him out of here last night, since I must have recognized him.
It was because I'd wanted to stay until the young woman
with the silver-gray fur hat left her table, in case I could learn
something. *The Bureau should do everything*, Zymyanin had
said, *to keep those people under surveillance.* Apart from that,
he'd given me almost nothing. That could have been because
he didn't know anything yet, anything major.

Perhaps this woman did.

They were there tonight, the men I called the generals,
six tables along the aisle. Did she know, Tanya? Did she
want to look round to see if they were there, if *he* were there,

Vilechko? They weren't talking; they hadn't been talking last night; they sat with their food, eating it as a necessity, looking up from the table very seldom, when someone went past them along the aisle; they were the sort of men who'd want to know what company they kept, but here they didn't show concern: they had their bodyguards.

I didn't think Zymyanin had noticed Tanya Rusakova last night, except as a woman, as any man would—look at the eyes, the cheekbones, the infinitely attractive mouth—but he'd been concentrating, with his oblique and casual glances across the dining car, on the three men, and hadn't caught, I believe, the expression in Tanya's eyes when she'd looked at Vilechko.

"I'm going to spend a night," I said, "in Novosibirsk." This chicken really was bloody awful; God knew what they'd done to it down there in the galley, wiped it all over the floor, conceivably; she was taking her time, perhaps wouldn't say anything at all.

"Yes?" She didn't look up. She was wondering how to ask me the question that was burning to get out—*why had I mentioned General Vilechko, quite out of the blue?*

"Just to break the journey," I said. "I wouldn't think there'd be much to do, in a place like Novosibirsk. Would you?"

The *Rossiya* blew its whistle just then and the sound came with the shock effect of a scream in the night and she almost flinched, and I wanted to comfort her in some acceptable way, put my hand over hers just for an instant; she wasn't having much fun, Tanya Rusakova, sitting here with her nerves like an open wound, sensitive to loud noises, to the sudden mention of a name.

"There's an opera house," she said.

"Oh really?"

Then she covered it, too late. "So I believe."

An attempt to disassociate herself from the city of Novosibirsk, to be noted.

"Are you fond of the opera?"

"I quite like it, yes. *Prince Igor.*" She put her knife and fork together, her chicken unfinished, and got her gray leather bag, giving me a glance in passing with nothing in her eyes except perhaps distrust. "Good night," she said, and slipped gracefully between the bench and the table.

"It—" *was a pleasure,* but I broke off, starting to rise and then stopping at once but not before she noticed it—I caught a look of surprise. It was so easy to forget and it could be so dangerous. . . . *Behave* like a Russian, *be* like a Russian, *think* like a Russian. . . .

She walked down the aisle, and I watched—I watched very carefully—the man sitting six tables along, heavy-faced, broad-shouldered, impressively tailored. He glanced up as Tanya Rusakova passed him, and by his expression I could see that there had once again been a smile for the general.

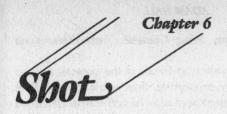

Chapter 6

Shot

"**T**hey have asked for a new compartment." Galina stood watching me. "I'm relocating them from Car Number Twelve to Car Number Four. They say they're too near one of the lavatories."

The dark was coming down on our second day out from Moscow; the *Rossiya* had plowed through nearly two thousand kilometers of steppes and the Ural mountain range and now we were running through forests of birch and pine and cedar standing draped in snow under the endless leaden skies. We were due in Novosibirsk tonight.

Galina had shown herself in the doorway of our compartment a few minutes ago, glancing across Slavsky—who was reading as always—and giving me the slightest movement of her head. I had followed her to the *provodnik*'s station.

"They object to the smell," she said, simmering. "So what do they expect? Look what the passengers do in there all day, are they rose gardens? Would our friends perhaps prefer the smell of roses? So would I!"

"But you've agreed to move them?"

She lit a cigarette, its black tobacco glowing as the flame of the match went out. It smelled of forest fires. "I have decided to accommodate them, yes," she said. "There are three compartments in Car Number Four, nearer the locomotive, occupied by Chinese tourists." Her small eyes kindled sparks of light. "Certain favors were exchanged, as you will understand. Our friends are not ungenerous, and the

Chinese are indigent, being Chinese. Thus there is no problem."

She had started yesterday to talk of the generals as "our friends," without my prompting. She would train well, if she ever wanted to enter the shadowed netherworld of covert operations.

"You're moving their entourage," I asked her, "as well?"

"But of course." She watched me steadily, squinting in the smoke from her cigarette. "I thought you should be informed."

"Yes. Do you think their reason for wanting to move was genuine?"

A shrug. "With men of their kind, who knows what is genuine, and what spurious? They had power, once. Now they have no power. But they think they have. Their ways are devious."

I drank some tea with her as the train plunged into nightfall through the dizzying snow that drove past the windows, piling against the frames. She told me that she had personally chosen to supervise the switching of compartments, and would report to me anything she observed or overheard.

In the evening I shared a table in the dining car with Boris Slavsky, and listened to his views on the future of Russia, if—as he said—it could be considered to have one. He spoke well, marshaling his facts, but my attention was less with him than with General Vilechko and his companion, Tanya Rusakova, smiling and attentive, at the table for two we'd been sitting at last night.

Galina searched me out an hour before I turned in; she had nothing to report except that during the changing around of the compartments she'd learned that the former General Vilechko had been made a Hero of the Soviet Union for gallantry in Afghanistan, and had then been stripped of his rank and honors following the coup.

I didn't see her again until soon after dawn the next morning, when she came to our compartment bringing tea for us, and the news that one of the passengers in Car Number 9, Nikolai Vladimir Zymyanin, had been found shot dead.

He was lying on his back with his face to the ceiling, and there were powder burns around the blood-filled entry wound in the right temple. Flecks of blackening flesh and splinters of bone were scattered across the floor from the exit wound: the bullet had gone straight through his skull. The gun also was on the floor, not far from the open drain, a short-barreled heavy-caliber revolver, perhaps army surplus.

"He shouldn't be in here," one of the security officers said to Galina. He was looking at me. We were in the lavatory for Car Number 9, and the security people had got the *provodniks* to rig up a makeshift curtain of sheets around the door to give them more room and keep people out; there was a piece torn from a cardboard box pinned onto one of the sheets with instructions chalked on it: *Out of order. Use lavatory in Car Number 8 or 10.*

"He is an important journalist," Galina told the officer, "from Moscow. He is known for his crime reports in all the papers." They were young, the security officers, and her tone was perfectly pitched: she spoke not as someone in uniform with responsibilities on this train but as a stern and implacable mother, the ultimate authority.

I squatted down, and the reek of the disinfectant burned inside my nostrils. I was looking for signs of torture on the face and hands and wrists, burn marks, the red pinpoint of a needle puncture anywhere. It had been set up as a suicide, but that wasn't in character, and Zymyanin had been left-handed and the entry wound was in the right temple. What I needed to know was whether he'd been put under pressure, very great pressure, to talk before they shot him, and whether to expect the same kind of thing if in fact they'd broken him and he'd blown my cover. But there weren't any marks, and the conjunctivae of the eyes that stared at the ceiling showed no damage.

I made notes, for the look of things—Jane had put a shorthand pad into the briefing bag—but I didn't ask any questions. Now that I'd seen what I'd come here to see I wanted to slip back into low profile and disassociate myself from the dead man.

I thanked Galina and pushed the curtain aside and started back along the corridors. The snowstorm had moved south, and a wintry sun was hanging above the pines on the east horizon like a Chinese lantern.

He'd died scared, Zymyanin. The Bucharest thing had shaken him, and more than he'd shown, though he'd shown a little: there'd been a note of panic in his voice when we'd been talking about Hornby's fatal incompetence—*And what guarantee have I got that I can trust you? How do I know how competent you are? How do I know you haven't brought half a dozen opposition hit men onto this* fucking *train because of your incompetence?*

That hadn't happened. I'd been totally clean when I came aboard the *Rossiya* in Moscow; there'd been no one surveilling me on the night flight, no one tracking me from the airport when I'd got into Jane's car: I'd made absolutely certain of that, had *needed* to make absolutely certain, because if the shadow executive for *Meridian* had landed for briefing in Moscow with even the smell of the *Longshot* thing on his shoes we would have gone into the mission compromised and endangered at the outset.

I hadn't brought any opposition hit men onto the train, but Zymyanin had. He must have done. I hadn't contaminated him, but he could have contaminated me in his last hours. Not his fault: *That is all I can tell you for the moment. When I've got something more, I'll contact you. In the meantime, keep your distance.* I would slip Galina another hundred rubles when I saw her again, tell her to play down the fact that I'd wanted to view the body. It had been a risk I'd had to take, a calculated risk; there'd been no choice.

I sat down to some eggs in the dining car when the first calls for breakfast came; I wasn't hungry but wanted to take in protein. There was only one topic of conversation among the other passengers, and they spoke in low voices.

"You mean he'd been lying there all night long?"

"But surely someone would have heard the shot!"

"Poor man, and we were all sleeping peacefully. I don't think I can manage any more, Julia, do you mind if I leave you here?"

I went back to my compartment soon after eight o'clock and found Boris Slavsky with sheets of writing paper laid out on his bunk like cards in a game of patience. He looked up at me, his eyes wide behind the thick lenses.

"What have they found out?"

He meant the security people.

"Nothing, as far as I know." I hadn't told him I'd been to look at the body.

"They still think it was suicide?"

"I don't know. I haven't asked them."

He went back to his papers. He was a professor of biology, he'd told me, at the Academy of Sciences in Akademgorodok, south of Novosibirsk.

Just before ten an announcement was made over the public address system. *This is the chief of security. We shall be stopping briefly in half an hour from now, at thirty minutes past ten o'clock. Nobody will be permitted to leave the train, and passengers are instructed to keep away from the doors. I will repeat: no passengers will be permitted to leave the train.*

I was reminded again that if anything went wrong with the mission, if I needed continued freedom of movement to keep it on track and make progress, I might be forced to do it in the confines of these narrow corridors, and might find that I had walked into a trap. The only way out of it, even if I could reach an unattended door, was across the limitless wastes of Siberia.

"There'll be a full inquiry," Slavsky said, "I imagine."

"Yes," I said.

In twenty minutes the huge momentum of the *Rossiya* began dying, and the beaker of water on the small collapsible table slid gradually toward the edge. A distant scream came from the locomotive ahead of us, and the steel couplings began banging as the tension came off.

"Would this be a town?" I asked Slavsky. He'd said he did this trip three times a year.

"Yes"—looking up from his papers—"a small one. There are several between Tyumen and Novosibirsk."

Small buildings swung past the windows, many of them with their blue or green paint faded and peeling away. We heard geese raising a clatter, and the faint shout of a farmer's boy. Inside the train, people were crowding along the corridors, staring through the snow-encrusted windows.

We will repeat our previous announcement. No one will be permitted to leave the train when it comes to a stop. Passengers must keep the doors clear.

Boris Slavsky was shuffling his papers into some sort of order and stuffing them into his big leather case. "I hope this inquiry won't hold us up," he said. "They've got a little dinner party planned for tonight in Novosibirsk." He trailed off with a modest mumble—"Celebrating my homecoming."

"How nice for you," I said.

There wouldn't be any celebrating in London tonight if I could send a signal through from Novosibirsk when the *Rossiya* made its stop. The board for *Meridian* would be looking bleak under the floodlights: *Russian contact deceased. Opposition hit suspected. Executive assumed in hazard.*

That would depend—the hazard thing—on whether any serious notice had been taken of the fact that I'd talked to Zymyanin not long before he was killed. It would also depend on whether the opposition had in fact struck some kind of spurious deal with Zymyanin—perhaps for his life—and had got him to talk before they killed him. And finally it would depend on how well or otherwise my cover would stand up to a homicide investigation.

"I have two grandchildren," Slavsky said. He was perched on the edge of his bunk and looking up at me with his eyes magnified by their glasses.

"You don't look old enough," I said.

"Thank you." He looked down, modestly.

I'd begun to find Boris Slavsky rather charming, and it would have been nice to talk to him some more between here and Novosibirsk.

I didn't think that was going to be possible.

The couplings out there raised a whole peal of bells as the carriages started shunting, and I braced myself against the bulkhead as the train came to a halt. I got a towel and cleared a hole in the fogged glass of the window and saw two police cars standing in the snow beyond the rustic platform, their colored lights revolving. Dark figures moved about; I couldn't tell whether they were in uniform.

A generator began running and hydraulic pipes hissed. The people lining the windows of the corridors were talking, their tones quietly excited, reminding me of a murmuration of starlings along a telephone wire. Then there was a tramp of boots on the platform and voices sounded, some of them from inside the train; then finally a door was slammed shut.

"Are they the police?" Slavsky asked.

"Yes," I said.

It was 2:14 when a *provodnik* put his head into our compartment, a man, not Galina.

"Shokin, Viktor?"

"Yes." I got up. I'd been looking at one of Slavsky's books, at a colored illustration of the nervous system of the *Drosophila melanogaster*, while I was mentally going through the details of my cover.

I followed the *provodnik* along to the dining car. The corridors were almost empty: there'd been repeated announcements asking passengers to keep to their compartments unless it was essential to leave them. The *Rossiya* had taken on a different atmosphere since we'd stopped at the small town, something like that of a ship running into trouble in midocean.

We were now halfway from the town to Novosibirsk,

and moving into the half-light of darkening skies. It was said there was another snowstorm, a big one, hanging over central Siberia.

The tables had all been cleared in the dining car except for their white linen cloths, some of them still stained. The smell of sour cooking seeped in from the galley.

"You are Shokin, Viktor Sergei?"

"Yes."

There were something like twenty uniformed policemen dispersed among the tables, sitting in the booths opposite the passengers with big yellow notepads between them. Some of the train's security guards were protecting the exits.

"Sit down, please. I am Chief Investigator Gromov."

A man in his fifties, thick-bodied and square-faced, a black mole near the side of his nose, his eyes bland and patient as he studied me. He'd left his greatcoat on, despite the steamy heat in here.

I sat down.

A *chief* investigator. This table was at the end of the dining car, the one where the major interest was centered, perhaps. They'd been sifting through probably two or three hundred passengers since they'd come aboard, and hadn't even reached Car Number 9, two along from my own.

I'd been specially selected.

"Do you know what has happened on the train?"

"Yes," I said.

"Tell us what has happened, please."

Two other investigators were at the table, one sitting beside me and the other opposite. The one opposite was quite different from his chief: lean and pale-faced with colorless eyes, a thin line for a mouth, a sharp nose bone. He was also much younger, would have come up fast through the ranks, to be sitting here with the chief of homicide investigation.

"A dead man was found," I said, "early this morning."

"Was it an accident?"

His eyes were a nutty brown, the chief's, with gold lights

in them; they could be the eyes of your favorite uncle, the one who always brought you things when you were a whippersnapper and he came to visit. But sometimes, as he watched me, the eyes of Gromov deadened, and the light in them went out, and that was when I felt worried, because he was slipping a mask over them.

"There are a lot of rumors," I told him. "Some say he committed suicide; others say he was murdered."

"And which do you think is the truth?"

"You're asking me to choose between rumors?"

He picked up a pen, a cheap red ballpoint with a tuft of frayed string on it; perhaps he'd pulled it away from something. He began making notes on the big yellow pad, not all the time, just now and then as I went on giving him the answers to his questions as best I could. He talked to me as if this were the first time I'd heard of any incident on the train, and I understood why: he wanted to see if I knew something that none of the other passengers did, and hoped I'd let it out unintentionally.

"Did you see this man Zymyanin when he was alive?"

I'd already told him I'd asked Galina to let me see the body and make some notes, and he'd thought it not unreasonable for a diligent journalist to do that.

"I saw him a couple of times," I said, "along the corridors. His carriage was two away from mine—or that's what I assume, since he was found in Car Number Nine."

"Did you ever speak to him?"

"Once."

Gromov looked up from his pad.

"Oh?"

"I think he was—"

"Where was this?"

"In Car Number Seven. I think he was waiting to go into the lavatory there, because someone came out while we were talking."

"What were you talking about?"

I told him Zymyanin had asked me what I thought of

the new economic bills they'd just signed in parliament, whether I thought they'd do any good, get any food on the shelves. He kept on circling this incident, Gromov, wanting to know the time when I'd talked to the deceased, what I'd thought of his demeanor—did he seem depressed, anxious about anything?

The other man never took his eyes off me, never made notes. Chief Investigator Gromov made quite a lot, covering half the first sheet of his notepad. Then he switched to a different subject, and I didn't know how well or how badly I'd done so far. It hadn't actually been a hurdle, the question of whether I'd ever talked to Zymyanin: several of the cleaning women had seen us together and so had the man who'd come out of the lavatory, one of the generals' bodyguards. I'd had no chance of lying.

"Do you know," Gromov asked me suddenly, "how the body of the deceased was discovered?"

I said no.

"But you saw the body."

He left his patient brown eyes on me.

"That didn't tell me how it had been found."

He looked down again at his notes. I didn't like these little traps he was setting for me, giving me a chance to say yes, the deceased had looked very depressed, possibly suicidal; asking me to choose the truth between rumors. It was quite probable that he'd spent his whole career as an investigator setting little traps, did it in his sleep, because he'd found they sometimes paid off; but he wouldn't have done this with the other passengers—unless they were already suspect.

I was right: this was the table where the action was, where they brought people straight through the line as a matter of doubtful privilege, to be put under intense examination, however patient his eyes, Gromov's, however they reminded you of your favorite uncle's.

I was suspect.

He was saying nothing, waiting for me to volunteer

some kind of information, waiting for my nerves to set little traps for myself on their own.

Wasting his time.

The younger man, the thin one, didn't take his cool pale eyes off me: they were fixed at the edge of my vision field, and if they moved I'd see it happen. I turned my head a little and looked through the misted windows. The world had become black and white out there, with the sky toward the east brooding in darkness and the snow-covered flatlands beneath it catching the last of the daylight. By the rocking of the train I would have said we were running flat out again at something like 150 kph, according to Slavsky's figures.

"You have nothing more to say?"

I looked back at Chief Investigator Gromov.

"I'm here," I said, "to answer questions."

"Of course. Let me tell you, then, Comrade Sho—excuse me—Mr. Shokin, how the body of the deceased was discovered. It might prompt your memory. The—"

"My memory's very good, Chief Investigator. My work demands it."

He inclined his large square head. "I was forgetting," he said. He wasn't. "The deceased was found in a lavatory, as you know. The door was not bolted from the inside, though it was closed. One of the passengers tried to go in there, since the sign was set at VACANT—the bolt being in the withdrawn position—but they found what they described as some kind of obstruction, and assumed that someone was inside and had forgotten to bolt the door and was simply pushing against it to ensure their continued privacy. This happened with three of the passengers, and after a time one of them told a *provodnik* that they thought someone might have passed out in the lavatory. The *provodnik* then used his weight against the door and managed to get it halfway open, and saw the deceased lying on the floor. He raised the alarm."

I waited. I was here to answer questions.

The two security guards at the far end of the dining car

stood aside to let one of the passengers leave—a short man, almost round, in a dark coat that hung from him as if someone had thrown a black cloth over a ball. Another passenger was brought in—Tanya Rusakova, no coat, a white heavy-knit polo sweater and black leather skirt, fur-lined boots, a gold chain swinging from her neck, as she slipped into the booth and looked at the investigator there, her eyes guarded.

"Does this suggest anything to you?" Gromov asked me. "The fact that the door had not been bolted from the inside?"

I leaned back, resting one arm on the table, at my ease. "It's still a question of taking your pick, isn't it, Chief Investigator? It could suggest homicide, since nobody could have shot the victim and then bolted the door from the inside when he left. But a suicide wouldn't necessarily have bolted the door either before he shot himself. The kind of evidence you're looking for is quite outside my knowledge, even though I viewed the body."

"And what kind of evidence is that?"

"Circumstantial. The basics. You'll have got it by now, of course: were there fingerprints on the gun that weren't the victim's or was it wiped clean or did it look as if his fingerprints had been impressed on it by someone else? Was the deceased left-handed, according to the measurements you've had taken of the musculature on both arms, since the shot went into the right side of the head? Things like that. Of course I can't give you the answers."

His eyes deadened, the tiny gold lights going out. "And you are not trying to teach me my job, I assume."

He wasn't being stupid; he was trying to get my goat, that was all, start an argument in the hope that I'd trap myself in the heat of the moment.

"You had me brought here to answer questions, Chief Investigator. You asked me what kind of evidence it was that I considered was quite outside my knowledge. That was my answer."

I waited again. It still worried me that he was setting traps, because it looked as if he'd been given some kind of evidence against me and had got me here to pick at my brains until I broke and confessed, and I'd have to watch it, watch every word, every move. I hadn't shot Zymyanin but I'd been seen talking to him and I'd asked to view the body and I couldn't afford—I could not *afford*—to let this man put me in handcuffs and under guard on a charge of suspicion. *Meridian* was running and Hornby had been killed and the Russian contact had been killed and the *only* lead I had would be taken away from me if Gromov took away my freedom.

"Your answers are appreciated," he said in a moment, and looked at his assistant, the thin man, and back to me. "You speak well, Viktor Shokin. You answer questions . . . adroitly."

I let that one go.

The thin man got up and left the table, his thigh catching the corner and sending Chief Investigator Gromov's red ballpoint rolling across his notepad. He picked it up and wrote three more lines, his large head tilted as he watched the thin spidery script forming along the lines on the pad. Then he looked up at me again.

"There are two witnesses," he said slowly, "who have given evidence concerning you, Viktor Shokin, that I find significant. They—" Then he broke off as his assistant came back, bringing two people with him: the generals' bodyguard who'd come out of the lavatory when I'd been talking to Zymyanin, and Galina Ludmila Makovetskaya, the redheaded *provodnik*. "This man," the chief investigator said, "claims that when he came out of the lavatory in Car Number Seven yesterday he saw you talking to the deceased, as you have admitted. But he says that your voices were raised, and that you seemed to be threatening him. What have you to say to that?"

I looked up into the face of the witness, saw no expression, a nondescript face, the eyes giving nothing away, as I would have expected of a former Red Army general's bodyguard, possibly a former member of the GRU, trained to keep his thoughts out of his eyes.

I looked down again. "He's lying," I told Gromov.

The large head tilted a degree. "He also claims that shortly before midnight last night he heard what he thought was a shot coming from somewhere in Car Number Nine, and that he saw you in the corridor there, hurrying away from the lavatory. What have you to say?"

"He's lying. You should check his story, Chief Investigator. You should check it very carefully."

Gromov dropped the red ballpoint onto his notepad and swung his heavy head up to look at Galina. "This *provodnik* has also stated that she saw you in Car Number Nine—which is not where your compartment is—immediately after she heard what sounded like a shot." He looked down at me. "What have you to say?"

I felt a vibration on the air, created by the nerves, I suppose, as I heard in my mind the bang of the trap shutting.

"She's lying," I told Gromov. "They're both lying."

"Perhaps," he said. "Perhaps. But until I have satisfied myself of that, I am placing you under arrest, Viktor Sergei Shokin, on a charge of suspected homicide."

The officer beside me nudged my arm and I made a token of protest as would be expected of me and then let him put the handcuffs on and snap them shut.

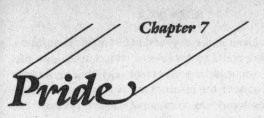

Chapter 7

Pride

"**W**hat was the town back there? Where the train stopped?"

"If you talk," the officer said, "you may incriminate yourself."

His name was Konarev: that was what Chief Investigator Gromov had called him. He was my guard, and he had the key to my handcuffs; it was on the bunch dangling from his polished black belt. His gun was in its holster; I couldn't see whether it had a safety catch. He was in his thirties, his leathery face still pocked with the ancient scars of adolescent acne; he'd sliced his chin this morning, or perhaps yesterday morning, with his razor. His eyes were hard, so hard that they had surely never softened even when he met his first love, or his last love, or his wife, whatever. If the question ever arose of his having to shoot, he would shoot to kill.

There were two other officers in here; they were sitting on one of the benches going through sheafs of paper, the first statements made by the passengers, conceivably. Two security guards were in the corridor, both wearing holstered guns. The train was moving at optimum cruising speed, or close, by the feel of things.

It was 4:17 by my wristwatch, the Kanovia watch that Jane had bought for me, a Russian model. Everywhere else on the *Rossiya* the clocks would be showing seventeen minutes past noon, Moscow time. They would be showing Moscow time when the train rolled into Beijing.

The time wasn't critical but I noted it, because it could

become critical later in the day, and in the night. Everything, in this situation, could be considered critical in the extreme. If there were going to be a chance of regaining my liberty, it would probably be the result of my having noticed something, perhaps something very small. Officer Konarev had a slight cold, for instance, and his reaction time would be a few degrees slower if he had to move quickly.

"Do you live in the town where we stopped?" I asked him, "or in Novosibirsk?"

"If you talk, you may incriminate yourself." He blew his nose again. I appreciated his official consideration, couldn't fault it.

We were in a compartment not far from the locomotive. The bunks had been ripped out and the bulkheads were partially repainted. I think there'd been a fire in here: there were areas of discolored and bubbling paintwork, and the lingering smell of burning. There was no heating; either it had broken down or the cleaning staff had turned it off, wanting to cool down after their labors in the rest of the train, where the heating was tropical. This was a staff carriage, and the banging of buckets and the light cries of the women's voices above the rumbling of the train were a constant background.

I'd put on my padded jacket over the tracksuit. The gloves were in the pockets. There'd been a penknife in one of the tracksuit pockets but they'd taken it away, also the cheap plastic-handled knife that Jane had packed for me in the food bag. The rest of my baggage was in here with me: two officers—one of them Gromov's thin and pale-eyed assistant—had searched it in front of me. A man in a blue coat and trilby hat had come in with a small attaché case and opened it up and taken my fingerprints, giving me a small sealed alcohol swab to clean my fingers with afterward.

I had no alibi.

The sky out there must have had some light left in it to the west, in the track of the train; perhaps the sun had found a hole in the overcast on its way to the horizon; it was leaving a pale unnatural light across the snows that I could see to the north through the window, making them seem like frosted glass faintly lit from beneath. Above them the sky was just as unreal, not quite dark but with no light in it, an awesome shroud across the evening, thrown by the coming of night. It looked inhospitable out there, not a place where one would think of going, of setting out alone, not in the ordinary way; but then of course one must on occasion leave room for the extraordinary, mustn't one, when the devil drives.

No alibi at all.

Slavsky had gazed wide-eyed at Chief Investigator Gromov, a dry nervous hand adjusting his glasses, and said no, he didn't hear me leave our compartment after ten-thirty last night when he'd gone to sleep, leave it or come back to it or leave it again, nothing, he'd heard nothing, he slept soundly, always, and was used to the noise of the train. It wouldn't have mattered much what he'd said, because the general's bodyguard and Galina Ludmila Makovetskaya had both sworn to having seen me near the scene of the homicide and having heard a shot.

I had been outbid. She hadn't had much time for the generals, Galina—*They had power, once. Now they have no power. But they think they have. Their ways are devious.* But they still possessed the power of money, and it had talked, it had said that she'd seen me there last night where the dead passenger was found.

With the generals' bodyguard there'd been no money involved. The *Podpolia* had put Hornby out of the way in Bucharest and they had put Zymyanin out of the way on this train and they had driven me into a trap that I wouldn't get out of, and whatever I said against them, whatever I knew about them, couldn't do them injury: it would be seen as an attempt to clear myself. They'd needed a scapegoat, someone for hanging, to draw attention away from themselves over the shooting of Zymyanin, and one of them had seen me talking to him in the corridor within hours of their killing him, and I had become a suitable candidate.

And Galina was dead wrong. The generals, the clandestine and omnipresent *Podpolia*, had power besides money, immense power in the land. This had been the thrust of Zymyanin's mission—itself clandestine: to attack that power. *I'm also here because there's a cell in Moscow, a completely unacknowledged, unofficial cell whose purpose is to seek, find, and expose the active members of the* Podpolia *wherever they may be.*

"Are you married?" I asked Konarev, my guard. "Have you got children?"

He told me I could incriminate myself.

But they'll usually start talking about their children, give them long enough. Of course he might not have any, or even a wife, could well be devoted exclusively to his police work. I watched the other two for a moment, at work on their papers, and then the noise started, a distant but enormous *whoomph* like a heavy-caliber shell bursting, and then just the rumbling of the train for a second, two seconds, before the big steel couplings began banging and the carriages started shunting and the iron buckets in the cleaners' quarters went wild and I saw Konarev, caught off balance, do a half-turn and hit the wall with his hands going up to save himself as I pitched sideways and crashed into him and he got his gun out very fast and pushed me away while the other two policemen hit the long plate-glass window and bounced off it with their papers whirling upward and then drifting like leaves as the red came, the huge red glare spreading across the snows through the windows of the corridor outside.

The women were screaming, and one of their buckets came rolling past our compartment door as the whole train went on shunting and Konarev and the other two found their feet and I got off the floor with a certain amount of caution because of the gun—he was still holding it on me but with both hands now: I think he'd knocked his head when he'd crashed against the wall and was feeling a bit dizzy, didn't want me to take advantage and try something fancy, but that was out of the question because the *Rossiya* was rolling like a ship in heavy seas and nothing looked certain: it had been doing 150 kilometers an hour before the explosion and there was a fire raging back there, half a dozen carriages away or perhaps closer than that: all I could see was the bright orange glare across the snowfields and its light flickering on the faces of the two security guards in the corridor as they picked themselves up and stared into the compartment with their mouths open.

The floor shifted again under our feet and we landed against the forward bulkhead as the train went on decelerating in massive jerks—obviously the carriage back there had blown up and jumped the rails and pulled the adjacent ones with it, and the locomotive was under the brakes as it dragged the train behind it like an injured snake through the snows. One of the women went staggering past in the corridor with blood running from her face, perhaps in shock and moving instinctively away from the fire.

"*Don't move!*" Konarev shouted above the noise and I noted this too: as well as having the beginnings of a cold he was more nervous than I'd thought, didn't want me to get too close while hell was breaking loose like this. I'd lurched into him, that was all, couldn't help it, and there was nothing I could do in any case—bring the link between the handcuffs down across the gun, yes, but I'd only get shot in the leg when his trigger finger reacted. And he wasn't the only armed man here, there were four others, and he didn't seem to realize I hadn't the slightest chance of getting away.

The train was still shuddering, the carriages shunting as the speed came down more progressively now as small buildings began swinging past the windows, dachas, I think, and a pall of smoke started rolling across the snow with its shadow meeting it. The last time I'd looked at my watch it had shown 4:48 and the city of Novosibirsk would have been a hundred kilometers to the east; I would now put it at something like thirty, perhaps less, and that was why we were running through scattered buildings on the outskirts, though none of them had lights in the windows.

A *lot* of noise as something smashed behind us, closer than the explosion; it sounded like the whole side of a carriage being ripped away, could have turned over, snapped the couplings. The speed was right down now: we were crawling, and smoke began blowing through the corridors. The two police officers went out there and one of them shouted *Oh my God* and they started running aft to help people and the security guards followed them as the shunting got a lot worse for half a minute and then we stopped and Konarev and I hit the bulkhead again and I kept my distance as best I could because he might pull off a shot by mistake: his finger was inside that bloody trigger-guard.

"Don't move!" he said again and I shook my head and stayed exactly where I was, my back to the bulkhead and pain moving in on the nerves now there was time for the organism to pay attention: the left shoulder had taken the worst of the impact when I'd hit the bulkhead the first time. There was an iron bracket sticking out of the wall where the bunk had been ripped away for replacement and I must have torn my thigh on it, because there was blood creeping down my leg, I could feel it, but it didn't worry me because it wouldn't stop me running if I had to, if I *could*, it's the only thing we think about when we're in a trap—if we can get out of it can we run?

People were coming past the doorway now, more security guards and *provodniks*, some of them with blood on their hands or their faces, one with her uniform ripped off at the shoulder. The smoke was thicker along the corridor and a man went past with a handkerchief pressed to his mouth and Konarev looked at me and jerked his gun and said—"*Out!*"

It was very cold.

We were standing, Konarev and I, a hundred yards from the train. He was behind me and had prodded me with his gun as a reminder that in spite of everything that was going on I was still a prisoner under guard.

The security people and the *provodniks* and some of the cleaners were bringing the dead and injured out of the train onto the snow, making a temporary first-aid station while people still inside were pulling sheets and blankets and pillows off the bunks and passing them down to the others. The carriage that had blown up—the twelfth back from the locomotive—was still on fire, and small figures in the distance, black against the snow, were forming a chain brigade with water buckets and waiting until they could get close enough to use them. Smoke still lay in a dark swirling shroud to the north of the train, and above the distant snows the sky hung black and enveloping, part of it rust-red from the glow of the burning carriage.

A kind of silence had moved in now that the train was standing still, and voices carried through the freezing air, mostly those of the rescue crews. The train staff was shouting instructions and information as they herded the passengers across to the comfort station they were setting up—no one was allowed to go back into the train even to fetch their belongings, since it was possible there might be further explosions. A radio message had gone to the army barracks, hospital staffs, and emergency services in Novosibirsk, and medical rescue helicopters were already known to be airborne. There would shortly be enough blankets available from the train to provide warmth for every passenger, and a soup kitchen was being set up.

Something was on my mind.

"Are you injured?" Konarev asked me.

"What?" He was looking down at my fur-lined boot: the blood had reached there now. "No."

When I looked up again and across at the train I realized it was Galina, the large woman I'd been watching as she helped with the rescue work, her back braced to lift the smashed bulkhead that had come down across a passenger's legs while someone pulled him clear; she would be good at that, Galina, the morals of a toad but with a streak of crude humanity in her that was brought out by crisis, but it didn't excuse her, the bitch, I was standing here with these hand-cuffs on because of her odious greed—and I could have raised the bidding if only she'd asked me, given her double what she'd been paid by the generals, wouldn't she like to know *that*?

Something was on my mind and I knew what it was now. The burning carriage was the twelfth one back from the locomotive, and that was where the generals and their bodyguards had been before Galina had moved them, at their request. *I'm relocating them from Car Number Twelve to Car Number Four. They say they're too near one of the lavatories.*

Two *provodniks* were swinging one of the huge copper samovars down from the train, smoke curling from its furnace underneath. Others were bringing wooden trays of cups, following the path of the samovar across to the comfort center, the sweat bright on their faces in the light of the fire.

Children were crying, their voices thin and piping, shreds of sound in the night, their cries torn from them, from their pain.

Would Zymyanin have done this to children?

Oh, yes. He'd been a man with a cause. When you set explosives you know you won't be there when they go off; it gives you the same feeling of remoteness a bomber pilot has when he watches the patchwork streets of the enemy city come into the sights: he too is a man with a cause and the cause is his country and that is enough.

But I didn't think it was Zymyanin. His business had been intelligence, not terrorism or political assassination. It was someone else, and he wouldn't have wanted to take the risk of getting killed if the whole train ran amok, and if he'd been on the train he would have known that the generals had moved out of Car Number 12.

Somebody screamed and went on screaming as part of the wreckage collapsed, and two or three people went over there from the rescue squads but there was too much to do and not enough hands.

"For Christ's sake," I said to Konarev, "can't we make

ourselves useful instead of just standing here? You can leave these things on me."

"No." It was the first time he'd said anything except to warn me that I could incriminate myself if I talked. "Stay where you are."

"Look," I said, "you can *keep* your fucking *gun* on me while I'm working, what more do you want?"

"No."

Bastard.

He was nervous because I was on a capital charge and he'd be entirely responsible if I got away from him; Chief Investigator Gromov and his team were helping with the rescue work: I'd seen two of them carrying a body in a sheet over to the place where they'd set up a morgue—Zymyanin's, possibly.

The screaming went on and I turned my back, it was all I could do, and Konarev told me to stay where I was and I told him to fuck himself and I added that in front of the whole court I was going to let it be known that while people were trapped in that wreckage and dying for the want of help he'd been content just to stand here and do nothing, *nothing,* but he just went back to his broken record, I could incriminate myself, *bastard.*

You could turn your back on the train but there was nowhere you could look where there weren't people injured or in shock or crying or standing with their arms round someone else and trying to comfort them. I'd seen Tanya twice, Tanya Rusakova, she'd been helping one of the stretcher-bearers, and then I'd seen her working with some other passengers, pulling wreckage clear where someone was calling for help.

I hadn't seen the generals.

The Bureau should do everything *to keep them under surveillance,* Zymyanin had said.

Then I would have to do that. Get rid of this bloody *peasant* and look for the generals and keep them in sight wherever they went; it was all Zymyanin had left for me as a focus for the mission. I looked into Konarev's flat square face and saw the nerves in his eyes, listened to that man screaming over there, the one who was trapped.

"Haven't you got any bloody *humanity*?"

It would have been dangerous, I think, if he'd warned me again about incriminating myself, because that would have blown all my fuses and I would have incriminated myself all over the stupid *bastard* and he would have ripped off a shot and that would have brought people running, people in uniform, end of mission, *finis*.

He didn't say anything, watched me with his eyes flickering slightly, worried about me, he should be, I can tell you he bloody well *should* be.

Then people began looking upward as the first flakes of snow came drifting out of the dark belly of the storm. The *Rossiya* had been running into it when the bomb had gone off and the train had come to a halt, but the storm itself was moving westward across the city and into the open steppes, and the snowflakes were big ones, eddying out of the silence of the sky. Then in the distance I saw the faint flashing of strobes as the first helicopters came in low, guided by the glow of the fire where the *Rossiya* was lying crippled.

Gypsies had wandered in from their camp near the town and stood watching the scene, their dogs barking in excitement. Two of the security guards passed us, going to talk to them, possibly to ask if they could bring some of their tents here to give people shelter. Someone was trying to break into one of the darkened dachas, shouldering the door until the lock broke with a bang. They were summer places, shuttered for the long winter season; none of them had lights in the windows.

The strobes glittered in the east, much nearer now and lower still, and the beam of a floodlight came fanning across the scene from the leading helicopter.

People called out to one another, and some of the children waved.

I would have to do something soon now, if I could do

anything at all: time was becoming critical. Investigator Gromov would bring his team away from the train as soon as the reinforcements arrived, and I would again become the center of their attention, and when that happened there'd be nothing I could do, nothing at all.

The chopping of rotors came in and shadows shifted across the scene, swinging as the floodlight turned and the helicopter put down in a whirling flurry of snow. Two more landed—three—and the snow became blinding until the rotors came to a stop.

I could kill Konarev but there was no case for that: it couldn't be justified as self-defense. I could overpower him but there was the risk of his gun going off and if that happened it would bring down *Meridian* in the instant because I wouldn't have any chance left of finding the generals and keeping them under surveillance.

Another helicopter put down near the compound where most of the passengers were huddled against the cold, and the snow whirled upward, blotting them out of sight. Two of the machines were military, with the insignia of the Russian Air Force on their sides; the other two carried a red cross.

Konarev was watching them, and I looked at him, at the angle of his head and the set of his body, left hand hooked into his belt, right hand with the revolver in it, finger inside the trigger guard. There was no safety catch: it was ready to fire. I would have to use both arms together for whatever action I could take because of the handcuffs, and that would make things more difficult, but not impossible. I was just running the whole thing through my mind, that was all: I probably had another few minutes before I actually needed to do something, if the risk was worth it.

I didn't think it was. Gromov and his team were less than a hundred yards away, still working with the rescue parties and close enough to hear a shot. They'd turn and start running across here and they'd be within optimum target range within fifty yards and when they saw me trying to get clear they'd shoot and they'd shoot to kill.

Two more helicopters landed, huge machines with twin rotors, troop carriers, and the dark figures of their crews came running from the haze of snow.

Then I saw the generals, recognizably, moving in a group with their bodyguards away from the train and toward the helicopters. They were thirty or forty yards away, their faces not distinct but the cut of their greatcoats clear enough, and their air of purpose. The three leaders were moving slightly ahead, with their bodyguards holding off on each side; it was almost a miniature parade.

I sensed Konarev, tested his aura, let my nerves pick up his vibrations, but the information I was receiving, fine as gossamer, was simply that he wasn't relaxed, wasn't just standing there. He was ready for me if I made a move.

The generals were talking to one of the military pilots, showing him papers, the snow drifting across their dark coats and settling on them as the edge of the storm reached us. The pilot was looking at the papers, turning them to catch the light from the helicopters that was still flooding the scene.

I didn't need the light. I needed darkness. I needed to be able to get clear of this man Konarev and follow the generals: they were asking the pilot to lift them out with the first of the passengers and the injured, what else would they be asking him?

The gun was six inches from my body, Konarev's gun.

That was too close.

The Bureau should do everything to keep them under surveillance.

Noted. But the pilot was giving the generals their papers back and pointing to one of the helicopters with the air force insignia on its side, then cupping his hands and shouting to one of the crew. Then he turned back and nodded and the generals began moving toward the helicopter, their bodyguards closing in.

There's an edict taught at Norfolk, and even repeated to senior and experienced shadow executives during refresher courses, on the subject of risk-taking in the field. At a crucial phase of any given mission when the executive is tempted to take a risk that would seem likely to place that mission in hazard, he is expected to bear in mind that his life is to be counted more than the mission itself, on the premise that he may well survive to bring future missions to successful completion and recoup the loss.

To strip this edict of its bureaucratic terminology, we are asked to sink our pride and not to act the bloody fool but to get out with a whole skin if we can, and leave the mission to founder. But it's extraordinarily difficult to put into practice, and we argue the toss about it in the Caff and the briefing rooms, quoting from the records, which show that the executives have so far got away with something like fifty percent of the decisions made in hot blood and carried the mission with them, sometimes with a bullet in them somewhere but not where it could incapacitate, sometimes with a flesh wound and blood loss but nothing critical. And the reason why this kind of decision-making is so difficult is nothing to do with the risk itself, nothing to do with its technical configuration or the balance of its calculated profit-and-loss. It's to do with personal pride.

I watched the generals.

They were picking their way across the snow, their bodies leaning forward, their shadows thrown by the floodlights as they neared the air force helicopter. Other passengers, some of the walking wounded, were following them as the pilot beckoned them on.

Chief Investigator Gromov was still working in the vicinity of the train, his officers with him. The man had stopped screaming some time ago: either they'd got him clear of the wreckage or he was unconscious or dead. I watched the injured passengers—one of them Boris Slavsky, blood soaking into the bandage round his head. When eight or nine of them had reached the helicopter I saw the generals and their bodyguards go aboard; then the pilot helped the injured to climb the short iron ladder.

So it wasn't Konarev's gun that was the danger here: it was personal pride.

Above the cabin of the military helicopter the rotor had started turning, and a puff of dark smoke clouded from the exhaust.

The Bureau must do everything . . .

But the Bureau could do nothing. I, the appointed agent of the Bureau in the field, could do nothing. Perhaps I had ten seconds left to deal with Konarev and get across to the helicopter and go aboard if the pilot would take me, but the risk of this man's gun going off and sounding the alarm was too high, and even if I could reach the chopper the bodyguard who'd given false evidence to the police would recognize me and I'd be back in a trap, *finito*.

The rotor was spinning now and the whole machine vanished in a vortex of flying snow and then its strobes lifted and traced an arc across the night sky before they were slowly blotted out by the storm as I stood there watching with my life vouchsafed and my pride in rags as *Meridian* died its death.

Chapter 8

Execution

"*A*djutórium nostrum in nómine Dómini. . . . Qui fecit caelum et terram. . . ."

The priest made the sign of the cross again and moved on to the next body, a nun following him, a thick woolen robe over her habit. A voice sounded faintly from nearby, and she went over there. He's coming, she told them, the father is coming. Other priests were working here, other nuns.

They had arrived in the police vans and the ambulances and on the fire trucks, finding what transport they could. The snowplows had got here first, an hour ago, clearing the cinder roadway alongside the track for the other vehicles to follow. Two bulldozers were working at the wreckage aft of Car Number 12, and a crane was lifting debris from the rails. Someone had cried out as one of the carriages was rolled back onto its wheels, and a doctor went over there, taking a nurse with him: there were still people buried under the wreckage.

The snow was heavy now, driving from the east and covering the length of the *Rossiya* and the passengers still huddled in the compound waiting for transport into Novosibirsk. There were no more helicopters airborne now: two of them had collided soon after takeoff, and one of the snowplows had swung in a half-circle and begun clearing a path for an ambulance.

"*Dóminus vobíscum, et cum spíritu tuo. . . .*"

The priest and the nun moved on.

I was looking for Tanya.

She'd been working on the wreckage of the train with the rescue crews until half an hour ago, and then I'd lost her. But I must find her again, and stay close. Tanya Rusakova had become important, could perhaps offer me a chance in a thousand. That was my thinking.

I went across to the head of the transport line where the trucks were still coming in to evacuate the able-bodied passengers. She hadn't left yet, Tanya: I'd watched every truck as the people had piled onto them. I'd watched from a distance, because Chief Investigator Gromov was there with a cadre of his officers, checking the people too as they clambered across the tailboards, looking for me.

I had a scarf across the lower half of my face; many of us did, it was quite the fashion, because of the bitter cold.

"Where's my mummy?"

"What?" I looked down.

"I can't find my mummy!"

A small, pinched face with tears frozen on it, a look in his eyes beyond desperation. I picked him up. "Don't worry, she's here somewhere." I carried him across to one of the nuns and left him with her and went back to the head of the transport line, watching from a distance.

I had not been gentle, my good friend, with Konarev. He had got my goat, if you remember. I had needed a diversion of some kind, had been waiting for it, waiting with great patience, and then the helicopters had collided and people had started screaming and the snowplow had swung round and throttled up with a roar and I brought the handcuffs down across Konarev's wrist and the gun fired once and missed the target and I smashed my head into his face and fell across him when he went down into the snow and used a sword hand to the carotid artery with enough force to stun and felt for the keys on his belt and tried five of them before I found the right one.

No one was looking in this direction; the only people I could see were half lost behind the dazzling curtain of snow in the floodlights, so I bent over Konarev and brought down a measured hammer fist to the frontal lobes to produce concussion and got him across my shoulders and took him to the ambulance station where they were putting the injured on board, told them it was a head trauma case.

That had been thirty minutes ago and it was then that I'd started to watch the pickup trucks, looking for Tanya, and by now I was beginning to think I'd missed her, but that idea was unthinkable, because of the last possible chance.

Drowning man.

Shuddup.

Clutching at a straw.

Shuddup and leave me alone.

Then I saw Tanya: she must have gone back to the train to find her suitcase; they were helping her swing it aboard the next truck in line. I turned and walked across the area ahead of it where the snow had been packed down by the vehicles coming in, had to watch my step, it was like a bloody ice rink now, they'd have to start breaking it up with a bulldozer. I went fifty yards and saw the truck coming at a crawl, slewing all over the place, and when it was close enough I clambered over the side and they made room for me. I still had the scarf across my face and I don't think Tanya recognized me, didn't want her to; she was at the rear and I faced forward, getting down behind the cab to keep out of the wind as the truck found better terrain and gunned up with the headlights dazzling against the curtain of snow. They hadn't seen me, Gromov and his men, but they'd go on looking for me and when they finally gave up and made for the city they'd fill the streets with militia patrols to help them. And there was the other thing—I didn't know how long it would be before Konarev regained consciousness but when he did he'd let out a big squeal and that wouldn't help, I'd have to be very careful, go to ground if I could, find some kind of a bolt hole.

Ferris wouldn't be waiting for me at the station in Novosibirsk as arranged: he'd have got the news by now and sent off a signal to London: *Reports are that* Rossiya *has crashed. Whereabouts and condition of executive unknown.* He'd look for me in the town wherever the transports were going to drop us off and I'd watch for him too, but I didn't think much of our chances in a crowd this size; we'd have to do it the other way, through Signals, try and set up a rendezvous.

"It was a bomb."

"What?" The scarf was round my ears.

"It was a bomb, back there on the train."

He was a youngish man, but with his face prematurely weathered by the Siberian winters, his eyes squeezed almost shut against the wind of the truck's passage, his nose leaking mucus.

"Was it?" I said.

"No question. I am a linesman. I work on the track. It doesn't take much, you see, at that speed, at a hundred and fifty kilometers an hour, for the wheels to jump the rails. We were lucky it wasn't worse."

"Very lucky," I said.

"Revolutionaries." The truck hit some ice and we grabbed each other as it slid and found some cinders and came straight again with a jerk, people calling out behind us. "They should be shot. If I found out who it was, I would shoot them."

"Yes," I said.

But I didn't think it had been revolutionaries. The target had been Car Number 12, where the former Hero of the Soviet Union, Vilechko, had been earlier, and it could be that the bomb, like the smile, had been for the general.

The city's authorities had commandeered a public gymnasium for the passengers of the *Rossiya*, those who hadn't already been taken to the hospitals, and women were carrying mattresses and blankets inside, unloading them from trucks with the municipal insignia on them: CITY OF NOVOSIBIRSK. The transports just in from the scene of the train disaster were dropping people off in a small square near the gymnasium, and loudspeakers were announcing the immediate and gratis availability of shelter, bedding, food, and limited washing facilities for those who preferred not to go to a hotel. The loudspeakers were crackling and cutting out altogether a lot of the time, and upwards of five hundred people—the uninjured survivors of the crash—were crowding around the entrance doors, and it looked as if it were going to be hours before there'd be enough bedding in there for them all.

The blizzard had stopped as the storm moved on to the west, but snowplows were in the streets, and emergency vehicles with chains were moving in behind them. Above the buildings the sky was black and the stars glittering. But it was cold: *In winter,* Jane had noted for me, *the night temps can go down to minus thirty degrees, so be prepared for closed streets and frozen plumbing.*

But the main streets in this area were open, their surfaces rough with sand, and the plows were working through the smaller ones, their engines booming among the buildings and their headlights flickering. I was on foot, and had so far made two turns to the right and three to the left: Tanya seemed to know her way and was walking quickly wherever she could, though her suitcase looked cumbersome for her. I could have brought one or both of my bags from the train—Konarev would have allowed that—but there was obviously going to be the need to travel light.

She turned to the right again and I moved faster until I reached the corner: we were now on Ob Prospekt, named after the river that had turned Novosibirsk into a major inland port. Halfway along she crossed over, dropping her suitcase into a snowdrift and heaving it out again. She looked back for the first time since we'd left the square, but I just kept on walking: the distance was adequate and there were other people in the streets: in this time zone, more than three thousand kilometers from Moscow, it was now 9:03, and the lights in most of the hotels were still burning.

The one she was making for was the Hotel Vladekino,

a small three-story red-brick building at the corner of two side streets, and I went past and came back and gave Tanya five minutes to check in and went up the steps.

"The hotel is closed," the woman behind the counter said, and watched me with eyes tired of looking at strangers. The lift was still moaning, and as I got my wallet out I heard it stop. Tanya was known here, had been made welcome. In the stairwell I heard the lift doors opening on one of the floors above.

"You're in the best place, Mother," I said, and put a fifty-ruble note on the counter. "It's cold enough to freeze a brass monkey out there." The Russian translation was less coarse, could be used in talking to a woman.

"Are you from the train?" She eased her bulk out of the worn red velvet-covered chair and came to the counter, folding the note and tucking it away.

"No," I said. I'd used snow to wash the blood off my boot.

"It was blown up. It was terrible. Have you heard?"

"Yes. Terrible."

"People killed," she said, and opened the register. The last entry had been made out for room 32. "You must fill in the form," she said, and I picked up the pen tied to a big brass paperweight on the counter. "And I must see your papers. You are from Moscow?"

"Yes."

"You have the accent." I couldn't tell from her tone whether it was a compliment or a reproach.

"Is there a phone in the room?" I asked her.

"There are no telephones in the rooms." A distinct reproach this time, as if I'd said I needed to contact a call girl.

I completed the registration form and she pushed my papers back across the counter. "Where do I phone from, Mother?"

"In the corner there." She copied my name into her book and put down the room number: 35. It was too close for safe surveillance work because Tanya would recognize me if she saw me, but I didn't ask the woman to give me a different room because it would bring questions and I didn't want that: she'd be one of the people in this town who'd be asked by the police if they knew anything of a man named Shokin, Viktor Sergei, perhaps a few minutes from now, a few hours from now, certainly by the morning. I'd taken the lesser risk, using my cover identity rather than alert her at the outset by saying I'd lost my papers.

"Where is your baggage?"

"They're still looking for it at the airport."

I'd seen three jetliners lowering across the city since I'd left the *Rossiya*, and two taking off, so they'd managed to keep at least one of the runways clear in spite of the snow; they must be used to it, had got things worked out.

"I need to make a phone call," I said, "to London, in the United Kingdom."

Her eyes widened. "To where?"

I told her again. "I'm a journalist, as you know." It was on my papers. "I want to file my story on the train disaster— I've heard there were some British passengers on the *Rossiya*."

In a moment: "You speak English?"

"A little."

It was another shocking breach of security but there was no option: I had to phone London and I had to do it from here because if I went to another hotel to put the call through I'd miss Tanya if she left here, wouldn't know where she'd gone, and she was the *only* chance I'd got of putting *Meridian* back on the board in London, and even then I couldn't do it without a safe house and a director in the field and they were here for me somewhere, Ferris was in this city, or should be, let's hope to God, let us hope, my good friend, to God.

"What number is it?" the woman asked me.

I wrote it down for her on the curling sheaf of old registration forms she used for a notepad. There was no risk this time: the number was protected, untraceable.

"It will take time," the woman said. "It's long distance."

I put another fifty rubles on the counter and said, "Tell them it's urgent, Mother, give them some of your tongue, you know how to ginger things up. This is a *news* story and I could be the first with it in London."

She watched me with her eyebrows raised and her faded blue eyes wide open; she'd got a face like a withered apple, round and red and wrinkled, but she wasn't your favorite aunt, any more than Chief Investigator Gromov was your favorite uncle: her eyes had the stare of studied innocence, and she could recognize a golden goose when she saw one.

"I'll do my best," she said, and lumbered across the creaking floorboards to the telephone in the corner, where a dead plant dangled from a chipped earthenware pot.

Through the glass entrance doors I saw a militia patrol car bumping across the ruts in the frozen snow, but it didn't stop, not this one, not this time; I had a few more minutes, a few more hours, before one of those patrols would stop and they'd come in here with snow on their boots and ask to see the register.

"It is urgent," the woman was saying and not for the first time, "it is *urgent*, I tell you," earning her fifty rubles as best she could while I stood halfway between the telephone and the glass doors, ready to move if one of those cars pulled up outside the hotel and started spilling uniforms.

There was a corridor off the lobby, lit by one glass-shaded lamp in the ceiling, and there were two recesses, one of which would lead to the rear of the hotel: there was no way out of the lobby except that one, the corridor; the stairs and the lift didn't interest me. I would cripple my chances at that moment, inevitably, when the militia came up the steps and opened the glass doors; I would bring them even closer as I got clear of the hotel, by the very act of vanishing. But I'd have no choice, if they came.

"*You are the newspaper?*" the woman was shouting into the phone.

They'd say yes. The switchboard in London will say yes

to anything when a call comes in from overseas, because they know the ferrets in the field can't always use a telephone in privacy and may have to throw them any name or the name of any organization on the spur of the moment. You can ask them if they're Tootsie and they'll say yes and tune in and take it from there, listening between the lines.

"It is the newspaper," my little mother said, and I went across to the telephone and thanked her and stood half-turned so that I could keep the mirror in sight, the huge pock-marked mirror with its gilded plaster frame that gave me a view of the glass doors and even patches of snow in the street below the steps.

"This is Shokin," I said into the telephone.

It smelled of garlic.

"Have you got a story for us?"

"Yes, I have story. But shall I tell now, or give to your agent here in Novosibirsk?"

It was a hundred-to-one shot that the woman knew any English, even though she worked in a hotel, and a thousand-to-one shot that she knew it well enough to tell whether I was fluent or only spoke "a little," but you keep to your cover when you can, as a routine exercise.

"You can give it to our agent," the man in Signals told me. I recognized Matthews' voice. "He's at the Hotel Karasevo. Ask for T. K. Trencher."

Ferris.

A snowplow went past the hotel and everything vibrated: the tarnished brass shade of the lamp over the desk, the glass front of the fire-extinguisher cabinet, the chandelier in the ceiling. In the mirror I saw that the woman was watching me.

"Then I will give to agent," I said. "Story is about train crash. The *Rossiya*. Very bad. People dead."

Matthews would be watching the signals board as he spoke to me, and Croder would be standing somewhere close, listening to the low-volume amplifier.

"Including the subject?" Matthews asked me.

"Yes." The subject was Zymyanin, the Russian contact. Dead.

This wasn't the time for details: the chief reason for this call was to find out where Ferris was, my director in the field. I would fill them in later, through him: Zymyanin hadn't died in the train crash; he'd been shot, probably on the orders of the generals.

In a moment: "And how are you?"

"Thank you. Very good. Except arthritis. Cold here."

In the established speech-code vocabulary "arthritis" is a signal to Control that the executive is wanted by the police of the host country. We can run the gamut from arthritis to rheumatism, but rheumatism's not often used, because it means the executive has finished up with his back to a wall somewhere with his escape routes cut off and the opposition forces closing in on him and this is the last signal London is going to get.

"Will you be sending in more stories?" Matthews asked.

I thought it over carefully before I spoke.

"Perhaps. Not sure."

It's in the book at Norfolk: *The executive is required to give as accurate a picture of his situation as he can when threatened with any opposition action, whether it be from the operations of a private cell or the police, intelligence or military forces of the host country.*

Sometimes an apprentice spook will ask for it to be spelled out, and the instructors play it straight: "It just means that if you're in the shit then you've got to tell Control exactly that. We've had cases where the shadow's got himself right up a creek but he'll try and put a bold face on it and tell Signals he hasn't got any problems, and that's just plain bloody stupid—we've lost people that way. If you don't tell Control you're in trouble, how can you expect him to help you get out of it?"

What Matthews had asked me was whether I thought there was any future—"more stories"—for *Meridian*, since my Soviet contact was dead and the militia were hunting for me, and I'd had to give some thought to his question because if I lost track of Tanya Rusakova, no, I didn't think there'd be any future for the mission. I would have reached a dead end and the only thing left for me to do would be to try getting out of Siberia through the militia net and report back to London.

It all centered on Tanya: she was the key.

"But there is chance," I said into the telephone. "There is perhaps chance of more stories."

"All right," Matthews said. "In the meantime, is there anything we can do for you?"

"No. You have agent here. That is good."

We shut down the signal and the concierge looked up at the clock that hung at an angle on the wall.

"Five minutes," she said, and came heavily across to the telephone, her massive bunch of keys jingling where they hung from her waist against her black silk dress. The call had been much less than that but I wasn't going to argue: the more I let her pluck the golden goose the more value I'd have for her. It occurred to me that there could even be a price we could put on her silence, on her passive cooperation when the militia came banging in here with their boots scattering snow: a thousand rubles? I had that much in cash and Ferris would have more available, five thousand, possibly ten. But she'd have to make an alteration to the register and they'd be looking for things like that, and in any case this woman, my apple-faced little mother with the faded blue eyes, could take the money and still expose me to the militia without even blinking. Galina Ludmila Makovetskaya wouldn't be the only Jezebel in Siberia.

"Five minutes," I nodded, and left her asking the operator the rate for the United Kingdom. I pushed the worn brass button for the lift, and heard it begin whining inside the shaft.

Novosibirsk is a modern city but it sprang up around older buildings, and the Hotel Vladekino had fanlights above the doors of the rooms. Three of them were showing a light as I walked down the corridor on the third floor; one of these was room 32. When I used the big deadbolt key in the door of room 35 it turned with a lot of noise, but the door hinges didn't squeak when I went inside, and that was much more important. The single window overlooked the street where the hotel had its entrance; a truck was bouncing over the ruts, its tailboard banging, and a militia patrol car was behind it. It didn't stop outside the Vladekino, but it could have. This place was a trap, and I went out of the room and left the door unlocked. The boards squeaked in the corridor but there was nothing I could do about it. The light still showed in room 32 and it was still on when I looked up at the third floor from the bottom of the wrought-iron fire escape that ran down outside the building.

I didn't think Tanya Rusakova would leave her room until morning, but I had to keep her under constant surveillance in case she did. The steps of the fire escape were covered with snow from the storm that had driven across the city tonight, and the small square yard down here was the same, with crates and refuse making humps against the building. There was a light on in the ground floor at the back and I kept clear of it, pulling open the door in the wall of the yard that led to the street. It opened only an inch or two and then the snow blocked it, and I found part of a broken crate on one of the rubbish heaps and worked in silence and with care, checking the light in the window of room 32 at intervals.

When I'd cleared enough snow away from the door to the street I latched it again. This wasn't the street where the hotel had its entrance; it was at right angles, and there were three cars and a truck parked there, offering cover.

I went back to my room and pulled down the blind on the window to keep out the light from the street: I'd left the door an inch ajar, and through the gap, from the bed, I could see the door of room 32 and would hear it open. Tonight I wouldn't be sleeping.

The pipes behind the wall banged and juddered when I turned on the hot water; it ran cold for half a minute and then turned scalding hot. The paper around the small cake of soap was printed in Chinese, and the soap was dark brown and smelled of tallow.

Ten minutes later I was lying on the bed with my back to the wall and my boots off, watching the door across the passage through the gap in my own and slipping into the limitless repertoire of the memory, at first working over the events that had taken place since I'd boarded the *Rossiya* in Moscow, then analyzing them, looking for insights, then taking a break and starting a search through the memory for the stimulus I would need for keeping sleep away.

The pipes banged again behind the walls, and I heard voices from the hotel lobby rising in the stairwell as some people came in. One of them sounded indignant: was my little mother telling them the hotel was closed? I would think so. They weren't the militia, these people. The militia would send a different and distinctive sound through the stairwell, with their boots and their sharp questions, their tone of authority. I would recognize them. I have lain on beds like this one, their springs musical under the slightest movement, their sheets reeking of strong soap or camphor or disinfectant or the stale scents of the human animal in sleep or at play, have lain listening so many times, God knows how many times, for the sounds of my pursuers, the baying of the hunt.

The people below in the lobby went away, a man's voice raised enough for me to understand that first thing in the morning he would be reporting my apple-faced little mother to the Inspectorate of Hotels and Lodging Places. She made no answer that I could hear.

In the room next to mine there was a commercial traveler counting his samples, which were made of glass and had glass lids. I welcomed the sound; it would help to keep me awake, though by midnight the hotel would have fallen quiet, and then would come the need for mental concentration. I was not here to throw away my thousandth chance of keeping *Meridian* alive by going to sleep on the job.

But then she surprised me, Tanya Rusakova, because

when the door of room 32 came open and the light was
turned off I looked at my watch and saw it was still only
10:41, local time. I saw her briefly in the passage as I pulled
my boots on, and when I reached the top of the fire escape
I could hear the moaning of the lift.

The night was still clear, with the galaxy strewn like
gossamer across the tops of the buildings and the moon low
in its third quarter. The air was numbing to the flesh. From
the corner I watched Tanya going down the steps of the hotel
and turning along the street toward me, so that I had to
move back and use one of the parked cars for cover. Then
she passed the end of the street, her gray fur gloves held
against her face and her boots slipping sometimes in the
snow, and I followed.

She was standing in a doorway, her gloves still protecting her face, and it was quite clear that she was waiting
here for someone. It was an intersection of two minor streets,
one of them Kurskaja ulica by the sign below the lamp, and
I had taken up station obliquely across from her in a doorway
much like hers but deeper in shadow.

The night was not quiet. A snowplow was on the move
along the major street that we'd crossed on our way here; I
could see its warning lights reflected in the windows of a
laundry. Trucks were still rumbling, perhaps delayed by the
snowstorm and working late. She was not only waiting here
for someone, Tanya Rusakova, but the rendezvous was clandestine, precisely pinpointed on the map at the intersection
of two minor streets but otherwise without identity or land-
marks: no hotel, no café, no building even with any lights
still burning.

A clock had begun chiming the hour of eleven, its strokes
booming from the gilded dome of a church two streets distant, and as the last note died on the air a Russian Army
staff car turned the corner and pulled up, sliding a little in
the frozen ruts, and Tanya came into the light and walked
across to it as the front passenger door came open.

She looked inside the car, saying something—I could hear her light clear voice—and it seemed she was about to get in, but a figure broke from the shadows and reached the car and snapped the other door open, dragging the driver out and using a vicious stomach blow to soften him up; then he hauled him across the ruts and threw him against the wall and pulled a gun out and took aim. I thought it was Vilechko, the man reeling against the wall, General Vilechko, and he was trying to say something, asking for mercy, I believed, his hands flung out, but the man with the gun was talking to him, not shouting but spitting the words out— *Pig!*—as the first shot went into the general's body and he tried to cover his face with his hands, then something about *my father*—and then *pig!* again, *bastard!* as the next shot banged and blood burst from the general's face and he staggered with his arms flying out as the third shot blew half his head away and his legs buckled and he pitched across the snow.

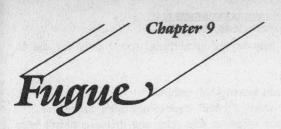

Chapter 9

Fugue

"**T**he airport," I told the driver, and he set his meter going.

Tanya Rusakova sat with her head back against the upholstery and her eyes closed. Her face was so pale that even her lips had no color. One of her legs was straight out in front of her, the fur-lined boot against the back of the driver's seat; the other was bent at the knee. She was sitting sideways a little: I'd noticed it in the dining car on the train.

"Why are we going there?" she asked me, her mouth moving as if it were numbed. I only just heard her: the taxi was running on chains, making a lot of noise as we hit the ruts of piled snow and bounced out again.

"Trust me," I said.

I didn't think she did. I wasn't even sure she understood the danger she was in. When the general pitched down onto the snow she'd turned away and started running, and that was when the militia patrol had swung round the corner, its headlights flooding across her. It hadn't been responding to the scene, couldn't have been, unless they'd been tipped off, given the location of the rendezvous and told that something might happen there. But I doubted that. Even if Vilechko's companions had suspected anything they would only have warned him; they wouldn't have exposed the assignation— he would have killed them for that.

He has a reputation as a lady's man, Galina had told me, Galina Ludmila Makovetskaya, that perfidious *bitch*.

Tanya was saying something, too quietly for me to
make out.

"What?"

"I am not leaving Novosibirsk."

"Don't worry," I said, "we're not flying anywhere."

With our voices at this pitch the driver couldn't hear
anything; in any case I thought I heard him singing to himself, just below the noise of the chains, not a care in the
world; I'd caught a whiff of his breath when we got in.

There were no lights in the mirror, not yet. Two more
patrol cars had passed us going the other way, flying their
colors. I didn't want to think of what our chances were of
getting clear tonight: Chief Investigator Gromov would have
heard by now that I'd made it as far as the city and he would
have concentrated the hunt with the Vladekino hotel as its
epicenter. A second hunt would have been mounted with
its focus on the rendezvous point where General Vilechko
had lain slumped against the wall only three or four blocks
away. I'd told our driver the airport simply because it was a
good hour's run on a night like this and we needed distance,
as much as we could get. I also needed a telephone.

She had run into an alley, Tanya, and I'd intercepted
her at the other end; she'd just been running blindly, not
away from the militia, I thought, but away from the man
lying back there with his face on the ruddled snow, away
from what had suddenly happened in her life; this was my
impression. She'd struggled when I'd held her and tried to
make her understand that she was in the most appalling
danger and that I wanted to help her, help get her away.
She hadn't listened, until I'd told her she had to go with me
for her brother's sake.

She had listened then.

Once, when we were slipping and lurching across the
snow, we'd passed the end of the street where the hotel was,
the Vladekino, and seen three or four militia patrol cars outside with their lights flashing. So one of the crews had gone
into the hotel earlier to look at the register, and seen the

name *Shokin, Viktor Sergei* there, and got on his radio.

The taxi had been outside another hotel, the first in the rank, and Tanya had got in without protest.

The traffic was light at this hour, 11:14 by the clock on the dashboard, but there were snowplows still churning through the streets, and late trucks still running.

Tanya was saying something, and I leaned closer. "I'm sorry?"

"How did you know I have a brother in Novosibirsk?"

"A *provodnik* told me."

"How would a *provodnik* know?"

"They know everything." Galina had telephoned Moscow from the train.

She still hadn't opened her eyes. She was trembling: I'd heard it in her voice. I pushed myself forward on the seat and spoke to the driver.

"Have you got a drop or two of vodka on board?"

He swung his head round with a look of great surprise. "I'd get arrested!"

"Look, we've been freezing to death out there trying to find a taxi, and my wife's starting a cold. Come on, be a hero, ten rubles a shot."

He reached for the glove compartment and fished out a plastic flask from among all the camouflage and passed it to me. I got the cap off and wiped the neck on the end of my scarf, best I could do, and nudged Tanya to get her eyes open.

"No," she said, "I don't want any."

"This is medicinal—you're in shock."

She took the flask in her gloved hands and tossed some of the stuff back and choked on it but I made her have another go; then I gave the flask back to the driver and he put it away.

"There's no more flights tonight," he said. "I suppose you realize that."

"Yes. We work at the airport. We thought we'd have a night on the town and then the car broke down."

In a moment Tanya spoke again. "You said I was in danger. Why?"

The lights changed and we slid to a stop halfway across the intersection, and when we got the green and the chains started thrashing again I moved my head close to Tanya's.

"You're in danger because that militia patrol back there caught you in its headlights and when they found that man lying there they would have started looking for a woman walking alone in the streets, walking or running or trying to hide. Your name is in the registration book at the Hotel Vladekino, where you saw those other militia patrols crowding around outside, and the concierge would have told them you'd left there fifteen minutes before—because they'd have asked her a *lot* of questions and that would have been one of the answers, and by this time they'll have made the connection between the young woman leaving the hotel on foot and the young woman seen running from the scene of a shooting only a few blocks away. You also made a statement to the investigators on the train, and that too will be on record. Did you tell them you've got a brother in Novosibirsk?"

"Yes." Then she saw the problem and said defensively, "I had to. They asked me if I had any relatives, so what else could I say? If you lie to those people they can find out and then you're in trouble."

I didn't say anything.

The driver was singing again, and the sound of his voice against the demented percussion of the snow chains lent eeriness to the night.

"Why are you helping me like this?" Tanya asked me. She hadn't closed her eyes again after drinking the vodka; she was sitting straighter now, watching me, the green shimmer dulled by the shock that was still going through her. But a bit of color had come into her cheeks, and the trembling had stopped.

"Because I need information." There were lights flashing

ahead of us and I watched them. "I need information about General Vilechko and the other two."

In a moment she said, "Is this for a story?"

"A what? No."

"You told me you're a journalist."

A whole circus of militia patrols along there, half a mile away, some kind of roadblock. I didn't tell the driver to take a side street because he'd wonder why, and if anyone along there saw us running for cover they'd send out a patrol to cut us off and ask questions and the only papers I had on me were in the name of Shokin, Viktor Sergei.

"Yes," I told Tanya, "I'm an investigative journalist with political interests."

"I don't know very much," she said, "about the generals."

But enough to want one of them killed. "What was Vilechko talking about," I asked her, "when you had dinner with him on the train?"

"He was telling me," she said with contempt, "about his heroic deeds in the war with Afghanistan."

"Nothing else?"

"No." I heard something in her voice, and when I looked at her I saw she was frightened because of the lights up there.

"Don't worry," I told her, "there's probably been an accident." There were still three stationary patrol cars ahead of us and I leaned forward and got a hundred-ruble note from my wallet and held it out to the driver. "I should have asked you before—this is the smallest I've got, do you have enough change?"

He broke off his singing and turned his head. "Not for a hundred, no."

"Well look, hang on to this and we'll work something out later."

He hesitated, then took the note. "If you say so."

I sat back again. It had been simply routine: we might need him as a friend. "Is that a roadblock up there?"

"Looks like it. They're always cluttering up the streets one way or another, don't give us no peace, we're fair game, see, taxi drivers, when they want to pick on someone."

I felt Tanya's hand on me. "Can't we turn off somewhere?"

"No. It's too late for that."

Her eyes were still frightened, and there was something I'd been trying not to think about: this woman had exposed herself to tremendous risk when she'd set up the general for assassination, but she might have got away with it if my name hadn't been next to hers in the hotel registry. The militia would still be on the watch for the woman they'd seen in the headlights but she might have been able to get back to the hotel and go quietly to bed: the concierge wouldn't have faced a barrage of questions if Viktor Shokin, wanted for murder, hadn't followed Tanya Rusakova to the Vladekino.

They were a quarter of a mile away now, the flashing lights, and the driver began slowing. I leaned forward again and spoke into his ear: "What's your name, my friend?"

"Nikki."

"Listen, Nikki. She's not my wife, as a matter of fact. This is a pickup, and I could get into a lot of trouble, you know what I mean?" He had his head turned to listen, and gave a nod. "So what about just keeping mum, Nikki, if those buggers ask you any questions? I mean forget about our car breaking down and everything—all you know is that we got into this cab and I just asked you to drive us round a little, how does that sound?"

He began slapping the rim of the wheel softly with his gloved hand, and said in a moment, "Nothing about going to the airport?"

"Nothing about that." He was still slowing, his head turned a little but his eyes on the street and the flashing lights. I told him again: "We just got in and I asked you to drive us round a little. Nothing else." He gave it some more thought, but there wasn't time for that. "And you keep the change, Nikki, all right?"

He jerked his head round another inch and then nodded.

"Fair enough."

There were things he still didn't understand, but those were the ones I'd paid for.

"You're a good friend, Nikki," I told him, and sat back again and looked at Tanya, gave her the briefing: "This is the story—yours, mine, and the driver's." I went through it twice and she said she understood.

Then I saw the flashing baton ahead of us and we began sliding across the packed snow as the militiaman directed Nikki into a side street, shouting something about a detour, and I saw a whole mess of telephone posts and wires blocking the street behind him with the snow piled in a massive drift after the storm, and when I looked at Tanya she was sitting with her head back against the upholstery and her eyes closed and tears of relief streaming on her face as we throttled up again and the flickering light from the patrol cars faded against the buildings.

"Can I look at your phone book?"

He was still half asleep, a boy in a rumpled uniform, the collar unbuttoned. I'd woken him when we came into the hotel. It was a mile from the airport, as far as it was safe to go.

I found the number and gave the boy some money and asked him to let me use the phone on his desk. Tanya was sitting in the corner of the foyer watching me, and I wondered what would happen if I turned my back for a moment, whether she'd slip out of the hotel and go her own way even though I'd told her that she was in danger, that I wanted to help her, that she had to stay with me for her brother's sake. She hadn't asked me what I'd meant by that, but she would.

The number wasn't ringing: there was just a click, then silence.

I dialed for an operator.

"This number is private?" she asked me.

"No. It's the Hotel Karasevo."

He's at the Hotel Karasevo, Matthews had told me when I'd phoned London this evening. *Ask for T. K. Trencher.*

Ferris.

There are times when you can get through half a mission, more than that, even the whole thing, without needing to call on your director in the field for help. This wasn't one of them. There was a meter running, like my good friend Nikki's out there in the cab, ticking away the time: it couldn't be long before we opened the wrong door, Tanya and I, turned the wrong corner and ran straight into the militia. We had to get off the streets.

"Did you say the Hotel Karasevo?"

The woman sounded as if I'd woken her up at the switchboard, as I'd woken the boy here: it was past midnight now.

"Yes."

I watched the street through the hotel windows, saw Nikki sitting there in his cab with his head back and his mouth moving, presumably in song. If I could pick up another taxi I'd tell him he was free, that we'd decided to put up here for the night. Fresh horses, break the scent.

"The lines are down," the operator said. "You cannot call the Hotel Karasevo." She sounded pleased.

"Try again," I told her.

Shocked silence, and then—"The *lines* are *down,* didn't you hear me? The snow has brought *down* the *lines* in that area."

"How long has the hotel been cut off? This is Colonel Mashakov, Novosibirsk Militia Headquarters."

There was another silence. "There has been no communication by telephone, Colonel, since seven o'clock this evening. I regret that the Novosibirsk Telecommunications Utility was unable to disperse the snowstorm, Colonel, before it could damage our system. But we shall try harder in the future, in the name of the new *demokratizatsiya!*"

The boy behind the desk had buttoned the collar of his uniform and pushed his fingers through his hair, was watching Tanya from the corner of his eye, seeing a plaything for his manly lusts.

"To your knowledge," I said to the woman on the telephone, "are there men working on the lines?"

She used her silences with skill, measuring them for their effect. "But you may be assured, Colonel, that we have men working on the lines. We do not expect, at the Novosibirsk Telecommunications Utility, the lines to restore themselves unaided to their former efficiency."

I put the phone down and spoke to the boy in uniform, tearing him from his licentious dreams. "Can I get a taxi from here?"

It took him a moment to work up interest in anything so mundane. "It's late," he said, "but I can try."

I put a twenty-ruble note on the desk and went over to Tanya. I couldn't tell what it was she had in her eyes as she looked up at me from the black vinyl settee: nothing I could read as trust. Those tears in the taxi had been of more than relief, I thought now; a few might even have been for the general: from the little I'd learned about her I didn't think she'd been involved in an assassination before, or even seen a man killed. She'd stopped trembling, but mentally she could still be in shock.

"There are militia patrols out in strength tonight," I told her quietly, "as you know. If they come in here, and there's time, you simply leave the foyer, take that passage over there. If there's no time to do that, don't come near me: I'm a total stranger." I heard the boy talking on the phone behind me; it sounded as if he'd managed to find a taxi. "That goes," I told Tanya, "for whenever we're in an open space like this. Keep your distance from me if you see any militia. How are you feeling?"

She didn't seem to know what I meant. It hadn't been a stupid question: she was feeling terrible, of course, but I wanted an answer of some kind, whatever kind, to find out at least something of what was going on in her mind.

In a moment she asked me in a dead tone, "Do you ever have nightmares?"

"All the time."

"That is how I am feeling."

The boy called from the desk—"I can get you a taxi. You want one?"

"When can he get here?"

"Five minutes."

"Yes, I want him."

The boy was watching the cab outside, Nikki's, as he spoke on the phone, the obvious question in his mind: we already had a taxi, so why did we want another one? It was the sort of thing he'd remember, but there was nothing I could do about it: we were going to leave a trail, Tanya and I, wherever we went tonight until I could raise Ferris and tell him we needed shelter.

It was tempting of course to go there, to the Hotel Karasevo, and call him from the foyer and tell him to get us off the streets. But unless your director in the field actually asks you to visit him at his base you can't go there, because you can never be certain you're not being surveilled, that you might not be leading the opposition or the host country's police or intelligence agents to your director's base, and that base is sacrosanct. The DIF can only run you from a position of total impregnability: he is the anchorman, the signals center, your only link with London and with the support in the field. Expose your DIF to the opposition and you'll cut your lifeline, and even if you can manage to limp home from the wreckage of a crashed mission you'd be advised not to do that, because if you've blown your DIF they'll flay you alive at the Bureau before they throw you into the street.

"He's on his way," the boy called from the desk, and I went outside and told Nikki we'd decided to stay here for the night and wouldn't need him anymore. He made a token gesture of getting me what change he had, but I sent him away.

Tanya had got up from the settee when I went in again, and was standing with her back to the boy at the desk. "I want to phone my brother," she said in an undertone.

I took her across to the far corner of the foyer. "For his sake you've got to remember that for the moment you're a danger to him. How long had you planned to stay in Novosibirsk?"

"Only for a few days. I have to get back to my job."

The lights of a vehicle swung across the windows. "When had you planned to see your brother next?"

"He just said when the smoke had cleared."

She spoke as if she were drugged, or disinterested. Sooner or later she was going to break: there was too much going on inside her and she was keeping it under too much control. The vehicle stopped outside the hotel: I could hear the tire chains grinding under locked wheels as it slid to a halt.

"There's your taxi," the boy called from the desk. "You were lucky to get it."

I gave Tanya my arm as we went down the steps, the ice crackling under our boots. She held my arm lightly, without trust, still afraid of me, of what I could do to her, do to her brother, because I was a witness to what had happened tonight.

"You are safer with me," I told her carefully, "than with anyone else in the city." It wasn't saying much, God alone knew, but it was still true, for what it was worth.

She didn't answer, glanced at me as we got into the taxi, that was all, didn't believe me.

It was a diesel, this one, shaking and rattling across the ruts and the patches of ice, the driver working hard to keep the thing more or less straight. I'd given him the name of a hotel I'd seen on the way here, the Great Siberian, a redbrick hulk with no lights in the windows, only a sign hanging above the doors with its capital S missing, almost certainly closed at this hour, possibly derelict, it didn't make any difference, there was nowhere we could stay tonight until I could raise Ferris, nowhere in this whole bloody city. Taking these cabs were bad enough: they'd be canvassing every driver all through the night, giving them my name and the description they'd have got from Chief Investigator Gromov, also advising that I might be with a woman companion, one Tanya Rusakova. I didn't think our good friend Nikki would hold his peace because I'd been generous to him; it had been worth trying, that was all.

"It's closed for the night," our driver said. "I suppose you know that?"

The big wrought-iron S was hanging from a railing; I suppose someone had picked it up and put it there, wonder it hadn't brained them. I looked at the meter and paid him. "I know the concierge," I said. "He's my brother-in-law."

Chips of ice flew against our legs as he gunned the engine, spinning the wheels until they found traction; the night reeked of diesel gas. I got Tanya to hold on to me for a while as we started walking, partly to persuade her that I was all right to touch, to trust; but she let go as we turned a corner and the wind came against us, and walked with her gloves against her face. The sky was black, the star fields strewn across it, the three-quarter moon casting stark shadows across the snow. The air was freezing.

She didn't ask me where we were going. She didn't speak.

There were snowplows still working, their din filling the night between the buildings, the drifts breaking into waves as the huge blades bit into them. We passed three abandoned cars and a truck, one of them skewed against a wall with its windows shattered and a fender torn away. Sometimes a taxi went by, but there was no other traffic until a militia patrol car swung out of an intersection in the distance and I pulled Tanya into a doorway before its lights reached us. It was there, after the patrol had gone past us without slowing, that she finally broke, and I stood holding her as the sobbing began, her body shaking with it, her tears streaming, jeweling the fur collar of her coat in the moonlight, all the fear and the misery and the loneliness coming out of her over the minutes until at last the force of her anguish broke through the protective shell of my reserves and reached the heart.

Chapter 12

Chapter 10

Phantoms

"*O*ur father was shot."

A siren had started up in the distance.

"Keep that door *shut!*" one of the women shouted from behind the admissions desk, and a thin boy in a tattered white coat went hurrying past the line of people and there was a slam that echoed around the dog-kennel-green walls, and another flake of paint floated to the floor, spinning like a leaf in the glare of the big tungsten lamps.

A young peasant woman came through the doors, holding a baby wrapped in a red shawl, only its face visible.

It was hot in here, airless. We'd been freezing out there in the streets only minutes ago; now we were baking. Tanya had taken off her sheepskin coat but still couldn't sit up straight on the bare wooden bench; she'd walked with her arms crossed in front of her on our way here, gathered into herself, and I'd thought it was against the cold, but now I realized it was to protect herself against the phantoms of the past that still came after her.

"He was taken to an underground room," she said, "and executed without trial."

Her father.

"Why?"

"For his ideals."

I listened to the siren. People were still coming in, and the thin boy—an orderly—was standing by the big entrance door, slamming it shut after them. A man went reeling to the end of the line, blood caked at the side of his head, the neck of a bottle sticking out of his pocket. The woman with the baby kept her distance from him; the baby's face was pinched, colorless, a wax doll's face; its mother's was haunted, her hollowed eyes looking from the child to the women at the admissions desk as she thought about going straight past all the other people because this was urgent, her baby was ill.

"When was this?" I asked Tanya.

"Four years ago."

"Four."

"You needn't think," she said with a look at me, "that everything like that stopped when Gorbachev took over. Even now there are secret executions. The worst of the Stalinists and hard-liners have been sacked from the KGB, but they've gone underground, and there are still scores to settle." She made an effort to sit up straight, pulling the hem of her white polo sweater down, leaning her head against the wall. "It's always like that, when a new regime takes over."

The siren was loud now, and lights colored the windows.

"You're talking about the *Podpolia*?"

She looked at me again. "Yes."

I'd seen intelligence reports going through the fax machines in London for a year now, since the days of the coup. The *Podpolia*—the new underground—was thought to have thousands of members, possibly tens of thousands, a lot of them still in office, going through the motions of embracing democracy and being reinstated. "Who the hell knows how many there are?" I'd heard Croder saying as he watched the signals coming in. "How can you count the heads in the cellars on foreign soil?"

"Was General Vilechko in the *Podpolia*?" I asked Tanya.

"Yes."

"But that isn't why your—why he was killed tonight."

"No. It was because he'd ordered our father shot. They were *his* orders." She straightened her right leg, spread her hands across her thighs, looking down at them, and a shudder went through her. "I thought it was going to . . . to liberate me, seeing him die, helping to make it happen. I thought the act of *revenge* would give me relief—I *wanted* to see it happen: my brother told me that all he wanted me to do was identify that man, make sure there wouldn't be any mistake, and then run away. But I wanted to stay there, and when the shots began I felt—I felt just a flash of the most bitter satisfaction, but then when I went on watching—" She broke off and squeezed her eyes shut and her body began shaking again.

"It was your father you saw."

Her head came lower and she clawed suddenly at her thighs—"Yes—*yes*—it was my father I saw. . . . "

A door banged open somewhere and the thin young orderly went scurrying past the line of people and into the corridor; the engine of the ambulance throbbed for a minute and then stopped, and I saw two men go past the doorway with a stretcher, a third holding a drip feed above it. I didn't know whether the hospital was normally as busy as this at two o'clock in the morning or whether the storm had brought accidents in the streets; it was too far north to take in people from the wreck of the *Rossiya*. I'd seen the lighted windsock of the helipad on the roof of this building when we'd passed the Hotel Siberian, and noted it; a hospital was about the only place that could give us shelter.

"What is your brother's name?" I asked Tanya. She didn't hear, was watching the man against the wall with the bullets going into him, her father, understanding for the first time that he was not only dead but had died, and like that.

The woman with the baby had made up her mind and gone to the admissions desk, and a couple of youths in black leather coats were chivying her, one with an arm in a sling; then some women began going after the youths in support of the mother, and I caught a glimpse of the waxen face of the child in the midst of the scuffle, its closed eyelids calm, as if it hadn't the strength to squeeze them tight against the light and the voices.

"Then my mother died," I heard Tanya saying. I didn't think it mattered to her if I were listening or not; she needed to say these things, hear them again for herself. "She drank cleaning fluid, a year ago, a year ago this month, on the fourteenth. They couldn't save her; she didn't want them to."

"It had been a long marriage," I said.

She turned her head, I think surprised to hear that I was listening. "They'd been together thirty-nine years when my father was killed."

"And she missed him too much."

"We all missed him too much," Tanya said, "or my brother couldn't have done what he did tonight. And nor could I. He—"

"What is your brother's name?" I asked her again.

She hesitated. "Vadim."

"You can trust me with *everything*," I said. "For your own sake, and for his, you *have* to understand that."

She stared at me for a moment and then looked down. "I want you to know that he is not the kind of man who . . . who kills other men without thinking about it. When—"

"As a soldier, he hasn't seen action?"

She didn't look at me but her mouth tightened: was there *nothing* I didn't know? "He was in Afghanistan, yes. But he has never taken a life in peacetime. It was a very . . . emotional thing for us, very impulsive." She swung her head to look at me. "Vadim heard that that man was coming here to Novosibirsk, where he is stationed, and he wrote to me asking if I wanted to help him, and I said yes, of *course* I said yes. It was only afterward, tonight, when I realized what we had done. I—"

"You destroyed a brute," I said, "and not only for yourselves. Your father wasn't the only one to suffer for his ideals, he couldn't have been, you know that. You did a great job, and so did Vadim. You're to be honored."

She watched me for a moment, and for the first time, I thought, there was no dislike, no distrust in the lambent green eyes. "I can't think of it like that," she said.

"I know, but you've got to try."

I got up and went across to the pay phone, telling her not to move. There'd been a man there for the past ten minutes trying to get through to someone, wanting to tell them where he was.

"There are lines down," he told me as he came away from the phone, "lines down everywhere."

But I put two kopeks into the slot and dialed the Hotel Karasevo for the third time since we'd got here, and stood waiting, looking across at the young woman in the fur hat and the white polo sweater, one leg straight and the other bent a little, her head down as she went over it all again, giving herself no peace, and I knew I'd have to let her see her brother Vadim as soon as it was possible, as soon as it was safe, because only he could do anything for her, help her battle the phantoms.

I checked the environment again: main doors, an archway behind the admissions desk—forget that one—the archway into the passage where I'd seen the stretcher case go by, the opening of the corridor six feet from the bench where Tanya was sitting now. They were the only exits; the huge windows were high in the wall with their catches rusted solid.

There was nothing but a faint crackling on the line and I pushed the coin return and went back to the bench. We had, with luck, until daylight before I would need to do something dramatic to get us both off the streets without Ferris's help if I still couldn't raise him; the three matrons at the admissions desk had their hands full and no one was likely to come across here and ask any questions. There were some other people along the walls, two or three of them lying on the benches trying to sleep until they could get some kind of attention, one of them a drunk spread-eagled on the worn linoleum with a bottle of blackish wine locked in the crook of his arm.

We were safe here but I didn't want to wait for daylight, to do anything dramatic, not with Tanya Rusakova in my care. Drama is the last resort when you're in the labyrinths, the desperate *sauve qui peut* that nine times out of ten will leave you dead on the field, *And above all*, I've told the bright-eyed and eager novitiates at Norfolk, *above all avoid drama*, *it's a one-way street and as often as not a dead end. Derring-do won't get you anywhere, you've got to* think *your way out.*

Easily said, yes, but what else can you tell them? When they're out there at last with the hags of hell at their heels they'll do whatever they have to, we all know that.

"Are you hungry?" I asked Tanya.

"No."

Her stomach was empty—the last time she'd eaten must have been on the *Rossiya*—but she couldn't even think about food, and that was understandable.

"You could sleep," I said, "if you wanted to." She'd have our coats for a mattress on the bench. "I'll be here."

"No."

That too was understandable; the phantoms of the delta waves would be worse than the ones who were haunting her now, and she'd have no control over them.

"You told me I had to go with you," she said after a moment, "for my brother's sake. I don't know what that means."

"It means that if you get arrested by the militia you'll give him away."

Her eyes flayed me. "I would never do that."

"Have you ever been questioned by the militia?"

She hesitated. "No."

But she knew what I was talking about. "By the KGB, then?"

"Yes."

"What did they do to you?"

She took a breath, looking down. "They beat me up."

"Because of your father?"

"Yes. I protested in public, after they'd shot him."

"Then you know what I mean, Tanya. The militia are no different, even now. They'll get *everything* out of you, once they start, and *that* is why you have to stay with me."

She didn't answer, still didn't believe she would give her brother away, even though she was sitting here with one leg straight and the other crooked and had scars on her body, must have, after what they'd done to her.

The big entrance door came open at intervals and I watched the people coming in, some of them injured and with blood visible on them, most of them sickly, shielding their eyes against the glare of the lights in here. Two doctors, one of them a woman, had come through the archway from the emergency unit where the ambulance had driven up, and were checking the people in the long straggling line. At three o'clock I tried the phone again and drew a blank, and soon after that I saw the woman doctor examining the white-faced infant at last and heard her say to the nurses behind the admissions desk, "But how long has she been here? This baby is dead."

The mother screamed once, twice, and then began moaning as they hurried her through the archway and a murmur of shock broke out among the people in the line.

I began trying the phone at thirty-minute intervals, but at half past four there was still nothing on the line to the Hotel Karasevo but a faint crackling and I thought *Jesus* I'd better start trying to raise London, see if the long-distance lines were down too.

Soon after five in the morning I pushed the two kopeks into the slot again and drew a blank and went through the archway to look for a lavatory and when I came back the entrance doors were both wide open and the place was full of militiamen and Tanya was gone.

Chapter 11

Sleep

"We're waiting for Dr. Kalugin," I said.

I'd passed a door with his name on it.

"He'll be another hour," the nurse said, "at least another hour, with all these accidents coming in." Her hair had come loose from her white cap and her eyes were red-rimmed from fatigue.

"Never mind," I said, "we'll wait."

"Olga!" a voice called, and she left us, saying we could go into the examination room if we liked.

There was no one in there. I left the door open, needing to hear distant voices, catch what they were saying, learn who they were and if they were coming closer, get out of here if there were time.

"What were they doing in there?" I asked Tanya. The militia.

She leaned her hip against the examination table, folding her arms, hugging herself, locked in with other thoughts. "I'm not sure," she said. "I didn't stay long enough to hear; but I think there'd been a bus accident and they'd followed the injured in there to take statements."

"Don't worry, then." I'd unnerved her, telling her they'd force her to expose her brother if she were arrested; but I'd had to do it because it was true, and if the worst happened she'd never forgive herself. It had also given her a healthy fear of a militia uniform: she'd followed the instructions I'd given her earlier out there in the waiting room: *if even one of*

*them comes in here, go down that corridor and wait for me at the
other end. Get out of his sight.*

There'd been five or six of them when I'd come back
into the waiting room, peaked caps, greatcoats and black
polished boots, belts, nightsticks, holsters and guns, five or
six in the waiting room and hundreds more outside in the
streets, right across the city, a minefield on the move.

I switched off the tubular lights to lower the stress on
our nerves by a degree. "It wouldn't hurt," I told Tanya, "to
lie down for a while."

"No. Anything can happen." She was watching my face,
listening to the voices of the militiamen at the far end of the
corridor, to the unmistakable tone of authority. Then she
surprised me: "Wasn't it terrible, about the baby?"

"What? Yes. Terrible."

I went to look for a telephone and found one near the
emergency rooms and got out my two kopeks again and
dialed and stood waiting, the sharpness of ether on the air
and the ring of a scalpel in a metal dish, the moaning of
someone in pain and then a click on the line and a woman's
voice and I asked to speak to T. K. Trencher.

In a moment, "Yes?"

"Executive."

"What can I do for you?"

"Get me off the streets."

His name was Roach and he was a small man with a
round pink face and baby-blue eyes that never looked at you
or at anything for more than a second or two, his attention
constantly on the move and his hands never still, their short
pink fingers playing with each other, the nails ragged and
bitten, a mass of nerves I would have thought and not therefore reliable, but Ferris had told me he was first class—he'd
worked with him before, in Moscow.

"More blankets in the cupboard there," he said, "if you
need them. The usual toilet things but not much soap—I
didn't know you were coming"—his eyes taking Tanya in

again but fleetingly, just a quick snapshot, nothing personal—"lots of tinned stuff in the kitchen, though, you'll be all right for grub. There's no heating or light because of the storm, no hot water, but if you feel like braving the shower turn it on slow or it'll blow you out of the bathroom. Anything else?"

"I don't think so."

"I'll be on my way."

I went into the passage with him and saw the door to the fire escape near the stair head and tried the handle to make sure it wasn't locked; then I went down the stairs with him and asked him where the nearest telephone was.

"It's in the building, the end of that corridor. You got enough coins?"

"Let me have what you can."

"I'm being picked up," Roach said, "so you can use my car, dark green Ford Escort out there." He gave me the license number and dropped the keys into my hand. "You want to debrief?"

"Yes."

"He said you probably would. Make a rendezvous?"

A woman in a bright red headscarf came out of one of the apartments and went through the main entrance, shouldering the spring door open.

"Yes," I told Roach. "For twelve o'clock." I needed sleep.

"That's in, what"—he checked his watch—"six hours' time, okay? How far d'you want it from here?"

"Make it a couple of miles."

He stood bouncing gently on his toes, tapping the tips of his middle fingers together as he stared through a window. "Okay, make it at Perovski Street and Volnaja, southwest corner—there's a pull-in for deliveries. You got a map?"

"Yes."

"He'll be in a black Peugeot, front offside fender bent in a bit—he'll lead the way, all right? Twelve o'clock."

We synchronized watches and I went back upstairs and

heard Tanya in the bathroom, the water running, and got out the map and checked the rendezvous point and folded the map again and put it away as she came into the room. She'd taken off her coat and boots and looked slender in her sweater and black leather skirt, would have seemed younger if it hadn't been for the fatigue in her face, the ravages of the long night's ordeal.

"Sleep," I said.

She didn't move, stood watching me. There was a narrow vinyl-covered settee with a soiled cushion on it against the wall, and I got the spare blankets from the cupboard and caught a whiff of camphor and thought briefly of Jane in Moscow and dropped them onto the settee, went over to the window and pulled the heavy velour curtains across to shut out the leaden sky.

"Turn off the light when you want to," I told Tanya. "I shan't need it."

I went into the bathroom and picked over the toilet things. The toothbrush had a wooden handle and real bristles and the plastic cups were in a bag from the Hotel Mokba and the soap was a dirty yellow, the same color as the stuff I'd seen the women washing the floors with on the *Rossiya*. The water was numbing and the copper shower head, rimed white with calcium, gave a kick when I turned on the tap, as Roach had warned; the blood from my thigh pooled rust-red, diluted, on the chipped ceramic tiles.

The light was off when I came back into the room and in the gloom I saw that Tanya was lying on the bed with her legs drawn up in the fetal position, hadn't felt able to get between the sheets with a stranger here, so I took the spare blankets off the settee and laid them over her.

Her head moved. "You'll be cold," she said.

"I'll be all right."

"No. You must share the blankets with me."

So I lay down with her back curved against me and eased my arms around her and felt her shivering; then after a while the warmth came into us and the shivering stopped, but later I felt her hands giving sudden little jerks as sleep came to her at last and she was dragged out of my reach and beyond my help into the first of the nightmares that would be lying in wait for her in the years to come.

Chapter 12

Debriefing

"Christ, what is it?"

I meant the smell.

"A dead dog," Ferris said, "probably."

Another rat dropped from the shelf onto the piled garbage; they were coming in through a hole in the wall, a gap in the boards. The garbage had been dumped in here from trucks, I would imagine, half-filled the place, it was a warehouse, though not quite that, too small, a bloody shed, then.

"Things don't look terribly good," I said.

It was gone noon. I'd left Tanya sleeping.

"They're not," Ferris said.

I'd meant that things couldn't be terribly good if this was the best he could do for a rendezvous, and he'd known that. He was squatting on a broken crate, thinning straw-colored hair and a pale face and amber eyes behind a pair of almost square-lensed academic-looking glasses, thin, bony, trussed in a surplus Red Army coat with the insignia torn off, you saw a lot of them now, he would like to be thought of, Ferris, as some kind of university professor, and that's more or less what he looks like, and you'd never believe he's got a reputation for strangling mice in the evening when there's nothing worth seeing at the Globe.

He was sitting there with his hands dug into the pockets of the coat, watching one of the rats. He wished he'd got a brick in his hand so that he could let fly with it and splash one of those little buggers all over the wall, and I knew this because I knew Ferris.

I found another crate and perched on it.

"It was meant for the markets," he said, "all this stuff, but it was already rotten when it finally arrived from the farms, so sayeth the sleeper who's in charge of this place; his adopted name is Vladimir Tchaikovsky, born in Birmingham, a real tease, but totally reliable. When a dog gets in here to stuff itself on the garbage the rats form a pack and stuff themselves on the dog, food chain thing. How much sleep," he asked me with a swing of his head, "have you been getting?"

"I've just had five or six hours."

"Ready for duty, then. Where is the woman?"

"At the safe house. Why aren't things terribly good?"

Ferris has what looks like the hint of a cynical smile on his pale face, the eyelids a fraction squeezed and the mouth a fraction compressed; I've never known whether it's just the set of his expression or whether there's a continual peal of hellish laughter going on inside his head as he surveys the human condition.

"Because Novosibirsk," he said, "has become a distinctly hot zone in the past few weeks. DI6 is here in force, working with local agents-in-place, and so is the CIA. All the government offices are under covert surveillance by plainclothes peeps and as soon as I got here I shut down the only two safe houses we had because they were no longer safe. Yours was established only two days ago, but as far as we know you can rely on it, at least for a while. As far as we *know*."

One of the rats screamed as they fought among themselves. The only light in here came from a square of cracked glass set high in the wall. When I'd got here the noon sky had been a dirty gray sheet, the wintry sun staining it with sulfur as smoke drifted upward from the docks and factories.

"Should I move the woman?" I asked Ferris.

He looked at me with that stillness of his that can be unnerving. "I've got surveillance on the place, of course."

"What the hell's the good of *surveillance*, if the militia

roll up in a bloody jeep and go in there?"

He waited until the slight echoes died, giving me time to listen to them and realize that I'd just thrown him a *lot* of information. "How valuable to you," he asked gently, "is Tanya Rusakova?"

I said it slowly for him. "She is the key to *Meridian*."

His narrow head tilted. "You mean that, of course?"

I didn't answer. He knew I meant it; he was just absorbing the information.

"Then we must try," he said in a moment, "to find her somewhere a bit safer. But I need to know things first. Debrief?"

"All right," I said, and got off the crate, moving around to keep the circulation going: it was freezing in this bloody place, in the whole of Novosibirsk, the whole of Siberia. I took it from Bucharest and he didn't interrupt because he would already have been called in on the debriefing of Turner, the director in the field for *Longshot*. Then I began filling him in on Zymyanin.

"He was tracking two former Red Army generals." I gave him their names. "They were with a former KGB general on the train. I'd say they had him shot, just as they had Hornby put away in Bucharest. They—"

"Zymyanin didn't set the bomb?"

"He couldn't have. He was out for information."

"The bomb was meant for the generals?"

"Yes."

"Why didn't it kill them?"

I told him. I told him why the generals' aides had set me up for the killing of Zymyanin: because I'd been seen talking to him.

"That was enough?" Ferris asked me.

"The whole cell's very professional, and their security's first class."

"They're in the *Podpolia*?"

"Zymyanin said so."

Ferris hadn't moved, was still perched on the edge of

the broken crate. I don't think he needs to keep his circulation going in the cold; I think he's cold-blooded. He said, "Who placed the bomb?"

"I don't know. But I think there's a rogue agent in the field."

He looked up sharply. "Oh?"

"The bomb could have been set and timed when the train was in Moscow, or anywhere along the line where it stopped. But I've been sensing an agent on the loose."

Ferris didn't ask me what I meant: he knew what I meant. There's a very great deal of tension in the air when a mission's running and you're close to the opposition, and your senses pick up things they'd normally miss, the shadows and the whispers and the faintest of scents in the labyrinth, the echoes and the wraiths of things gone by, warning of things to come.

"You sensed him on the train?" Ferris asked me.

"No, after the crash. I saw a man taking a lot of trouble to get past the checkpoint they'd set up and into one of the transports, just as I was doing."

This bloody smell was getting on my nerves. That dog must have been killed days ago. We support things like bad smells or too much noise with less tolerance, don't we, when the nerves are touchy, and mine were like that now because in any given mission the presence of a rogue agent in the field can burden our operations with the need to find out who he is and what he's doing, whether he's dangerous. It can sometimes crash the whole thing for us if he thinks we're getting in his way and manages to put a bullet into the shadow executive's back. They're difficult to see, those people, difficult to catch, because they haven't got a cell running them—hence the name we give them, "rogue"—and they flit from one sector to another like a bloody bat in the dark.

"So he must have been," Ferris said, "on the train. You just didn't sense him there."

He got off the crate and walked about—minced, almost,

taking tiny steps, head down and hands behind his back, your archetypical professor on the lecture platform. It had got him worried, this rogue-agent thing.

I said yes, he must have been one of the passengers. "I think I saw him later, in the town. He—"

"To recognize?" Ferris swung his head up.

"No. You don't see much of anyone's face in this weather. I think I recognized his walk, the way he moved." I'd seen him on the way to the hotel when I'd been tracking Tanya, but not after that, even though I'd started watching out for him.

In a moment Ferris looked at me and said: "Paranoia?"

It was a legitimate question: paranoia becomes part of your psychological makeup as you go through the missions: you see shadows, hear footsteps. "Possibly," I said. "But the man avoiding the checkpoint out there was real."

"Could have been anyone."

"Yes."

"I think I've got a gap," Ferris said, "in the debriefing. Why did you follow the Rusakova woman to that hotel?"

"I lost track of the generals when they were choppered out, and I thought there was the slightest chance that she'd agreed to meet Vilechko in Novosibirsk. She'd—"

"An assignation?"

"Yes. She'd been having dinner with him, and it looked rather cozy."

"Not a bad shot," Ferris said.

"It didn't pay off. The minute I caught up with him he was dead."

"Then why is Tanya Rusakova still the key?"

"Because she could put me in contact with her brother."

"He could know something about the other two generals?"

"He's in the army, and might have his ear to the ground—"

"Or might be persuaded—"

"Yes."

"You think the generals are here to meet some top brass in the Russian Army?"

"It's possible."

Ferris didn't answer, took a turn and minced for a while with his back to me, didn't want to point out how very thin our chances were of picking up the track again. I went over to the big timber door and found a gap in the boards and stood there with my nose to it, breathing in the sooty smell of the city instead of the sickening stink in this place, freezing my sinuses until my eyes watered, couldn't win.

A rat screamed and my scalp drew tight.

"How long have we got?" I turned away from the door and looked at Ferris. "Have we got any kind of a deadline?"

He stood still, feet together, thinking it out. There was a whole mass of undigested information in his head, culled from the stuff that had been flooding Signals and Codes and Ciphers in London since *Longshot* had crashed in Bucharest and every Bureau sleeper and agent-in-place had been called on to send in whatever they thought was useful. Ferris wouldn't be giving it to me en masse: it would clog my perspective in the field, and the field is *local*, and the executive must concentrate totally on local events. What Ferris would give me, if he decided to give me anything at all, would be a minuscule condensation of the heap of raw intelligence that was burying the analysts in London as the uncut rolls of print came out of the fax machines by the mile.

"Yes," he said at last, "we have a deadline. It's zero."

I listened to the echo of his voice. A zero deadline means just what it says: whatever we have to do will have to be done within every next minute. No leeway, no rest, and no respite.

"The generals were Zymyanin's target," Ferris said, "for information. That's what he told you before he was killed. They arrived here the night before last and two of them have been here all yesterday. We don't know that they might not have already finished what they came here to do. They could be leaving Novosibirsk tomorrow morning."

"Or tonight."

"Or tonight. Or they might be on their way out of the city now."

I waited until I could get some kind of conviction in my voice. "All right, we'll take it from there. I'll try to get Tanya to put me in touch with her brother."

Ferris watched me, didn't answer. We'd worked together half a dozen times and this is the man I always ask for as my director in the field but don't always get; he is the man those bastards at the Bureau offer me when they're trying to con me into a mission that nobody else will take on. I like working with Ferris because he knows how to get inside my head and I know how to get inside his, which is ironical because we both cherish privacy. But we can cut corners, he and I, dispense with the bullshit and the rigmarole and come down to the bone without touching the flesh, and I knew *exactly* what he was thinking as he stood there watching me in that reeking hellhole: he was trying to decide whether to let me go on running with *Meridian*, because the chances of making any progress with it were critically slight and the chances of my getting picked up by the militia before he could fly me out of the city were infinitely strong. Even the safe house he'd put me in was a hazard: you don't normally put surveillance on a place like that, there's no need.

There was something else on his mind, and I knew what that was too. If I had to work with a zero deadline I was going to feel the pressure and take risks.

When he spoke I think it was to break my train of thought.

"How do you feel," he asked carefully, "about Tanya Rusakova? Roach told me she's rather a stunner."

"Guilt," I said. "I feel guilt, chiefly."

"Because you exposed her?"

In the debriefing I'd told him we'd both checked in at the Hotel Vladekino, so he knew our names had been together in the registry.

"Because I bloody well exposed her, *yes*."

My anger against myself was information for him, and I meant it to be. He needed to know my frame of mind because his job was to handle me in the field, nurture and protect me as best he could, and pull me out alive if that were possible, and he would be quite aware that my anger would diminish my instinct for survival by a degree, and the risks I decided to take would be greater.

The obvious had to be put into words to give it weight, to offer me atonement, bring the anger down, lessen the risks. "But of course," Ferris said, "you wouldn't have checked in at that hotel if you'd known Rusakova was spotting the target for an assassin."

"All right," I said, "I would have kept clear, yes, but that isn't in point of fact what happened, is it?"

He paced for a little time and I waited, hoping for more sops for my conscience, but he did better than that. "See if she'll put you into contact with her brother," he said gently, "and then I'll do what I can to fly her out of the city and ask Control to keep her safe in London or in the country. Then you can clear your mind."

He was being too bloody *accommodating*.

"Listen," I said and went up to him, looked into those quiet honey-colored eyes that can conceal his thoughts so well that it seems he's not even thinking at all, that you're looking straight through and into an empty skull. "Are you going to let me go on running?"

Nothing changed, nothing in his eyes, even though I'd just asked him, in effect, whether *Meridian* had quietly crashed, here in this freezing rat-infested hole, because of the debriefing, because of his assessment of it.

He said at last, "That's a good question," and I took it in the stomach.

He turned away and watched a rat fretting with something at the bottom of the garbage, its big tail threshing as it worked; and then I saw what it was working on, the entrails of the dog.

I looked away, looked at Ferris. "For Christ's sake leave those fucking rats alone," I told him, and he turned to look at me with the faint cynical smile touching his mouth.

"Give a lot," he said, "for a brick."

"I know."

He turned his back on the garbage and took two seconds to put the whole thing into shape and said, "The thing is, I can't get you enough support. We—"

"I don't want support. You know—"

"Oh yes," Ferris said, "you do. If I let you go on running you're not going to bitch me about like you do other people. Remember me?"

All right, I'd agree to having support in the field since this man was running me; he knew how to handle things, how to keep them out of my way until I needed them, and how to get them to me in five seconds flat if things got sticky.

I didn't say anything, didn't tell him that. He knew it.

"We can't move too many people into this town because with all the frontier feuds going on across the whole of Eastern Europe there's been a drain on manpower—executives, directors, and support groups. You were lucky to get me for this one."

"You were a bargaining chip, you know that."

He left it. "The thing is, your chances aren't terribly good, are they?"

"Are you talking about timing?"

"Partly."

He meant the zero-deadline thing. "What else?"

"You're being hunted actively by the police and the militia and there's a murder charge on your head. That alone means that you can't even show yourself on the street without very high risk. You've also come close enough to the opposition—the generals—to be recognized by their aides, who in fact engineered that murder charge against you, and if you go closer to them again, which you'll have to if you're to pursue the mission, you'll be up against a group of military professionals, and if—"

"Christ, I've been inside Lubyanka and got out again— remember *me*?"

Ferris tilted his head. "You're very competent, I know. I also know from experience that you possess a pathological fascination for the brink."

"That's my problem."

He took it up, instantly: "I agree." He gave it the weight of silence, then: "Apart from the Russian police and militia and the generals' aides, you have a rogue agent in the field, if you're right about that—and I suspect you are. And a rogue agent, difficult to track and difficult to trap, can be more dangerous to you than all those other adversaries put to- gether." A beat. "You know this."

I didn't say anything. It was perfectly true: he wasn't telling me anything I didn't know. He was just telling me things I didn't want to know.

Ferris waited, then gave the slightest shrug. "To make contact with Captain Rusakov," he said, "without even being able to show yourself on the street is I think close to impos- sible, without the extreme risk of getting caught or trapped or shot out of hand. If you—"

"Look, I can't *work* like that. If I stopped to think of the bloody risks I'd never leave London."

Ferris took a turn and came back. He'd lost the stillness I'd seen in him earlier, and it worried me. For this man to get up and walk about was like anyone else climbing the walls with their teeth.

He sat down on the crate again, and I felt a *frisson*: he'd been reading me.

"Finally," he said, "your target for information—Cap- tain Rusakov—is at risk himself, and he'd also be the subject of a manhunt if his sister got herself arrested and they put her into an interrogation cell. He couldn't go near you and you couldn't go near him, and I would have to get you *both* off the streets."

A wind had got up, a light wind, and it was fretting at a bit of loose corrugated iron on the roof. It would also bring a chill factor across the city, and the air was going to skin us alive out there when we left this place. Extreme cold can work on your system in so many ways, numbing your hands and your thoughts and what's left of your ambitions—but it wasn't the cold, really, that worried me—it was simply that the director in the field for *Meridian* was telling his executive to drop the mission and go home. That was the real chill factor.

I looked at Ferris and asked him: "What are you going to tell London?"

He took his time. "What do you think I should tell them?"

"Say that if you don't keep me running I'll go underground."

I think he drew a deeper breath: his body straightened a degree as the lungs filled. Then he said: "You'd do that to me?"

"I've no choice."

But it had taken some saying. If I broke contact with him and got off the streets and went underground, found a foxhole somewhere and operated from there, they'd give him hell in London. The DIF is totally responsible for the man he's running in the field and if that man breaks off and goes solo it means his director hasn't done his job, hasn't protected him, hasn't kept him on track, hasn't even managed to bring him home.

"If you go underground," Ferris said, "you won't have a chance."

"Then keep me running."

Screaming broke out and slashed at the nerves.

"I'd have to tell London how things stand," Ferris said. "And you know Croder. He'll instruct me to pull you in."

It wouldn't work.

"You'd never find me," I said.

"He'll instruct me to *convince* you that you must break off the mission. You can still be useful to the Bureau. They're not ready to throw you out."

That wouldn't work either.

"Why should they be?"

"You're not easy to control, you know that. They like discipline in the field. This time you could blow your credit."

"That's a bloody shame."

He got off the crate and stood there with the light slanting across his glasses, and I couldn't see his eyes. It didn't matter; they wouldn't have told me anything.

"I want you to report to me," he said, "as often as you can. If I decide to put support into the field I want you to accept it. And I want you to bear in mind that the minute you let yourself fall for the death-or-glory thing I'm going to cut you loose and throw you to the dogs."

"I'll toe the line."

"No," he said, "you won't."

The wind cut between the buildings and blew flotsam across the snow, bits of paper and a milk carton and a plastic bag. I left Roach's Ford Escort on some waste-ground half a block away from the building where the safe house was, and approached it slowly, making a circle. The early-afternoon sky pressed down on the city, leaving the pale orb of the sun sinking toward the west as if through dark water.

Ferris had come with me to the door of the shed, and it had taken both of us to wrench it open on its frozen runners. "As soon as you've made contact with Rusakov, I'll get his sister out of Novosibirsk if it's possible." It was the last thing he'd said to me.

The wind brought the river smell from the east, foul water and coal smoke, tar and diesel gas. The Ob wasn't far from this part of the city, three or four miles; earlier I'd heard an icebreaker working, its engine roaring as the bows thrust and drew back and thrust again.

I moved in closer, completing the circle. Traffic was thin, most of it trucks; no one was walking in the streets: all I'd seen on my way back were a drunken militiaman throwing up in a doorway and a pack of stray dogs lurching from one garbage bin to the next, ravenous and out of luck—it was winter and times were lean.

The peep was standing in a doorway; he'd seen me from a distance and hadn't moved out of shadow, but now he lit a cigarette and in a moment flicked it away, the glowing tip tracing an arc through the lowering light before it hit the snow and went out. I kept walking and crossed the street, stopping when I reached the doorway. *I've got surveillance on the place, of course*, Ferris had told me. The man took a few steps to meet me.

"Everything all right?" I asked him.

"No," he said. "The woman's been arrested."

Chapter 13

Whores

What that man Roach hadn't known when he told me there was a telephone booth in the building was that the cord had been cut by hooligans, and I had to drive two miles before I found a booth that didn't have the glass smashed or the cord cut. I didn't expect to find a directory, took the phone off the hook and dialed Information, the wind fluting through the gap in the door.

"Yes?"

"Military Barracks."

"Which department?"

"Administration."

"Wait."

I waited.

Arrested. Mother of God.

I could look along the street from here, both ways. I'd left the Escort round the corner where I could see its reflection in the window of the Number 3 Dockworkers' Union of Novosibirsk Meeting Rooms.

Someone had carved some crude letters on the tarnished aluminum panel behind the telephone—WHERE IS THE FOOD?—jabbing at the panel, slashing at it with the force of desperation.

"Here is the number," the operator said on the line.

She rang off before I could repeat it or thank her.

I hadn't any one- or two-kopek coins so I used a ten and dialed.

Not at the safe house: she hadn't been arrested at the

safe house, Tanya. She'd left there soon after I had, the peep told me, when I'd gone to meet Ferris at noon. The peep had followed her. He was surveillance, not support: he would have told us where she'd gone—that was his function, and he'd had no instructions to stop her. But she hadn't gone anywhere, hadn't *arrived*.

"She was crossing the street," he'd told me, "down by the bus station, and the militia stopped her and checked her papers—"

"A patrol on foot?"

"Yes. Then he used his walkie-talkie and called a car and they put her inside and that was it. Eleven fifty-one. I got to a phone by 12:03 but the DIF didn't answer."

Because he'd been with me in that stinking shed.

Ten rings, twenty, they were taking their *bloody* time.

This was so very risky.

"Military Barracks."

"I want to speak," I said, "to Captain Vadim Rusakov."

"Wait."

So *very* risky because I couldn't get an introduction to Rusakov now from his sister; I'd be talking to him cold, and when I told him what had happened he could duck out and run for cover in case she broke and talked and exposed him. I wouldn't expect much chivalry from a man who'd talked a woman into spotting the target for him, bringing her right onto the scene of the shooting. Anything could have happened and he must have known that.

The wind gusted through the gap in the door, flapping at an official notice that said vandals would be arrested for damaging the property of the Intercity and International Telephone Service of Novosibirsk, that did not say that accomplices in the assassination of former Red Army generals would also be arrested and would face imprisonment for life, were they going to *answer* this bloody telephone or weren't they?

Steady there.

Yea, verily, but time was of the essence: once they put

Tanya Rusakova under the five-hundred-watt lamp in Militia Headquarters it wouldn't be long before she told them what they wanted to know, before she blew her brother and the safe house and *Meridian*.

I had to make contact with Rusakov before that happened.

"Ordnance Unit Three."

I asked again for Captain Vadim Rusakov.

"Wait."

It was going to be like this until at some hour in the future I would secure *Meridian* and keep it running and find the means of bringing it home, or leave its ashes here in this dark and frozen city and make my way out, with luck, with luck and nothing more, nothing to show them in London.

"Captain Vadim Rusakov is not present."

I cut in fast before she could ring off—"When will he be there? This is a matter of urgency."

"I cannot say."

"Do you know where he is? Is there another number I can try?"

"He is not here."

The line went dead.

I dug another ten-kopek piece out of my pocket, dropping a glove and bending to pick it up, caught my temple on the corner of the metal shelf and felt the freezing draft against my face from the gap in the door, straightened up and pushed the coin into the slot and dialed. It was the last one I could use in a telephone; I'd have to get change as soon as I could.

"Hotel Karasevo."

I asked for *Gospodin* T. K. Trencher.

"Yes?"

Ferris.

"You heard the news?" I asked him.

A brief silence, then: "Tell me."

He would have gone straight back to the hotel after leaving me because he was the signals center for the field,

but it could have taken him longer than I'd taken to reach
the safe house, and the peep hadn't yet made his second
call.

I told Ferris what had happened.

Silence again. Then he asked questions, but all I could
tell him was what the peep had told me.

A militia patrol car had turned out of the intersection
half a mile away and I watched it.

"What are your plans?" Ferris asked me at last.

"I'm trying to contact her brother."

"He could be at risk, yes, before long."

"I'm going to use him, if I can. He's in the military. He
might know where the other two generals are."

It sounded thin, a last desperate chance. It was.

"The safe house could also become hot," Ferris said. He
wasn't impressed with what I'd said about using Rusakov.

"Yes."

The militia patrol car was heading in this direction, going
slowly. But then all the traffic was going slowly because of
the snow and the ice.

"I'll find you a new safe house," Ferris said. "You'll need
somewhere to stay while I make plans to fly you out under
a new cover." He was speaking in a monotone. Tanya Rusakova had been the key to the mission, and he didn't expect
me to rope in her brother as an ally without her introduction.
Rusakov's hands were still red and he'd startle easily.

There was a man walking alone past the dockworkers'
meeting rooms, head down and hurrying, and when the car
was alongside it dipped on its springs and slid to a stop and
a militiaman got out.

"I'm not ready," I told Ferris, "to fly out yet."

"It'll take time," he said. "Your new papers will have
to come in through Moscow. We haven't anyone here who
can do that kind of thing for us."

The militiaman was asking the civilian to show his identity. Novosibirsk was a big city but the militia had thrown a
net right across it in the past twelve hours because Zymyanin

had been shot dead on the train and then the train had been blown up and the man who'd been charged with Zymyanin's death had escaped custody and General Vilechko had been gunned down, and a red alert had gone out to all forces: militia, police, investigative, and the army. It was understandable.

"They're stopping everyone," I told Ferris, "on the—" and broke off because of the click on the line.

"Don't worry," Ferris said. "I've got sniffers out." Line detector, bug detector.

"They're stopping everyone on the street," I said. "Checking identities."

"I know. Where are you?"

"In a phone booth."

In a moment Ferris said, "I've already ordered your new papers. I told Control it was fully urgent."

The civilian was walking on again, tucking his wallet away, and the patrol car had started off, was rolling nearer the phone booth. The glass hadn't misted since I'd come in here, because of the freezing draft. I had my back turned to the street, all I could do.

"Tell London," I said, "that I'm working on Rusakov."

In a moment Ferris said, "If you had the freedom of the streets I'd let you keep things running. But you haven't. You'd have to *trap* that man before he'd even listen to you."

I could hear the tires of the patrol car, ice crackling as it broke the frozen ruts; the smell of the exhaust came into the booth through the gap in the door. The nape of my neck was flushed; I stood as if expecting a bullet there. But of course there was no danger of that. They'd simply heave the door open and ask for my papers and all I'd have time to do would be to whisper *Mayday* into the phone and hang up. Ferris would know what had happened: I'd just told him they were stopping everyone on the street.

Ice crackling outside.

"If I can manage to contact Rusakov," I said into the phone, "I'll tell him his sister's been arrested, and that I'm going to get her out. If he's got any feelings for her, that should make him listen to me."

Ice crackling and tires slipping in the ruts. A shadow was moving across the scarred aluminum panel behind the telephone, not actually a shadow, the soft reflection of the patrol car as it came past the booth. I stood breathing in the exhaust gas.

"Give that to me again," I heard Ferris on the line.

"What?"

"You said something about getting Rusakov's sister out."

"Yes."

The shadow moved across the aluminum panel. The reflection.

"They'll have taken her," Ferris said, "to Militia Headquarters."

"Yes."

Exhaust gas, stronger now, and sickening.

"You're going to get her out of Militia Headquarters?"

"Yes."

Then the shadow moved on and the panel was clear again, and the crackling of the ice grew faint.

The line was quiet. He would tell me, Ferris, that he was pulling me out of the mission. He would instruct me to signal him again at thirty-minute intervals until he'd got a new safe house for me, then he'd tell me to go there and stay there until he had my new papers and a plane lined up. He would make quite sure that I didn't go through with what he called the death-or-glory thing and finish up chained to the wall in Militia Headquarters, a blown executive of the Bureau in London today, a prisoner facing trial in the months ahead, and after five years, ten years, fifteen, a remnant of humanity breaking stones and hauling timber in the far reaches of Siberia, a creature of the permafrost living out its token life until that too was gone, unknown by any.

"We have to meet," Ferris said.

"There isn't time."

The patrol car was fifty yards away now and still rolling, and I pushed the door of the booth open a bit to let the sickening smell of the exhaust gas out.

And then with a soft shock of surprise I heard Ferris saying, "All right, you'll have my full support."

The taxi slid to a stop with a front wheel buried in a drift.

"How far are you going?" the driver asked me through the open window.

"The nearest red-light district."

He hawked and spat. "You want class?"

"No. Just a country girl."

"Get in."

He had pointed ears like a gnome's, and shiny patches of ointment on his face, red raw fingers poking from mittens with the black wool unraveling. A watery blue eye watched me in the rearview mirror. They could all be shut, for all I knew, the brothels; in the early afternoon of a day like this the libidos would be frozen right across the town.

"There's a girl I know," the driver said. "Peasant girl. She's half—you know"—circling a finger against his temple—"but with a body like—" He tried a whistle but couldn't make it, his lips were too dry.

"I'm looking for variety," I said. "What's your name?"

"Mikhail. You could get her for—"

"Mikhail," I said, and passed him fifty. "I want you to stay with me, all right?"

"Keep the meter going?"

The front of the Trabant bounced and we slid off course, grazing a sand bin. "Dead dog," Mikhail said. "They got nothing to eat."

"Keep the meter going," I said, "that's right. Give me some change, will you? I want to make some phone calls on our way."

"You want twos?"

"Ones, twos, fives, whatever you've got."

He raked in his pocket, and the glint of metal came into his hand like scooped minnows. Ahead of us through the windscreen the sky leaned across the street like a fallen roof, heavy with winter. It suited me. I wanted the darkness to come down on the day. We are more used, we the brave and busy ferrets in the field, to the Stygian shades of night than the light of watchful noon.

I phoned the army barracks again at a booth on a corner, asked for Rusakov.

"He is not present."

"There were canned goods meant to be coming in on a freighter," Mikhail said when I got back into the car, "did you know?"

Told him I didn't.

"Salmon," Mikhail said, and hit the brakes as the truck in front of us slewed suddenly and wiped out a snow-covered Volkswagen, leaving it piled against a lamppost with a door burst open and the pink plastic rattle from a baby's carrier rolling on the ice.

"They're always doing that," Mikhail said bitterly. "Truck drivers are the sons of whores." He gunned up and spun the wheels and found traction on some sand and shimmied his way round the truck, which had gone plowing into a snowdrift. "The Office of Foodstuffs and Domestic Supplies announced there was a shipment of salmon coming in on a freighter from Kamen-na-Obi, but there's been no sign of it. They were lying. They're always lying. They too are the sons of whores."

I phoned the army barracks again from a sub-post office, where there was a woman squatting on the steps with her onion-pale face half-buried under shawls, handing out bones as clean as a skeleton's to a pack of dogs.

"He is not present."

In another mile we stopped outside a square sandstone block of apartments with some of the windows already showing warm pink lights behind drawn curtains.

"She is the best, this one," Mikhail told me, and got a

small round tin out of the glove pocket, touching his raddled
face with ointment. "She tells the girls to let the clients take
their time, get their trousers back on properly before they go
down the stairs. Her name is Yelena." He put the little tin
away.

I would *have* to make contact with Rusakov soon. If I
couldn't warn him that Tanya was at Militia Headquarters
they could drop on him at any time if she'd exposed him,
and throw him in there too. I couldn't get both of them out.

You can't get her out, even. You're mad.

Shut up.

I got out of the taxi and went up the hollowed steps of
the building.

You're out of your mind, you know that?

Bloody well *shuddup*.

The place smelled of woodsmoke and vodka and cheap
scent and human sweat; the heat washed against my face,
suffocating after the numbing chill of the streets. I stayed ten
minutes talking to Yelena, a woman with an auburn wig and
blackheads and a cough she couldn't control, but I couldn't
budge her, took it up to three hundred, four hundred, five,
no dice, she'd be scared, she said, and called two of the girls
as I was leaving, told them to show me their breasts. He
looked surprised, Mikhail, when he saw me coming down
the steps so soon.

"None I fancied," I told him, and the rheumy blue eye
in the mirror had puzzlement in it as he drove off again; he'd
always thought a whore was a whore was a whore.

I phoned the barracks again from a dockside bar and
asked for Captain Rusakov.

"He is not present."

She was getting used to me, that woman in uniform at
the switchboard for Ordnance Unit 3, getting tired of me,
couldn't I take no for an answer or what, and as I got back
into the Trabant I felt the onset of premonition and con-
fronted for the first time the fact that it was already too late:
Tanya Rusakova had been broken under the light and had

told them what her brother had done last night, and they'd sent a van with metal grilles at the windows to pick him up, *finis, finito.*

"You want another place?" Mikhail asked me.

"What? Yes. Another place."

I would go through the motions, in the mistaken belief that it wasn't already too late; I would follow this path through the labyrinth as if it could lead me somewhere, until the knowledge came to me from the other-world source beyond the senses that I was wasting my time, performing an exercise in futility.

Running around like a chicken with your head cut off.

Shuddup.

The draft from the open window cut across my face and I sat with my gloved hands covering it as Tanya had done when she'd walked from the Hotel Vladekino to the place of execution last night.

"Can't you shut that window?" I called to Mikhail above the din of the snow chains.

"It's got to stay open," he said over his shoulder. "There's a leak in the exhaust manifold, the gasket's gone, we'd both be found with our toes turned up if I shut the window, be a gas chamber in here." He reached for his little tin again.

She wouldn't hear of it either, Olga, sitting in watch over her gaggle of sluttish girls in the next place we stopped at. I took it to seven hundred and she wavered then, but I didn't press her because she could chicken out when the time came to go through with it and that would be dangerous.

"For God's sake," I told Mikhail, "they're like cows in there."

He shifted into gear with a clashing of cogs. "You said you didn't want class. You get what you pay for, this area. Now I can take you to—"

"I need a phone," I told him.

The sun had lodged among the black frieze of cranes along the dockside, their thorns cutting across its red swollen sac as the dark sky deepened; night would come soon now in the late Siberian afternoon, flooding in from the steppes.

There was a line of booths near a bus stop, one of them with the cord still intact, and the two kopeks rattled into the almost empty coin box.

Mikhail was watching me from the taxi. He'd asked for another fifty rubles to keep the meter going and I'd given it to him. He would be my companion in the coming night, providing me with wheels and shelter and a shut mouth: I'd mentioned to him that the militia seemed busy of late, and he'd said they were always sticking their snotty noses into other people's business, they also were the sons of whores.

She would be frightened, Tanya, as they worked on her at Militia Headquarters. She would be wondering how she could have ignored my warning, would have realized now that I'd meant what I said, that I knew—and should have been trusted to know—more than she did. It couldn't have been easy for her to leave that building and make her desperate run for the nearest telephone that would work, that would bring her the voice of her brother and the comfort she hungered for.

She would be frightened now, under the blinding light. I didn't want to think about that.

"Ordnance Unit Three."

I asked for Captain Rusakov, said it was a matter of urgency.

"Wait."

Mikhail had left his engine running; he'd said the starter dog was worn and that it had let him down twice, he couldn't trust it.

The booth stank of vomit: there'd been a drunk in here. I kept the door cracked open with my boot.

She would be frightened at the thought of what she might say, of what they might make her say, about her brother. Frightened and alone, and God knew how long it would be before I could reach her, if I could reach her at all.

Have you ever been questioned by the militia?

No.

By the KGB, then?

Yes.

What did they do to you?

They beat me up.

Then you know what I mean, Tanya. The militia are no different, even now. They'll get everything out of you, once they start, and that is why you have to stay with me.

The glass panels of the booth were filthy, and one of them had words scrawled on it by an angry finger—*Gorbachev murdered the Motherland.* Beyond it the sun was down, crimsoning the earth's rim as its sac burst at last and spilled its blood across the horizon.

There was so little *time*.

The line clicked.

"Captain Rusakov speaking."

Chapter 14

Lipstick

"**A**re you alone?"

In a moment he said, "I don't understand."

"Are you alone in the room?"

"Yes. Who is this?"

"Your sister has been arrested."

I heard him let out a breath, and then there was another brief silence before he asked me again, "Who is this?" There was caution in his voice now, and an undertone of shock; in the last few seconds his life had lurched.

"Write this down," I told him. "There's a rooming house with a bar at Pier Nine on the river, the west bank. The bar is called Harbor Light. Wait for me there at—"

"Where are they holding her?"

"Listen carefully," I told him. "We've got to cover the important things first, in case we're interrupted." A militia patrol car had crossed the intersection a minute ago, eastward toward the river. "You should know that I am your ally and that I'm going to try getting your sister free tonight. Now I want you to wait for me at a table at the Harbor Light bar at Pier Nine on the west bank of the Ob at eight o'clock this evening. You should—"

"Give me your *name*," he said.

Not too bright, this army man, trained to respect discipline, to have his life run for him on rails, didn't care for anonymous phone calls. But he'd at least had the imagination and the necessary passion to set up an assassination and bring it off, a private enough act, he hadn't done *that* to orders.

Or had he?

The thought came at me like a stray bullet and I filed it. That had been the *second* attempt on the life of General Vilechko.

"Rusakov," I said, "if you waste my time you could wreck our chances of getting your sister free. She'll be under interrogation *now* and may at any moment expose you, under duress, as the assassin of General Gennadi Vilechko. Are you prepared to cooperate with me?"

A huge shape was on the move beyond the filthy window of the booth, and I watched it.

What I didn't want him to do was panic and put the phone down and run for some kind of cover. He would have got the point by now: it didn't need a lot of intelligence. The instant his sister told the militia who had shot Vilechko there'd be a telephone call from the officer commanding Militia Headquarters to the officer commanding the Russian Army garrison with a request that Captain Vadim Rusakov of Ordnance Unit 3 be placed under immediate arrest on suspicion of murder pending the arrival of prisoner transport and an officer bearing information.

If Rusakov ran, I would lose the second key to *Meridian.*

The dark shape moved slowly past the gap between the rooming house and a stevedores' gantry, and its port riding light bloomed like a rose in the river fog. A freighter bringing salmon, perhaps, canned salmon from Kamen-na-Obi in the south for my friend out there in the taxi.

"I am going there now," I heard Rusakov saying.

"Going where?"

"To Militia Headquarters." His tone was strong, adamant. "That's where they must be holding my sister. I will give myself up—"

"Rusakov—"

"I will give myself up and tell them she had nothing to do with it!"

"Rusakov, listen to me. They won't take your word for that. They'll get at the truth and the truth is that she was an accomplice. She—"

"I must help her! She is my sister!"

God give me patience. "If you go there, Rusakov, you will *both* be held for inquiries and by midnight tonight they'll have got the whole thing out of you and there'll be *nothing* I can do for Tanya. You will have condemned her."

I waited.

Emergency numbers, it said on a panel by the phone. *01: Fire Service, 02: Militia, 03: Ambulance. It is not necessary to use coins.*

"Why should I believe you?" Rusakov asked suddenly.

"Why would I call you and warn you to lie low if I didn't want to help you?"

Waited again. Time was running out, would go on running out as the minutes and the hours measured the long night's passing and I did what I could, what I must, before it was too late. I wanted to shout at this man, force him to understand what he'd got to do; but that wouldn't work: I had to appeal to his intelligence.

His voice came again. "Why should you want to help me?"

"It would take too long, Rusakov, to tell you. I'm going to give you a last chance, and remember that the longer they keep Tanya there the worse it's going to be for her, and that I *alone* can hope to get her free. Now write this down." I went over it again, the name and location of the bar and the time of the rendezvous. "Go there in civilian dress," I told him, "not in uniform. You should—"

"I am on duty until midnight."

"Then request immediate compassionate leave: say that you've just heard that your sister was injured in the crash of the *Rossiya* and you must visit her at the hospital immediately. Can you do that?"

"Yes."

"Good. You should put on your oldest clothes: the Har-

bor Light is a seaman's hangout. When I go in there to find
you I shall look for a pair of slightly odd gloves lying on the
table beside you. Now give me your description."

He took a moment to think. "I shall be wearing a—"

"Color of eyes?"

"What? Green."

I took him through it—clean-shaven, height one meter
ninety-two, weight one-sixty, medium build, no visible scars.
I didn't need all that for the rendezvous in the bar but I might
need it later if he didn't show up or panicked and went to
ground or made things tricky for me until he was ready to
trust me.

"All right, you'll be wearing?"

Dark blue duffle coat, dark woolen hat with earmuffs.

"Don't forget the gloves. Now listen, I don't know if I
can make it there by eight o'clock but you must wait and
keep on waiting unless the bar closes—it could be open all
night, with shipping movement going on. Don't leave there
and don't go back to the barracks until I've talked to you."
I took a moment to check his thinking: "Do you know why?"

He found it difficult to say but he got it right. "If . . . if
my sister is made to talk, I would be arrested."

"Right, at the barracks or in the open street or anywhere
you go, but you'll be safe enough at the bar. If it closes, check
in at the rooming house next door and use a false name, give
them some money instead of your identity; there'll be drug
traffic on that river and they'll be used to people wanting
privacy." Then I told him, "If I haven't reached you by midnight either at the bar or the rooming house it'll simply mean
I can't, and you should then consider getting out of Novosibirsk by ship—they'll be watching the airport and the train
stations and the roads."

He thought about that but didn't take long. "I shall remain here and give myself up and try to help my sister."

I heard a warning note and thought of telling him to
shift the deadline to beyond midnight, but left it. If I hadn't
got Tanya free by then it'd be no go.

"When did you see her last?" Rusakov was asking.

"This morning. She was trying to contact you when the militia picked her up." Bite the bullet: "Rusakov . . . How do you think she'd stand up to interrogation?"

I heard him let out a breath again. "She . . . she had a bad time with the KGB, a few years ago. Since then she's been afraid of getting hurt again." He should have thought of that before he got her involved in an assassination. "That is why I tried to keep her out of . . . what happened last night."

"So why couldn't you?"

"She insisted. She's very obstinate. I'd seen his photograph many times but she said that wasn't good enough. She was afraid I would make a mistake." A beat. "She was also very . . . determined that we should go through with this thing."

I thought that was interesting. "Rusakov, do you know why those three men came to Novosibirsk?"

Mikhail shut off the engine of his taxi and silence came in. A tug's klaxon sounded from down the river like a night bird croaking.

"No," Rusakov said, but he'd taken a long time to think about it.

"Do you know where the remaining two of them are?"

Mikhail got out of the Trabant, stood stamping his feet, looking toward the phone booth.

"I think," Rusakov said, "I could find out. There's a lot going on."

I felt a booster kick in for *Meridian*.

"Be there at eight," I told him, "and remember—"

"There must be some way I can help you," Rusakov said quickly. "I'll go with you to Militia Headquarters."

"That would blow up the whole thing."

"You must realize how I feel. I love my sister. I'm not good at waiting, doing nothing, when—"

"Be at the rendezvous."

"If I'm not there," he said, "it will mean I changed my mind," and the line went dead.

"There's only one more," Mikhail said, "in this district. There's always a girl here and there in the bars, of course, if you—"

"Let's go to the last house."

There was another street closed, telephone wires festooned like a spider web across the snowdrifts and the small dark figures of men working on them, trapped like flies, warning flags hanging limp and a flare burning, black smoke standing in a thick column from the oil barrel; the wind had dropped and the night was quiet except for the rumbling of snowplows across the city.

The frayed wool at the wrist of Mikhail's right mitten trembled to the vibration of the Trabant as it rocked across the ruts with the ice popping under the tires.

She's very obstinate, Rusakov had said. *She was also very determined that we should go through with this thing.*

I thought that was interesting because all I'd known of Tanya Rusakova was that she was unskilled in subterfuge— had given General Vilechko, for instance, the name of the hotel where she was staying. Her obstinacy had shown itself perhaps when she'd left the safe house despite my warning, but the same trait, together with her determination, could help to save her now at Militia Headquarters by dragging out the interrogation process until I could move in.

You don't need to go there now. You're wasting your time.

Bloody little organism, starting to panic.

Of course I'm not wasting my time.

You should meet Rusakov now, as soon as you can. He thinks he can find the generals. That's your objective.

Dead wrong: he won't do a thing for me until I can get Tanya out of there.

You're rationalizing.

An icicle as long as a spear dropped from a roof gutter

and crashed onto the roof of a parked car, scattering rainbows in the headlights.

First get Tanya out, then work on her brother.

You should be working on him now. You should have told him to meet you right away. He's the key now, not her.

If I don't get Tanya out he'll try to help her by giving himself up, then I'll lose him and the mission's gone.

You haven't got a chance of going in there and coming out again, you know that.

Scares you, doesn't it?

You're doing what Ferris said you might, it's the death-or-glory thing, go dashing in there like a white knight on horseback and carry the maiden off, you want your fucking head tested.

You're shit-scared, that's all, I know you of old.

Walking into a lion's den, you'll get eaten alive.

Shit-scared.

Bloody little organism.

The tire chains dragged on the snow and the engine idled.

"Name's Marina," Mikhail said, his rheumy eye in the mirror. "Cunning old cow, you should watch it, keep your wallet in sight, know what I mean?"

She was sitting in a huge carved Ottoman chair, a woman with three chins and enormous breasts trapped in a rusty black satin décolletage and hips that bulged across the arms of the chair, four rings on her thick fingers, three dirty diamond solitaires and a black tourmaline, her feet squeezed into splitting patent-leather shoes on the stained Kazakhstan carpet.

"I have the best," she said huskily, "the best in Novo-sibirsk. The youngest."

The heat pressed against my face, sucking the moisture from my eyes and leaving them dry. The smell was the same here as it had been in the other places but with something added, sharp and indefinable, reaching from the lungs into the gut.

"I have Chinese girls," Marina said. "Thirteen, fourteen years old. You should see them. They are like porcelain. I'll show you."

She picked up a brass bell engraved with dragons, and the sound seemed half-muted in the stifling air.

"You can have two in a bed," Marina told me, her small eyes like sparks in the thick folds of her flesh. "Three in a bed, as many as you want. What about a boy? You like variety? Or I have whips here, chains. You like that?"

Perhaps it was stale blood, the sharp iron smell on the air.

I let her go on talking because I wanted to know what my chances were. Mikhail had said this house was the last one in the district and God knew how far we'd have to drive to find the next.

A whore came through the red velvet curtains and stood looking at me, her thick white body wrapped in a soiled nightdress and her coarse dyed hair lying across one shoulder, her lips parted to show the tip of her tongue, her eyes narrowed, fear in them, fear of the gross woman in the chair.

"She can go," I told Marina. "I'm not here for that."

I told her what I was here for.

"You must think I'm crazy," she said.

I started at three hundred, implying I would go to five.

A drunk was in there somewhere and a girl was squealing, and the sound pierced the nerves like chalk on a blackboard.

"How do you expect me to do that?" the woman asked me.

"Say it's your birthday. Come on, you're smarter than I am."

"I would lose my license," she said.

"You haven't got a license. Not for the whips and chains."

She offered me vodka.

"I haven't got long," I said. "One thousand, take it or leave it." I got up to go.

She watched me, still as a toad. "Are you on the run?"

"No."

"You'll have to tell me more about yourself."

"There's nothing to know. One thousand, cash."

"Fifteen hundred. I'll do it for that."

"A thousand's all I have."

I got as far as the door.

"And suppose I get into trouble with this?" she asked me.

"If you don't know how to keep out of trouble, Marina, nobody does."

"Let me see the cash."

She counted it. "All right." Her face began creasing, and a wheeze started coming out of her that almost sounded like laughter. "I would have done it for half," she said, and tears glistened in the folds of flesh.

"I know," I said, "but the other five is to make sure you don't double-cross me." I went close to her and smelled her foul body smell as I looked into the little black slits of her eyes. "If you cross me, you fat stinking bitch, I'll see that you croak, they'll find you sitting in this chair like a stuck pig with your throat cut and your blood running under that door and into the street for the dogs to drink."

I told Mikhail to drive me back to within two city blocks of the safe house and check for a usable phone booth on the way.

Ferris answered at once.

"I've got things set up," I told him.

There was a short silence. He hadn't known, before the phone rang, that I wasn't already in a red sector at Militia Headquarters and desperate for help.

"I haven't told London," he said.

He meant he hadn't told London I was going to try getting Tanya Rusakova out of Militia Headquarters. Control would have wanted to talk to me direct on the phone and I didn't have time for that; he would have said no in any

case, would have gone through the roof and ordered Ferris
to call me in, would have created a strictly monumental
fuss, and I'd started moving too fast now for London to
block my run; of *course* Ferris hadn't told them, he knew
better than that, he was a seasoned director in the field,
and quite possibly the *only* DIF who was in fact capable of
running this particular shadow executive through a mission
without calling on London for instructions, because this
particular shadow executive is difficult to control—as Ferris
himself has said—isn't amenable to discipline, so forth, is
not your most popular ferret in the Bureau, and that is a
bloody shame.

It hadn't surprised me when Ferris said I'd have his full
support. He'd had no choice. He's run me before, and
through some extremely sticky operations—*Mandarin, North-
light*—and he's learned to read what it says on the bottom
line: if I've decided to take a mission into a new direction
with some really significant risks attached I'm not going to
back off if the director gets cold feet, I'm going to do it anyway
and if I can't do it with his support I'll do it solo. Ferris
understands that.

But I felt for him. He wasn't going to get any sleep
tonight, and when I signaled him again he would pick up
before the second ring.

"What's the score?" he asked me now. His tone was
particularly cool, and I heard the control in it.

"I've made contact with Rusakov," I told him, "and
we've got a tentative rendezvous. There's no time to go into
details. Now here it is—I need two support men and two
cars. The first one is to pick up Tanya when she leaves Militia
Headquarters. The second one is to do a relay." To take
Tanya over from the first one and leave a cold trail.

"Timing?" Ferris asked me.

"I'll come to that." I'd have to work it out; it could be
two hours from now, three hours, four, midnight possibly,
even as late as that, it'd depend how things went. "You
should deploy the first car just off the square in front of Militia

Headquarters, out of sight and in a street with a clear run."
I went over the details with him, told him the car should be
parked facing away from the square, told him how I wanted
the relay set up, though it wasn't really necessary to spell it
out: a relay is a relay and it's designed to do one thing—to
throw off pursuit.

"What else?" Ferris asked me.

"That's all. We just need to get Tanya clear and into your
safekeeping."

"Will you be going with her?"

"No. I'll be making my own way out."

In a moment, "When do I send in the support?"

I gave it some thought. "Make it an hour from now. No
later than that."

"Five forty-one."

I checked my watch.

"Yes. I'm synchronized."

Tentatively Ferris said, "You know, don't you, that if
you get stuck in Militia Headquarters there'll be absolutely
nothing I can do."

I translated that in my mind: was I prepared to push the
mission right to the edge at this stage and risk sending it
over? Because the director in the field for *Meridian* would be
put through a rigorous debriefing when he got back to London, and Control would want straight answers. *Yes, I warned
the executive that there'd be nothing I could do for him if he placed
the mission in final hazard.*

"The thing is," I told Ferris, "there are no options. We're
working with a zero deadline and we can't slow up, we've
just got to go for it."

*The executive felt there was no choice but to proceed with the
mission, despite the risks.*

"I'm sure you'll do well," Ferris said, and I didn't like
the polite formality: it showed nerves.

I left it. "Final thing," I said, "I'm going to call the peep
off the safe house. It's going to get blown in any case, sometime before midnight."

He took it cold, didn't ask why. "But you still need a new one."

"Yes. With spare clothes, provisions, the usual thing."

"I've been working on it."

I didn't ask him where it was; I didn't need it yet.

"Then it's over and out," I told him and put the phone back onto the hook.

In the crown of the night sky the stars were huge, fading as they sank into the smog that clouded the city. The snow was brittle under my boots as I finished circling the block and closed in on the safe house.

"You're free to go," I told the man in the doorway. "Report to the DIF by phone."

He was huddled into his coat, his eyes peering from above the scarf he'd wrapped round his head. "No one relieving?"

"No. Go and get some grog."

He left a patch of bare wet concrete in the doorway where he'd cleared the snow with his heels. I walked on and checked the windows of the building and then went in.

The bedclothes were still rumpled and Tanya's bag was gone, but she'd left the toilet things in the bathroom and a message on the mirror scrawled in lipstick.

Thank you. Forgive me. Tanya.

I wiped it off with some toilet paper and flushed it and looked round; there were no other signs that a woman had been here.

The shower head in the bathroom was dripping, rhythmic as the ticking of a clock.

It was time to go.

You're mad, you know that? You've gone mad.

Shuddup.

You'll be walking straight into a trap.

Oh for Christ's sake shuddup and leave me alone.

I took a last look round and left the curtains almost closed and the light on and the door unlocked and went down the stairs and into the street and across to the Ford Escort and started it up, letting the engine warm while I scraped away the ice that had formed on the windscreen. Then I drove three miles east toward the suburbs and left the car on a vacant lot and locked it and had to walk nearly five blocks before I saw a militia patrol car and stopped it and told the driver I was Viktor Shokin, the man they were looking for.

Chapter 15

Violets

"**Y**ou are giving yourself up?"

"No."

The colonel looked at me, his head going down a degree and his eyes remaining on my own. The light wasn't too bad in here; this wasn't an interrogation room, just a holding cell by the look of it, with a small barred window and a steel door with a look-through panel in it. The door wasn't closed; there was still quite a bit of bustle going on out there, militia tramping about, phones ringing; I heard my cover name several times: Viktor Shokin was quite a catch.

"Then why are you here?" the colonel asked me.

He had an intelligent face, unsurprisingly in terms of his rank, and didn't seem to think I was playing the fool when I'd told him I wasn't giving myself up. If he'd thought I was playing the fool he would have given immediate orders to have me beaten into a different frame of mind.

"You've got a woman here," I told him. "Tanya Rusakova. Is that correct?"

He went on watching me while he thought it over. He was a big man, bigger still in his greatcoat, and had the kind of eyes that would be able to watch a war-trained Doberman tearing a fugitive to pieces, for instance, without showing anything except possibly a hint of amusement.

"Yes," he said at last. "That is correct."

"I want her released, Colonel."

I left it at that for the moment. I wanted to feed information into him slowly, so that I could catch and weigh his reactions, because this was the man who was going to decide, at some hour of this long and perilous night, whether he was going to let me walk out of here or hand me over to Homicide Investigation and start the machinery of justice rolling over me.

Someone in the passage outside was asking where Colonel Belyak was, and in a moment a junior officer was standing in the doorway, glancing at me and away again.

"Telephone, Colonel. In your office."

"Who is it?"

"OIC Catering, sir."

"Take a message. Are you monitoring my telephones?"

"Yes, sir."

"Then go on taking messages and don't come to me with anything unless it sounds urgent. Are those not the orders passed on to you?"

"Yes, sir. I'm—"

"Catering is not urgent, you clod. Get out."

Everyone brought themselves up an inch straighter— the junior officer and the two guards at the door and the sergeant who stood behind and to the left of Colonel Belyak. The sergeant was a short square man with a pock-marked corpse-colored face, the eyes lost in hollows, nose broken and jaw skewed. He hadn't spoken since I'd been brought in here ten minutes ago. He watched Colonel Belyak when he asked me questions, and watched me when I answered them. He would be the one, this sergeant, who would be ordered to beat me up if I looked like playing the fool, or refused to give the information the colonel was looking for, or in any way got out of line.

"So you want the woman released." Belyak watched me steadily with the polished black stones in his face.

"Yes."

"Why?"

"Because she's innocent of any wrongdoing. She was set up."

"Explain that for me."

"She was set up as bait in the assassination of General Gennadi Vilechko."

He brought his head down a degree and left his eyes on mine, a mannerism I was beginning to understand. I'd caught his attention.

"Continue," he said. His voice had the tonelessness of a surgeon asking for another scalpel.

I must have moved on the chair, because it creaked. It was a straight-backed kitchen chair and I'd noticed stains on it when the colonel had told me to sit down. I've seen chairs like this one before, stained and gone in the joints; professional interrogators all over the world use the same tricks, and one of them is to sit the detainee down so that he has to look up at the other people, which makes him nervous, and so that he's conveniently positioned if they decide to make him still more nervous by smashing him backward onto the floor, chair and all. They use the back of their fists or their boots or whatever they choose, and although I know how to stop that kind of thing right in its tracks, I never do unless there's a chance of changing the odds and getting clear.

Tonight there was no question of that: I'd come here of my own free will.

"I'm not going to tell you very much at this stage, Colonel Belyak. First the woman has to be released. We shall need Chief Investigator Gromov here, won't we, for his authority."

"He is on his way," the colonel said.

"How long will it take him to get here?"

"Why do you ask?"

"Because we've got to hurry."

Colonel Belyak lifted his head slightly, still watching me; I'd seen him do that before when I'd told him something he didn't intend to believe.

"We have all night, Mr. Shokin." He used *Gospodin*, as Chief Inspector Gromov had done on the train when he'd questioned me; its closest equivalent in the West is *Mister*. In Russia, *tovarishch* was out now, a quaint Leninist trapping.

"We have as long as I decide we shall have," the colonel said.

He was standing with his feet apart, the polish on his jackboots glinting in the light from the bare electric bulb overhead, his shadow huge against the wall. His hands were behind him, and there was nothing in them; they'd been empty when he'd come in here. There was nothing in the sergeant's hands either; he was a man who liked the feel of bone on flesh when he went to work, a former pugilist with the gloves off these days and real toys to play with.

"I want you to realize," I told the colonel, "that you're going to be very pleased indeed with the information I shall be giving you eventually, once *Gospozha* Rusakova has been released. I'm not setting any kind of deadline, you see; it's just a fact of life: we can't afford to waste any time."

Not in fact true. Certainly I was setting a deadline, because I had to keep up the pressure. If I gave these people all the time they wanted they'd simply put me through intensive interrogation and I'd come out days later with not much more than pulp where flesh had been, with a torn urethra and clouded conjunctivae and the kidneys contused and pouring blood into the urine and my sight gone and my brain out of sync and *Meridian* blown to hell.

There was also the risk of Tanya Rusakova's brother losing patience. *I'm no good at waiting, doing nothing,* he'd said on the telephone. *If I'm not there*—at the rendezvous—*it will mean I changed my mind.*

He could wreck everything I was trying to do.

"If there were any deadlines to be set," Colonel Belyak was saying, "I would set them myself."

"Of course."

He was touchy and I'd have to watch it. I had begun paying out a thread so fine that one wrong word could break it.

"Tell me what you know," the colonel said, "about the assassination of General Vilechko."

There was the sound of snow chains locking across concrete outside the building and the slamming of doors, so I took a chance and left the question unanswered, turning my head as the tramping of boots loudened and voices began echoing along the passage and Chief Investigator Gromov came in, shouldering his way between the guards and nodding briefly to the colonel and staring down at me with his hands dug into the pockets of his coat.

"So we have you."

Cold air was still coming in from the passage, laced with exhaust gas.

"Not quite that," I said.

"What, then?"

I missed the patience in his caramel-brown eyes that I'd seen on the *Rossiya*. He'd had all the time he needed, then, but now he was more energized: he'd thrown a net across the city of Novosibirsk and here suddenly was the minnow, squirming, and he wanted facts and he wanted them fast.

"I decided to come here of my own free will," I told him, "to obtain the immediate release of Tanya Rusakova. She did nothing wrong, intentionally, and I want her out of here." I spoke carefully, articulating; it wasn't a time for misunderstandings. "I will then deliver into your hands—if it's not too late—the man who shot Zymyanin on board the *Rossiya* the night before last, who also set a bomb in one of the compartments with the intention of killing General Vilechko, General Chudin, and General Kovalenko, and—having failed—shot General Vilechko to death last night in the street."

The cell was very quiet. There were telephones ringing in the offices along the passage, and boots sounded constantly over the bare boards.

"Shut that door," Colonel Belyak told one of the militiamen, "and stay on guard outside." He swung his head to look at Gromov, wanting to tap into his thinking, but Gromov had his eyes on me.

"In the case of Zymyanin," he said, "you had witnesses against you on the train."

"They were lying. But please remember that I just told

you I can deliver the actual perpetrator *if there is time.*" I gave it a beat. "When I last talked to him"—I checked my watch—"forty-two minutes ago, he was making plans to set another bomb."

Colonel Belyak was first. "Where?"

"I can't tell you. He thinks he knows where the other two generals are, and he still means to kill them."

"Do *you* know where they are?" Gromov asked quickly.

"No. I asked him but he refused to tell me."

Belyak: "Who is this man?"

I looked at my watch again. "With respect, gentlemen, you will have to use your *heads.* I can't give you this man if we stay here talking. Nor can you hope to stop another tragedy like the one on the *Rossiya,* with further loss of innocent lives. The responsibility is yours."

Silence came in again. It was warm in here with so many bodies, and the sweat was beginning to run on me. The thread was still intact, but I'd have to go on paying it out in the hope of drawing them with me, and there'd be a lot of strain.

"Why should we release this woman?" the colonel asked.

"Because she's done nothing. She—"

"That's beside the point. Why do *you* want her released?"

"She's been traumatized by the whole thing and—"

"The 'whole thing'?"

"Vilechko's death." He was right: I'd stopped choosing my words and we couldn't afford misunderstandings. "You may consider it beside the point that you're holding an innocent person here and putting her through further suffering but I do *not.* The release of Tanya Rusakova is my only condition, but if you don't meet it I won't deliver the agent into your hands. But of course he could have left his base by now."

They didn't react, wouldn't be hurried. If I finally got them with me, one of them would look at his watch. It hadn't happened yet.

"Are you in love with this woman?" Gromov asked me.

"No."

"She's remarkably attractive."

"Yes. I wish I had time in my life to fall in love with every attractive woman I meet."

I'd been listening for her voice in the building: she couldn't be far from here because she'd be in a cell too and this was the detention area. All other things being equal, a woman's voice carries more clearly than a man's. I'd heard nothing.

Gromov looked at the colonel. "Is this man your prisoner or mine?"

"He's mine at this point but I'm willing to hand him over. I don't want him."

Wasting *time*.

"Yes," I told Belyak, "you do."

He watched me with his polished black stones.

"Explain."

"The agent is a former militia officer, major's rank. He was sacked for persistent drunkenness and killing three men on the firing range by culpable negligence. Since then he's been taking on clandestine operations, one of which has *so far* included the death of Zymyanin on board the *Rossiya* and the bombing of the train and the shooting of General Vilechko here in Novosibirsk. If you don't pull him in as soon as you can, your head's going to be on the block and the people of Russia are going to lose a great deal of faith in their militia, whose job it is to protect the peace. The people of Russia are in a touchy mood these days."

Another vehicle pulled up in the forecourt of the building and I felt the thread in my hand grow taut as the door banged open and boots clattered along the passage. *I'm here to demand the release of my sister, Tanya Amelia Rusakova, and to make a full confession in the death of General Gennadin Vilechko.*

I waited.

"Why have you decided to betray this agent?" Colonel Belyak asked.

"I've been considering it ever since he bombed the train.

He took innocent lives. It's not my way. He needs stopping now, or God knows what he'll do."

Boots tramping. *I'm no good at waiting, doing nothing.*

The gallant Captain Rusakov.

"All right," Gromov said. "Tell us where we can pick up this man."

"I'll have to take you to him."

"Why?"

"He's violent. If you put him in a trap he'll try to shoot his way out."

Boots tramping, passing the door, not stopping.

"Others have tried that too," the colonel said.

"Look," I told him, "you can go in there with as many men as you like but you'll end up with a messy operation and get half of them killed unnecessarily. Or you can take me with you and I'll talk to him first and set him up for you and there'll be no bloodshed; I can promise an elegant, copybook operation, which I would think is more your style."

I waited again, watching the colonel and the chief investigator in turn, seeing first one and then the other start looking at his watch, seeing it again and again in my mind, but only there.

A cell door slammed shut along the passage and the boots sounded again.

Belyak opened his mouth but Gromov was first—"What is your connection with this agent?"

"We were collaborators."

"In what?"

"The same clandestine operation."

"Its purpose?"

"To sabotage the *Podpolia.*"

That got a reaction, as I'd known it would. The hardline Communist underground was known to exist and the Russian and Commonwealth police, militia, and MPS were known to be smoking out its leaders, but some of those leaders were firmly ensconced in the Russian and Commonwealth police, militia, and MPS, which made things difficult.

I'd glanced from Gromov to Belyak when I'd said what I had, but couldn't catch anything: they were both trained to remain deadpan whatever was in their minds.

Gromov—or Belyak—could well be a member of the *Podpolia*, unknown to the other, but it didn't make any difference: each of them had a job to do and he'd get a great deal of kudos within his department if he could pull in the man who had bombed the *Rossiya*, whether he was in the underground or against it. The charge against him would be mass murder.

"You believe, then," Gromov said, "that General Vilechko was in the *Podpolia*?"

"Yes."

"And you would furnish me with a full accounting of both your own actions and your collaborator's, once he is taken?"

"A full accounting, in the expectation of leniency for myself."

The colonel looked across at Gromov again. "We should confer," he said.

"I agree."

Then Belyak looked at his watch.

"I'm glad to see, Colonel," I told him, "that you're aware of the passage of time. It's critical, as I've warned you."

Gromov opened the door of the cell and the colonel followed him out and the door banged shut again, the look-through panel vibrating. The militia sergeant had come to attention when his colonel went out; now he was standing at ease. He'd been sorry, I knew, to hear I was ready to give a full accounting of my actions; he would have preferred orders to tear it out of me word by word as the blood came running. I thought of talking to him, asking him how the sweet peas were coming along, but he wouldn't have answered me: I was a dog brought in here from the streets, and he didn't talk to dogs.

It would have been pleasant to stand up and stretch my legs, and have him order me to sit down again, and refuse, and give him the excuse to drive his fist into my diaphragm, so that I could parry the blow to the left and open him up and go in with some fast center-knuckle jabs to paralyze the major nerves and finish up with a back fist to stun the pineal gland and take him gently onto the floor. It would have relieved the tension in me and I could have used that, but of course it wouldn't have done any good because when they'd come back, the colonel and the chief investigator, they'd have thought I'd been losing my temper, and wouldn't have trusted me anymore.

They'd been gone three minutes. I was sitting with my legs crossed and my left hand on my right thigh with the fingers spread out so that I could look down at my watch and check the time without moving. Three minutes was too long. One minute was too long, because we had two deadlines running: at any time at all, Captain Rusakov's patience could break and he could come storming into the building, or his sister could talk under interrogation and give the lie to everything I'd been telling these people, and in either case my fragile thread would finally snap, *finito*.

Four minutes, and the sweat came springing, itching on the scalp.

"You do much quilting, Sarge?"

"Keep your mouth shut."

"Yes, Sarge."

Five. Five minutes.

There was only one real chance of pulling this thing off and I started running it through my mind, over and over, to keep the nerves under control: they were crying out for action and in the quiet confines of this bloody cell there was the itch in me to provoke this sergeant and melt him down and that was dangerous.

The *only* chance of pulling this thing off lay in the fact that I'd given Colonel Belyak and Chief Investigator Gromov an offer they'd find difficult to refuse. They'd nothing to lose.

Six minutes. I could smell the sergeant. Feet, most of it, filthy socks, typical of the breed, they're not the ultrasensitive among us, these paid professional body-busters, I've known some, I tell you I've known some and I've left stains on their kitchen chairs and all I'm looking for is any excuse to plug this bastard's nervous system into some really high-voltage center-knuckle techniques and—

For Christ's sake watch it or you'll blow the whole thing.

Perfectly right.

Seven minutes.

They'd nothing to lose. They could let Tanya Rusakova walk out of this building and through those rusting iron gates and across the square and they could get her back in five minutes, deploy patrols and cover the environment: they'd be quite sure of that, wrong but sure, unworried. And they could escort me to where I would direct them and surround the place with half a regiment of armed militia before they let me in there, nothing to lose, they could pull me out again and slam me back into the patrol car or shoot me down if I resisted, whatever they chose to do, *nothing* to lose.

If they agreed to the deal at all, *that* would be their reason.

Eight minutes, and the sweat reached my chin and I brushed it off and the sergeant caught the movement and I saw him tense, the scarred leather-skinned hands lifting a fraction and the fingers forming claws ready to grab me and send me spinning backward on the chair, *you try that you stinking bastard and I'll*—steady, for the sake of God, you'll blow *Meridian.*

I want her out of here, that's all. She's had enough.

Nine. Nine minutes.

Are you in love with this woman?

No.

She's remarkably attractive.

Yes indeed, that is indeed so, you look into those green and shimmering eyes and watch the soft and subtle play of that perfect mouth as she speaks and you're moved, you can't help it, moved as a man, as a male of her species, this is the way it is with Tanya Rusakova.

But that isn't why I came, why I want her out of this bloody place.

She's innocent, you said, and she's had enough.

Well yes, but the main thing is that if they keep her locked up here long enough that gallant brother of hers is going to bare his breast for the bullet and I'll lose the only key I've got left for *Meridian*.

So you'd have come here, then, for anyone? A man? You'd have risked all this for anyone?

Keep your *bloody* questions to yourself.

Touchy, aren't we?

Shuddup.

Ten. Ten minutes.

Voices outside the cell. No louder, no nearer, just voices.

I could hear the sergeant's breathing, smell his breath, the taint of tobacco on his breath. He was standing with his arms hanging like an ape's and his feet astride, something on his boot, on his left boot, something he'd spilled, he'd been slopping soup around or this was perhaps vomit, another man's, a man in a stained kitchen chair, or it was something else, you couldn't hope to tell what sordid business had soiled this uniformed whoreson's boot.

You stink, you know that, you stink like a pig—

Steady, lad, steady.

Yes I know. I know.

"That's a nice cologne you use, Sarge, is it violets or—"

"Shut your fucking mouth."

"Sorry, Sarge."

Then the voices outside stopped and the door opened and they came in, Colonel Belyak and Chief Investigator Gromov, and looked down at me.

Chapter 16

Dog Pack

We were set out like men on a chessboard in front of Militia Headquarters, our shadows slanting across the concrete from the big wrought-iron lamps over the gates, Gromov and two aides standing beside one of the patrol jeeps, Belyak positioned near a prisoner-transport van drawn up at the front of the building. Its engine had been running but now it had been switched off, and it was quiet here in the forecourt, with only the roar of a snowplow in the far distance. It was very cold.

An icicle dropped from the eaves, flashing in the light and then hitting the ground with the music of breaking glass. A voice sounded over the radio of one of the patrol cars standing outside the railings, and a militiaman answered, and the night was quiet again. But there was the sweet-and-sour smell of carbon monoxide on the air: there was an engine running somewhere, perhaps on the other side of the building. That was to be expected.

Chief Investigator Gromov rolled his shoulders inside his greatcoat, as I'd seen him do before. I suppose the coat was a bad fit, or he was just trying to keep warm. He would have been awake for most of last night, supervising the city-wide manhunt for Viktor Shokin, and would be tired now.

The three-quarter moon clung to the heights of the southern sky, bone-white and mottled, its light casting prismatic colors across the snow-covered roofs. A horned owl was calling from the bare trees of the park, with the note of a bamboo flute.

She came out of the building, Tanya Rusakova, walking alone, not looking around her yet, taking care with the steps, her boots grating on the sand that had been thrown down over the hard-packed snow. Then she reached the bottom and walked a little way into the courtyard, looking round her now, confused, her face drawn and her eyes wary; then she saw me and came on again, and I took a few steps to meet her. This was what I had asked for, that she should have no escort out of the building and that I should be the only one to speak to her.

Her eyes had surprise in them now; the last time she'd seen me was in the safe house, and she couldn't understand why I was still apparently a free man, surrounded by uniforms but at a distance.

"Why are they letting me go?" Her breath clouded on the lamplit air.

I asked her quietly, "What did you tell them?"

She tensed, remembering the past hours, I suppose.

"Nothing about you, or my brother."

She's very obstinate, her brother had said. Perhaps it was that.

"Walk through those gates," I told her, "and into the park. A man will meet you there and look after you. He'll tell you his name is Georgi. Do everything he says. The militia will try to bring you back, so be careful this time."

I stood drowning for a moment in the shimmering green as she went on watching me, still confused. "You are not coming too?"

"No. Remember what I said, Tanya, and be careful."

I turned and walked a little way toward the building and then turned again and watched her going through the big iron gates. She looked back once, her face pale in the wash of the two big lamps, then walked on again across the churned snow of the roadway and into the trees of the park.

Somewhere on the other side of the building I could hear a vehicle of some sort moving off through the gears; it was

probably the one that had been sending the smell of carbon
monoxide across the courtyard.

"Colonel *Belyak*. Get that vehicle *stopped*."

He swung a look at me but did nothing.

"Stop that patrol car or the deal is off, you understand?"

He left the black stones of his eyes on me for a little
while and then made a quick gesture to the driver of the
prisoner-transport van, and we heard the squelch of his
transmitter. Belyak turned away, pacing with his head down,
hands behind him, pacing back. In the distance I heard the
patrol car halt and the sound of its engine die away. I didn't
believe Belyak could have ordered something so crude; we'd
made a deal, purportedly among gentlemen, the only kind
that would work. Perhaps some minion had thought of trying
it on, and Belyak had done nothing to stop him, seeing it as
a test for me, to find out how much confidence I had, how
I'd respond to the challenge.

"Colonel *Belyak*. Did *you* give the orders for that?"

He stopped pacing and looked up at me from under his
big round cap, said nothing for a moment, and then—"Let's
get on. We're wasting time."

I looked at my watch. "Ten minutes, remember? That
was all I asked for and you agreed."

He moved away from me impatiently, crunching across
the snow to talk to Chief Investigator Gromov. No one else
moved and there was no more sound of engines or anything
else, no sound of a shot.

One of the uniformed militiamen was stamping his feet,
over by the black iron railings. He was nursing an assault
rifle: they all were, slung low and at the ready. A dozen of
them were positioned outside the gates, facing the courtyard,
facing the prisoner, Viktor Shokin.

The night was quiet except for the snowplow in the
distance. Six minutes had passed and there was still no sound
of a shot. That was what I was waiting for, hoping against.

Seven minutes and the radio in one of the patrol vehicles

opened up and I went over there straight away to listen through the driver's open window.

Forty-nine to base, this is forty-nine.

Come in.

I'm stuck on the ice at Saint Petersburg ulica and Boronov Prospekt.

Base told him they were sending help and the call was shut down. It hadn't been anything to do with this driver here; the radio was on open network. I'd checked the call as a routine, and it was all I could do. If Colonel Belyak or Chief Investigator Gromov had set up a multivehicle tracking operation on the little park to keep Tanya Rusakova monitored, there'd be no signals on the air: they would have ordered radio silence.

Nine minutes and another big icicle came away from the eaves of the building, lancing through the lamplight and splintering against the bottom step. It touched the nerves a little because if the sound of a shot came from across the park it would be a signal that the support man couldn't get Tanya as far as the first car, couldn't get her clear, and if that happened there'd be no further options. If these people weren't prepared to let the woman prisoner go free in exchange for what I could do for them I couldn't force the issue.

I heard the horned owl call again from the trees, the *ushastaya sova*, its notes soft and echoless; the snowplow had stopped working over there in the distance, and the winter silence grew vast across the city.

There had been no shot.

Colonel Belyak turned to face me.

"Ten minutes—are you satisfied?"

"Stop," I told the militiaman at the wheel.

The safe house was two blocks from here, eastward toward the river.

Belyak spoke to the driver from beside me on the rear seat.

"Give the signal for deployment."

The man opened up his radio.

I'd counted seven unmarked patrol cars on the way here from Militia Headquarters, some of them tailing us and the others keeping abreast along streets running parallel to our route. I hadn't given directions when we'd started out: this too had been finally agreed. Belyak had raised objections at first but I'd waited for him to sweat it out because the situation was quite clear: if I'd given him the location of the safe house he could have left Tanya in her cell and put me back into mine and sent in a platoon and evacuated the building and taken it by storm.

"It's the concrete block of apartments straight ahead of us," I told him, "two streets down."

"We will wait," he said.

We'd agreed that I would take him to within two blocks of the safe house and give him time to deploy his forces in a ring at that distance from the building before I went in.

"Microphone," he told the driver, and the man passed it back to him. "Commander to all units. Keep your engines as quiet as you can. No lights."

He smelled of cigars, the colonel, cigars and boot polish; he was an easier man to handle than Chief Investigator Gromov; Belyak was paramilitary, trained within the narrow perspectives of the soldier. He'd be less likely to spring a surprise than Gromov, a subtler and an older man, more of a chess player than a tin-drum major. Gromov was in his own car but his radio would be linked with the colonel's network and he'd be listening to the moves.

Static came on the air.

Twenty-one to Station Six and halted.

Colonel Belyak sat with his bulk in the corner between the seat and the door, the microphone in his hand. He wasn't worried about my attempting an escape: this area was already a supertrap and if I'd wanted to escape I wouldn't have set it up for myself, and so far I'd got him to believe in that.

Thirty-four to Station Seven and halted.

Engines sounded everywhere in the quiet of the streets,

a background murmur. Normal traffic had been stopped, and there were no lights moving anywhere, only the blacked-out shapes of the patrol cars. Dogs loped past us, singly and in packs, hollow-flanked and with their heads down, scenting; this wasn't far from the big Number 3 Meat Market, closed because there was no meat but still attractive because of its smell.

Nineteen to Station Twelve and halted.

The time on the dashboard clock was 7:13.

The colonel flipped the mike open. "What units are still moving?"

There was only static and some faint Morse we were picking up from another band.

"If any unit is not yet deployed, report immediately."

Static.

Belyak looked at me. "You are ready?"

"Yes."

He got out of the car with me, bringing a walkie-talkie with the antenna extended, and I took him to within a block of the safe house.

"It looks," I told him, "as if he's still there. It's the fifth room along on the third floor." The chink of yellowish light showed clearly enough through the gap in the curtains. I looked at my watch. "Do you have 7:21?"

"I do."

"You're giving me fifteen minutes. That was agreed?"

"It was."

"Then you can send your men in at 7:36 if I haven't brought him out. If I can get him under control before then, you'll see the light in that window go out and you can expect both of us to leave the building by the main entrance. You won't need to order any rush: I'll have a gun at his back."

I couldn't see the colonel's eyes in the shadow of his cap, knew only that they were watching me.

"Very well. And whether you bring this man out or not, you understand that you will remain my prisoner. That also was agreed."

"Yes, I understand."

I turned away and began walking, and heard the sound of boots over the snow as my two escorts began tailing me at a distance. There would be others as I moved closer to the building, and once I was through the entrance door they would close in from all sides with their assault rifles covering every exit and every window.

The edges of the frozen ruts broke under my boots as I kept on walking. From somewhere over to my left I heard a radio come to life, and faint voices; then it was quiet again.

He had done well, Belyak. I could see only two patrol cars from where I was now and their crews were inside them, keeping a low profile, but there'd be upward of thirty vehicles forming the peripheral ring at two blocks' distance, because it would take at least that many to seal off the area effectively. When we'd left Militia Headquarters I'd counted five personnel carriers, and there could be others here, so that the actual number of armed bodies within and round the ring was probably in the region of two hundred. If I tried to break and run at any time, at any time at all, I would have as much chance as a rat in a dog pack.

It was 7:23 when I reached the building and kicked the worst of the snow off my boots and went through the entrance door and let it swing shut behind me.

*F*erris caught it before the second ring.

"Things went off all right," I told him.

In a moment he said: "I'll tell London."

He just meant he was pleased, that was all, because he hadn't believed I'd got a ghost of a chance of going into Militia Headquarters and coming out again of my own free will. There was nothing in point of fact to tell London. The purpose of the exercise had been to stop Captain Vadim Rusakov from going down there and offering himself as the sacrificial lamb in order to get his sister out. I needed him.

I hadn't advanced the mission; I'd simply averted the terminal damage that Tanya had come appallingly close to causing when she'd walked out of that safe house in spite of my warning. But that was something, at least; we hadn't crashed *Meridian*, though it wasn't the kind of signal the director in the field could flash to Control in London.

Novosibirsk's just come in, sir. We've still got a mission running.

Croder would freeze him with his reptilian eyes.

How nice.

We're expected to do rather better than that, we the brave and underpaid ferrets in the field. But I had felt something move softly within when I'd seen her look back, just that once, before she'd vanished into the trees of the little park; you could call it joy of some kind, I suppose, or as close as I can ever get to such a thing inside the cold and scaly carapace of my defenses.

As close as I'll let myself get? You read well, my good friend, between the lines.

"I blew the safe house," I told Ferris. "It was full of militia when I left there."

"They were looking for you?"

"Yes."

"What's your location now?"

"I'm about three miles away, at Iskitim Prospekt and— wait a minute." The glass panels were steaming up. "Iskitim Prospekt and Borodin ulica. And I've got the car here." I'd just walked across the patch of waste-ground where I'd left the Ford Escort earlier this afternoon. "You've got Tanya in safekeeping?"

"Here at the hotel."

"For God's sake try and make her understand," I said, "that if she goes off on her own again we won't be able to help her."

Lights swept across the telephone booth and I turned my back until they'd gone. I wouldn't have long: they'd be spreading the hunt.

"She's hating herself," Ferris said. "Feels she let you down."

"Then maybe she's learned." I tried to remember the names of the major intersections east of here, but a lot had gone on since I'd studied the map of the city on board the *Rossiya*. "Look, I'm still a bit too close to things at the moment, so I'm going to start driving eastward from here as soon as we shut down. Have I got a new safe house?"

"Yes. Nothing posh."

"I'll take anything. I need someone to intercept and lead me there. You should also send someone to the Harbor Light bar on the river." I gave him the location. "Captain Rusakov should be going there in a couple of minutes from now." I repeated the description Rusakov had given me of himself and told Ferris about the recognition mark: the odd pair of gloves. "He should be told as soon as possible that his sister's free and in safekeeping and that I'll meet him there as soon as I can. Where's the safe house?"

I could hear the faint crackling of a map on the line. "Five kilometers from the Harbor Light, downstream on the river."

"What sort of place is it?"

In a moment, "It's an abandoned hulk. We didn't have much time to find anything better."

"No problem."

But it wasn't good news. If the best the director in the field could find for his executive was an abandoned hulk on the river it meant that the local support people were not only spread thin on the ground but couldn't come up with anything safer. It was the nearest they could get, I suppose, to a bloody cellar.

"There'll be a change of clothes for me there?" I asked Ferris. The collar of the uniform was rough and my neck had started itching.

"Clothes," Ferris said, "food, oil stove, oil lamp, bedding, the usual supplies."

There hadn't been a trace of satisfaction in his tone but I said, "More than I could have hoped for, considering."

"Thank you."

"Look, I'm still a major target and they'll start spreading out from the safe house as soon as they find out I'm not there, so I want to get off the streets as soon as I can. Let Rusakov know that I'll try and meet him at the Harbor Light by nine o'clock."

"Noted."

"And tell the support man I'll start driving east from Borodin ulica along Iskitim in two minutes from now and I'll expect him to flash me when he intercepts."

Ferris acknowledged and we shut down the signal and I shouldered the door of the booth open against the heavy spring and waited until a dark blue van went past, only one of its headlamps functioning; then I walked across the street to the patch of waste-ground and got into the Ford Escort. The clock on the dash was three minutes slow and I adjusted it to read 8:02 and started the engine and moved off along Borodin, sitting with my neck forward a degree to keep it clear of my collar, not *my* collar in point of fact, the whole outfit belonged to the sallow-faced and brutish-looking militiaman who'd come sliding in there an hour after I'd finalized the deal with that fat stinking bitch.

She'd looked shocked at first when I'd told her what I wanted, sitting there like a great female Buddha in her rusty black satin dress, her rings glinting on her fat fingers and her mouth hanging open. "But I couldn't ever do such a thing!" She'd get arrested and shot, so forth, hamming it up because she'd already scented money in it, perhaps quite a lot if she played hard to get.

I'd had to start from there.

"But they come in here, don't they? The militia? Just for a quickie?"

"It has happened," she said cautiously.

"All right, I'll give you three hundred rubles for the uniform off the first militiaman my size who comes in here, the hat and the boots included, the whole kit. Three hundred."

The huge Ottoman chair creaked as she shifted her weight in it, settling herself for the struggle. "How could I possibly get such a thing for you?"

"Oh come on, Marina, how long have you been running a whorehouse? Tell him it's your birthday, give him two or three girls and a bottle of vodka and slip in a Mickey Finn."

Her fleshy mouth opened in shock. "You want me *arrested*?"

Rhetoric. I didn't answer.

"Can you *imagine* what they would charge me with? Physical assault on an officer of the law, attempted—"

"Bullshit. He couldn't tell them where it had happened, you know that. Tell them he'd gone into a brothel and got drunk on duty and they'd give him a year in the brig."

Her right foot began tapping on the stained Kazakhstan carpet. "And how would I get him out of here? You expect me to—"

"Wrap him in a blanket and dump him into a taxi."

She looked as if I'd gone out of my mind, and the price went up another hundred.

"And how would he ever find another uniform?"

She couldn't care less but I said, "He'd buy one or steal one."

The door from the street opened and a man came in, turning to look behind him before he shut the door, a gross creature with the veins on his face broken into a purple network and one eye dulled, unseeing, the other too bright by far, too hungry.

Marina jerked her head and the man parted the slit in the heavy red curtains and pushed his way through them. *I have Chinese girls,* this woman had told me, *thirteen, fourteen years old. You should see them. They are like porcelain.*

But this is a man's world, my little slant-eyed alabaster loves, and there's no hope in it for the likes of you. "I'm waiting," I told the woman, and though I'd said it quietly I saw a leap of fear in her eyes at something she heard in my tone.

"It's too big a risk," she told me.

"Five hundred."

"I would lose my license."

"One thousand," I told her, "take it or leave it."

I'd given her cash and she'd counted it and it had been an hour before the sallow-faced militiaman had come through the door, and now I could smell the vodka on his uniform as I drove east along Iskitim, watching the mirror, a blade of freezing air cutting through a gap where the window rubber had rotted away, the heater pushing oil fumes into the car from the engine compartment, the mirror trembling to the vibration.

Two militia patrols, both coming past me from the opposite direction, two militia patrols and a bus crowded with fur hats and featureless faces behind the steamy windows, a truck lurching half across the pavement to keep out of its way, ten blocks, eleven, twelve, and support still hadn't intercepted. A dog loped into the roadway and I felt the bump and the front end of the Escort slid across the ruts in the snow and I brought it back again, thirteen blocks, fourteen, until I could see the red lights winking at the top of the radio masts where the land rose toward the river and fell away again.

He found me at the twentieth block and flashed me and I put a hand up to steady the mirror and took a look at him and slowed and let him go past and took up station fifty yards behind him; he was in a two-door Trabant with most of the paint gone and a strip of adhesive tape slanting across the rear window and one of the taillights flickering, nothing posh, as Ferris would have said, dear Jesus, I was beginning to realize the kind of operation London had thrown that man to direct in the field—*Meridian* was not your fancy West European parlor game with elite supports and backups and courier lines and signals facilities by courtesy of the British embassies in Berlin, Paris, and Rome; this was a strictly cut-rate package trip through the frozen hinterland of Siberia at a time when even the dogs were too thin to be thought worth catching for the pot.

Something appeared in the mirror and I held it steady and saw the front-end profile of a truck against the glare of its lights. I was checking it from habit, that was all, because the rogue agent I suspected was in the field may have been interested in me on board the *Rossiya* and could have closed up on my movements since I'd arrived in Novosibirsk, but when I'd taken Tanya Rusakova under my protection after the Vilechko killing I'd gone through the rest of the night in a complex travel pattern that no one could have tracked unseen, and when Roach had picked us up at the hospital in the Ford Escort we'd been absolutely clean, I knew that. So lights in the mirror now wouldn't mean anything, but we always check them, we the paranoid ferrets in the field, with a devotion to ritual worthy of a priest.

The Trabant turned south and east again and the mirror went dark. I found the switch for the heater and turned it off. The air inside the car was thick with oil fumes and I cracked the window open on the passenger's side. Another militia patrol car passed me, this time at right angles across an intersection. I didn't know if they'd taken the name of Shokin, Viktor, off the all-points bulletin board at Militia Headquarters when I'd reported there, but it wouldn't make any difference because by now they'd have taken the whole building apart where the safe house was and set up the hunt again and put my name back on the board. It didn't worry me: at this point I was running unseen and within reach of shelter and my main concern was to get out of this bloody uniform.

But I mustn't complain: it had served me well.

I'd asked that elephantine harpy for something to carry the uniform in when I left the brothel and she'd given me a brown paper bag, and I'd put the whole kit, still unwrapped, in the wardrobe of the safe house and left it there when I'd gone to find a militia patrol and turn myself in. When I was taken back there under escort I'd told Colonel Belyak to give me fifteen minutes before he sent his troops in but it hadn't taken that long to get into the uniform, and I'd stowed my clothes under the handbasin in the bathroom and was down the stairs before the headlights of the vehicles outside came flooding through the windows and I heard a chorus of shouted commands.

I was in a janitor's room at the end of the main corridor on the ground floor when they hit the entrance doors open and filled the place with the clatter of boots.

I gave them time.

There was a picture on the wall of the room where I was waiting, a faded photograph of former President Gorbachev of the USSR being greeted at Novosibirsk airport by girls in white skirts belled out around them as their leader presented him with a huge bouquet of flowers. One little girl, among the youngest, stood watching the presentation with a contemplative finger up her nose, which I thought gave the whole scene a unique charm.

"Plekhanov, take the stairs!"

By the sound of their boots the corridor was filling up and I could hear doors opening and a woman's shrill voice and then a man's, demanding to know what was going on, and I waited until the first wave had passed the janitor's room and then went out and joined the tail of the advance group and started hammering on doors, telling people it was the militia, open up.

The vanguard of the group on the ground floor was spilling at right angles into a passage leading to the yard outside: I'd checked the layout of the building after Roach had left us here this morning.

"Kuibyshev, take your men into the yard and stake out the perimeter and leave two men guarding that door!"

I went out with the main group and took up station by the gate. The whole street on the far side of the building was a blaze of light as the militia vehicles were brought in from the surrounding streets by radio to complete the total containment of the area, and through the ground-floor windows I could make out the civilian residents of the apartment block being lined up for questioning.

"Open this gate!"

People banging at it from the other side. I didn't do anything; we'd need a sergeant to order it done.

Glass smashed somewhere and I looked up and saw what looked like a struggle going on in a room on the second floor: a man was trying to get out onto the fire escape and they weren't letting him. *Let me go,* so forth—I suppose that if you turned any given apartment block in this city upside down and shook it you'd find the odd drug dealer or black-market *capitano* with evidence he couldn't get rid of at short notice. *I haven't done anything,* so forth, and I felt a touch of queasiness because when I was growing up I'd seen flies on a web and had watched them buzzing and buzzing as the spider darted from its lair and the delicious chill of horror had trickled down my schoolboy spine.

"Sergeant in charge, open this fucking gate, come on!"

The NCO heard the order this time and gave a shout and two of us went for the wooden bar and swung it back and got the gate open and I stood clear as a body of men came plunging through and split up and started climbing the fire escapes against the wall of the building while I went through the gate and turned and held my revolver at the ready. Two men were bringing the civilian down, going against the stream; I suppose it was the quickest way out of the building with all that fuss going on inside, and when they'd got him as far as the gate I turned again and took up the rearguard in case he managed to break loose.

We took him to one of the vehicles half a block away; I think it was the prisoner-transport van that had come with us from Militia Headquarters earlier. There was less light here and I left the escort party and took up station at the end of an alley, facing the street to watch for anyone attempting to escape; but the focus of action was still down there at the apartment block and nobody was looking in my direction so I turned and walked into the alley, the boots a bit on the loose side even though I'd pulled the laces tight; it's important in this trade that our feet are comfortable because sometimes we need to run and run flat out and if we're not fast enough we can lose the whole thing.

That had been at 7:31 and it was now 8:20 and they wouldn't give it much more than an hour down there, Gromov and Belyak, and there was something I'd have to remember: there'd been only one way I could have got out of that place and as soon as they gave their minds to it they'd put Shokin, Viktor, back on the a. p. bulletin board, described as possibly wearing militia uniform.

They were there again, the lights.

The support man was driving cautiously and I liked that.

You could wipe out the front end of whatever you were driving on streets like this one if you didn't watch it, clouds of steam and rusty water pouring onto the ice and the timing gear pushed through the cylinder block, and in these boots I didn't feel like walking.

That was the second time.

I edged the throttle down a fraction to pull up on the Trabant in front of me and watched the mirror. It was the second time the car behind had gone through a red light, oh quite possibly, yes, with so little traffic on the streets after the storm there wasn't much attention being paid to the lights, just slow down a bit and take a good look and off you go again if there are no police around; on the other hand it's the first intimation you get when a tracker comes up on your tail: he can't afford to stay too close and go through the intersections with you but he can't afford to lose ground to a red light and watch you sail away.

All I could see from the profile of the vehicle behind me was that it was a private car, not a van or a truck or anything with emergency lights on the roof, unlit or otherwise.

But you said you weren't worried about lights in the mirror.

I wasn't.

You gave us all that bullshit about watching mirrors with the ritualistic devotion of a priest, just because you thought it sounded good, and now—

Bloody well *shuddup*.

There was *no* way that *anyone* could have tracked us last night from the Vilechko killing site to the hospital without my knowing, but I used the throttle again and fought the ruts and pulled alongside the Trabant and signaled the driver to stop. His fender caught the side of my door as he skidded on the snow but it wasn't more than a bump, and then we were stationary side by side and our windows were down and we started talking.

"I've got some lights in the mirror," I told him.

They were still there in the distance, but the car had stopped.

The support man was watching me, a stubbly face with unsurprisable eyes under a black leather ski cap. "Was he there before I intercepted?"

"He could have been." There'd been more traffic, earlier.

"He's not mine," the support man said. "I got there clean." There was a note of censure in the tone, as if he'd just noticed I hadn't washed. He was also puzzled by my uniform.

"Where's the safe house?" I asked him.

"You peeling off?"

"I might have to."

Our engines idled, echoing from the wall alongside.

"Two kilometers east of here, and you're on the river. It's the wreck of a coaster, single mast with four deck hatches and the starboard bow stove in, the MV *Natasha*, but you can't make out the name very well. She's on the west bank, three berths down—that's south—from Number Seven Granary, Novosibirsk, black clapboard with the Russian flag painted over the main doors, recently done."

He waited, watching me, his eyes in the shadow of his cap.

"Vessels on either side of the wreck?"

"Another coaster, north, and a dredger with a list on it. Place is a graveyard."

The lights were still in the mirror.

"All right. Stay where you are, and if I'm wrong I'll be back and we can keep going. Give me half an hour."

"You need help?"

"No."

It had better be done solo.

I knew what had happened now, and the chill of the night air was creeping through the skin and reaching the nerves, because it might not just be a case of throwing off the tracker and resuming operations without him. *Meridian* had been compromised, and even Ferris could be in hazard. It was perfectly true that no one could have tracked us through this city last night, that we'd been absolutely clean when Roach had picked us up at the hospital. But the lights back there were still in the mirror, and now I knew why.

There must have been surveillance on the Ford Escort when I'd picked it up twenty minutes ago, and they'd started tracking me, were behind me now. But they couldn't have found it there by chance on that patch of waste-ground in a city this size: they'd been surveilling this car since I'd brought it away from the safe house, *and before then*; they'd been surveilling it when it had been standing outside the apartment block after Roach had left it there for me to use, *and before then*: they'd tracked Roach to the rendezvous at the hospital, must have got onto him when he'd started out for there. The thread went back, and back, as far as the unthinkable.

I looked across at the support man.

"Change that," I called to him above the drumming of the engines. "Don't wait for me. Get away from here *and watch your tail*." He'd caught my tone, lifted his head an inch like an animal scenting. "Signal the DIF as soon as you can," I told him. "Make sure the line's not tapped. Tell him I think your whole support base could have been blown, and tell him to look after Roach, if it's not too late."

Chapter 18

Blood

*L*ights flashing.

It looked like a militia patrol crossing the intersection behind us and coming this way, so I got into reverse and tucked in behind the support man's Trabant. The colored lights began filling the mirror.

It should be noted that the wanted man is possibly wearing a militia uniform at this time.

I'd taken off the fur hat as soon as I'd got into the Escort, but if a patrol took an interest in me and looked down through the window he'd see the uniform.

But they couldn't be onto me yet.

Oh yes they could. They've had quite enough time to—

Shuddup and sweat it out, you sniveling little bastard.

Flashing lights, filling the mirror and reflecting in the windows of the factory and the bus garage opposite, coloring the night.

Then it was passing us and I heard banging and a voice raised, a muffled shouting, a drunk perhaps, trying to break out of the car, giving the boys a hard time.

The support man waited until it was out of sight and then started up and wagged his tail a bit over the snow and found traction and took it away, skidding into a side street and vanishing. The car behind me hadn't moved, was still standing a hundred yards away, its lights shining in the rearview mirror.

I reached across and put the window up on the passenger's side and got into gear and left the back end to dig for

213

traction with the chains and then got a grip and moved off,
going three blocks before I started playing with the gears
and looking for patches of sand and using them for acceleration while the headlights fanned from side to side across
walls and doorways and parked and stranded trucks, cars,
and carts and the characteristic bric-a-brac of the dockland
environment, while the tracker fell behind for a minute or
two before he saw I was onto him. His own lights began
swinging across and across the mirror as he went into a series
of slides and then got a grip and lost it and found it again
and started to close up a little.

I chose a side street where the snow had piled into a
drift against the wall of a warehouse and used it to get me
through the ninety-degree arc, letting the rear end hit the
snow and kick the Escort straight again as I found traction
in patches and put fifty yards behind me before the tracker's
lights came flooding into the narrow street and threw my
shadow ahead of me against the snow.

It happens. It happens sometimes: the director in the
field sets up a model deployment of his shadow executive
and his support group and his contacts and couriers and
whatever he needs for a given mission, spinning his small
and delicate network of resources and testing it out for
strength and making changes where potential danger threat-
ens, sitting back in his inner sanctum plugged in to his communications system with its portable scrambler and its bug
monitor and taking signals from the shadow out there and
relaying them through the mast at Cheltenham to the signals
board in Whitehall, the whole thing running like silk through
a loom, and *then* one man and one man alone can suddenly
send the web shaking because he's made a mistake, talked
to the wrong people, exposed a password, missed the half-
seen face in a doorway or the figure humped at the wheel
of a parked car or the broken hair across a drawer in the
hotel room, and the network becomes an alarm system and
all we can do is shut down signals to prevent interception
and get out of the safe house before it's blown, run for cover,

go to ground, hole up somewhere as the smell of the smoke starts drifting through the field where the fuses have blown and someone reaches for the chalk in the signals room in London and writes it up on the board: *Mission compromised, clear all channels and stand by.*

It was happening now.

The shadow of the Escort was flitting across the snow and the buildings ahead of me like a bat out of a nightmare as both vehicles swung and corrected and swung again over the treacherous surface. There wasn't any question of pushing the speed to more than thirty or forty kph through streets like this with dead traffic all over the place, parked or abandoned or stuck in a drift; there was only a question of the leading car's ability to outstrip the one behind, and it was already becoming clear that whatever the tracker was driving it was more potent under the hood than the Escort, possibly a Merc or a Porsche or a Mazda with tight suspension and a pinpoint steering system. All I could hope to do was let him close in and then try to fox him with tricks.

I kept seeing Roach, a short man with bright blue eyes and a round pink face, his fingers playing with each other as he transferred nervous tension, nails bitten to pieces—I'd wondered about him when he'd shown us into the safe house, but Ferris had told me he was totally reliable and had worked with him before. He wasn't a mole, Roach. He wasn't a changeling. We don't have any people like that, in the normal way of things, because the Bureau is conceivably the most elite intelligence organization in the Western Hemisphere, officially nonexistent and responsible directly to the prime minister of the UK, and there are as many traitors in our ranks as there are in the SAS, whose number is reputedly subzero.

I didn't think Roach was a traitor. I thought he'd made a mistake. But in practical terms it didn't make a lot of difference: *Meridian* was in hazard.

Don't think about Roach. Think about survival.

The side street opened onto a major road and I touched

the brakes, trying to get as much deceleration as possible out
of the drums before they locked, but the speed wasn't coming
down all that much and I'd have to do better than this because a truck was passing the end of the street and there'd
be other traffic on the move and I didn't want to splash this
thing all over the side of a heavy-duty haulage rig or anything
else for that matter, so I put the nearside front wheel into
the deeper snow along the curb and felt the drag and touched
the brakes again but the surface was more or less pack ice
and we spun full circle and fetched up with the back end
clouting a sand bin. That was all right because it brought the
speed well down and the major road was fifty yards ahead
and it didn't look as if I still had enough momentum to hit
anything out there, but I was losing ground in terms of getting clear of that *bastard* and if I led him into the major road
he'd overhaul me without any trouble because his car was
out of an elite sports stable of some kind and the Escort was
made for taking the kids to school in comfort and running
Aunt Gertrude home, so I did the only thing that was available to me and sighted him in the mirror and swung the
wheel and bounced the Escort against a drift and swung
through a hundred and eighty degrees and gunned up and
got smoke out of the rear tires as they bit through the ice
and reached solid macadam and pushed the car back the way
we'd been coming.

Part of the whole thing was going to depend on luck
but I found enough steering to take the Escort through the
gap between the other vehicle and the sand bin—there was
a lot of blinding light as we closed up and I think I heard a
shout, he hadn't been expecting this and I suppose it worried
him. We missed a total head-on but the sand bin was solid
and the Escort ricocheted to a certain extent and tore a door
away from the other car and smashed quite a lot of glass and
I felt the sudden drag of deceleration and the Escort spun
half round and I saw the other car swinging much too wide
and much too fast, and one of the wheels came spinning
past me as his front stub-axle sheared and he hit the wall of

a building and bounced back and then went into a slow roll with the engine screaming and the bright red of a flame popping from inside the engine compartment as a fuel line was torn apart and a spark from the ignition found it.

The engine went on screaming until the fuel in the injectors gave out and then there was silence of a kind and when I hit my door open it raised an echo in the narrow confines of the street. He was still inside, the tracker, sitting there like a crash-test dummy with blood coming bright from a head wound, seeping across his face. Black smoke was rolling from underneath the car as spilled engine oil took fire and I went for his seat belt but it had snapped at the buckle so *that* was what the head wound was all about. I dragged him out of the car and across the snow and pushed him into the front seat of the Escort on the passenger's side and got in and spun the rear wheels to get the chains through the snow and finally got moving and started looking for cover as we drove, any sort of cover where I could pull up and talk to this man, I wanted information.

"Can you hear me?"

He didn't answer, just keeled over a bit, that was all, so I had to push him upright again. I realized now that his head was a mess and by this time most of his face was covered in blood. Lights washed across the buildings from behind us but there'd be no traffic coming this way: the burning car was on its side and blocking the street.

"Can you hear me?"

Nothing, only the metallic smell of his blood filling the car.

The warehouse we'd passed coming the other way had a wide entrance and I pulled in there, cutting the engine and feeling for the carotid artery in the man's neck, finding it and sensing, shifting my fingers and trying again, finding no pulse, trying again, watching his face, seeing how pale it was now between the streaks of blood, moving my hand inside his coat and sensing again over the heart, shifting and sensing and finding nothing, nothing at all.

There was mostly sand on the ground where they'd cleared the entranceway and I got him out as gently as I could and laid him on his back and held one hand behind his neck to tilt the head and put my mouth over his and began breathing for him, his blood sticky on my face, sticky and cold now, dear Jesus I wanted *information* out of this man.

Lights again and a pickup truck rolled past the warehouse, no chains, the tires crunching across the ruts as the driver slowed, seeing the wreckage ahead of him along the street.

Breathe one . . . two . . . three . . .

Heel of the hand on the chest.

Someone was running down the street, boots clumping across the snow, two people, two youths, their voices excited, *breathe* one . . . two . . . three . . . and *press* on the rib cage . . . the sound of an engine, the pickup truck reversing, couldn't get through, his mouth cold against mine, the man's mouth, two . . . three . . . *Come back, you bastard, I want to talk to you* . . . *press* on the chest, his blood glutinous and pulling at my mouth as it congealed, *I want information*, two . . . three . . . as the pickup truck went crawling past the entrance in reverse, the smell of its exhaust gas on the air, *don't go yet you bastard I want to talk to you* . . . the back of his neck cold now under my hand, his eyes open, a pair of black buttoned boots behind his head, standing there on the snow and I looked up at the old woman, dumpy in her shawls, her eyes staring down at us, at our faces, at the blood.

"Babushka," I said, "go and phone, get an ambulance, *Babushka!*"

The black boots turned quickly, scattering snow.

Press on the rib cage and *breathe* . . . two . . . three, but I believed now that I was wasting my time. I would have liked to leave him there but they might have some basic resuscitation gear on the ambulance so I kept going, using deeper breaths, deeper and slower as he watched me, two . . . three . . . as he watched me perhaps from a little distance, puzzled by my efforts and already wishing not to be pulled back to it all by this busy stranger, *press* on the rib cage until at last I heard the ambulance klaxon echoing between the buildings and felt for his wallet and found it and straightened up, lowering his head gently and going down on my hands and knees like a dog at a water hole, scooping up snow to wash the blood off my face and rinse the rich salt taste out of my mouth.

I went back to the Escort and got into motion and reached the end of the street and did a skid turn and gunned up through the gears as the ambulance arrived on the scene with the blare of its siren filling the night with alarm.

Chapter 19

Christmas

Night and silence.

I stood in shadow, smelling the river smell.

Ice drifted on the water, breaking away upstream and floating down through the channels gouged by tugs and dredgers and coasters big enough to make headway. The ice made soft xylophone music as the floes touched and bumped together.

I had left the Escort half a mile away, buried under an iron roof that had slid at an angle when the walls of a shed had collapsed some time ago, perhaps under the weight of snow, to lie like a broken box in the thickets of weeds. It was almost invisible, the Escort, but I had no illusions. That was a hot car. It had been under extensive surveillance ever since Roach had blown his cover and got into it and picked up a tracker without knowing. I'm not blaming him. Support people don't get the training they give the shadow executives at the Bureau, though some of them apply for the higher echelons and graduate.

Dark shapes moved as I watched: a small high-decked freighter with coal smoke curling behind it on the motionless air, to lie in skeins along the water; a truck on the far bank, sliding among the wharves, its diesel rattling. Nearer to where I stood, nothing moved, but I had no illusions about that either. Watchers keep still. The motor vessel *Natasha* lay in her berth some sixty or seventy yards distant from the stack of rusted freight containers that I was using for cover. I needed to know if the *Natasha* was being watched.

The sensible thing to have done would have been to phone Ferris and ask him to send someone out with another car, leave the Escort back there in the side street and take over whatever they brought me. But the time for doing the sensible thing had run out now because *Meridian* was compromised, and the new car they brought me could be hot too, the subject of undetected surveillance. I would think that Yermakov had been the only man tracking the Escort, and that it was therefore safe to use for the moment. It was still hot, because it could be recognized later, but it could only be by chance, and that chance I was ready to take.

That was his name: Dmitri Alexandrovich Yermakov. His wallet was still in my pocket. I didn't think he'd been the rogue agent loose in the field. The surveillance of the Ford Escort had been the work of a cell, at least of a cell, possibly of an organization. It had needed at least two peeps to maintain the operation, because the car had been watched for more than twelve hours, from the time when Roach had picked it up to the time when I'd driven it away from the patch of waste-ground at two minutes past eight tonight. A rogue agent would work alone: It is their nature.

A night bird screeched and a ring of light flashed inside my skull and died out like a firework. I'd seen cormorants, earlier, wheeling under the lights of a warehouse crane. I had been here for twenty minutes and hadn't moved; I too was a watcher, and kept still. There are good and bad among the ranks of the peeps; some can stay silent for hours on end, moving only by indiscernible degrees when they have to, flexing the leg muscles to keep the blood flowing and the brain supplied, turning their heads as slowly as the hands of a clock, sweeping the environment continuously. Others, less professionally trained, can't go for long without needing to release tension, and they'll shift their feet or yawn or cough or even stretch their arms, and they're blown.

Night and silence, who is here?

A rat ran squealing in the shadows and the light flashed again behind my eyes. It didn't worry me: it was reaction, that was all. I hadn't expected to get out of that place, out of Militia Headquarters, but I was only aware of that now: the heat was off and the blood was cooling, and looking back at the whole enterprise it seemed as if I must have been clean out of my gourd to have taken a risk that size.

I told you. I said you'd gone mad, but you wouldn't listen.

Nor will I ever, you little shit. You can get away with things in hot blood that'd never work if you thought about them. Ask any tightrope walker—they never look down.

The broken ice rang like a peal of bells in the distance as a tug moved upstream towing a barge, blacking out the lamps along the far shore and then relighting them. But nothing was moving, had moved, closer than that. I believed the *Natasha* was clear, and I broke cover and walked across the snow-covered boards of the quay. The gangplank had been cleared by whatever support man had brought the provisions here for me, and he hadn't found it an easy choice: to leave evidence that the hulk was in some kind of use, or to leave me to make footprints on the snow and testify to the very same thing.

I dropped onto the deck and stood there, watching and listening again. The cabin had been wrecked and there was no door, just a hole through smashed timbers; I thought perhaps a crane had toppled or the boom had run its brake disks, coming down on the cabin. Snow had drifted inside the wreckage, its minuscule facets diamond-blue under the light of the moon.

Something splashed into the water and I swung my head and saw ripples crossing the surface some distance away, near the third vessel downriver, a sailing boat with the mast lying like a dead tree across the quayside. Yellow light came from its dark hulk, burning steadily, and I turned my head away. Watchers do not burn lamps to mark their presence, or throw garbage out.

The support man had dropped a rope mat over the snow where the lower part of the steps was still solid, and I went down into the smell of rotting timber and rope and lamp oil, ducking my head under a beam and seeing the glow of a night-light showing the way to the stairs down to the lower berths. I stood listening again, hearing nothing but the slap of water against the vessel's beam. The light grew stronger as I went below: there was a brass hurricane lamp burning with a good flame on the table of the main cabin below deck, with supplies stacked around it: black bread, cheeses, canned milk, dried fruit, half a dozen military-issue cans of self-heating soup, a *Christmas cake* ... and I felt a moment of warmth for Ferris: all he'd been able to scrounge in the way of a safe house for me was a rotting hulk among the ice floes, but he'd told the support man to raid the black market for what he could find to make it look like Christmas, on this unholy night.

I could still taste that man's blood in my mouth and I got the little black iron kettle and filled it and put it on the butane stove for warm water to wash with and brush my teeth, we are not here to stint ourselves, my good friend, it's Christmas, remember, and have you ever tried to clean your teeth by biting on bloody icicles?

Eight forty-three on my watch and I did only the necessary, getting out of the uniform and putting on warm sweaters and sheepskin boots. There were no rats here but they wouldn't be long in coming once they caught the scent of human habitation; I stowed all the vulnerable food packages in the cupboard with the torn poster on the door, girl in a fur hat and slacks and fur boots to the knee, I think it says a lot for a country where the women can look sexy in the depth of winter without a single bikini in sight.

I turned down the wick of the lamp and looked around for a bit of rope and took the militia uniform and boots up on deck, burying the standard-issue *Malysh* "Little Boy" automatic pistol inside the clothes and weighting the whole bundle with a rock I'd marked out when I'd crossed from the Escort to the ship. Then I crouched at the quayside watching the bubbles break surface under the light of the moon.

* * *

At 9:14 I signaled Ferris.

"Location?"

"The Harbor Light."

I'd taken fifteen minutes to check the environment when I arrived here, but it was simply an exercise in security: any danger would come from inside the bar.

"Have you met Rusakov?" Ferris asked me.

"Not yet. I've just got here." Then I said, "There's a man gone. Dmitri Alexandrovich Yermakov. He was tracking me." I told him what had happened. "He's down as a pipe fitter on his papers. He couldn't have been operating solo. I'd say he was in the *Podpolia*." Two men came from the quay, hands buried in the pockets of their padded coats, boots clumping across the snow. "I'm surprised you're still there," I told Ferris.

"I'm taking all precautions."

The two men hit the door of the bar open and bundled in. This phone booth was outside, at the end of the wall where the door was. There weren't any windows on this side.

Taking all precautions, well all right, but God knew where Roach had picked up that tracker—it could have been outside the Hotel Karasevo, where Ferris was. I didn't want him blown from under me.

"We lost Roach," I heard him saying.

Merde.

"I thought we might have," I said.

"They trapped him and there was a shoot-out."

Those shifting eyes, yes, and the nervous fingers, trigger-sensitive. We don't often get a shoot-out because weaponry isn't normally part of our stock-in-trade; we prefer silence and shadow, the soft-shoe retreat. But Roach would have carried a gun, yes, I could believe that, had spent his life looking over his shoulder, had found sleep difficult, until now.

"As long as you think you're safe there," I told Ferris, meaning for Christ's sake don't blow the nerve center for

Meridian and wishing instantly I hadn't said it, because when the executive starts worrying about the safety of his director in the field it can only mean he's starting to feel mission pressure.

"Relax," Ferris said quietly on the line.

"Did I say something?"

"Not really."

Someone had used his finger across the grime on the glass panel of the booth, *Fuck Yeltsin*. "Many kind thanks," I said to Ferris, "for the cake."

"Nothing too good."

I made the effort and asked, "Where is Tanya Rusakova?" It had taken an effort because I was worried about her too, didn't want to hear him say we'd lost her again.

Relax, yes.

"I've put her in a room on the same floor here, only three doors along, two people on watch." He'd heard the effort I'd had to make. He hears everything, Ferris, if the line's good enough; he can hear you taking too deep a breath to quiet the nerves; he can hear gooseflesh rising under your sleeve.

"I need to talk to her," I told him.

"I know. She's waiting here now."

He'd known I'd have to debrief Tanya before I talked to her brother, to find out what she'd said in Militia Headquarters, what his situation was now, and Ferris had brought her into his room to wait for my call, saving a few minutes' delay as I stood here in a telephone booth with glass panels and no identification papers on me that I could show anyone, now *that* is direction in the field.

"Hello?"

Her voice soft, her green eyes shimmering behind the notice that said you didn't have to put coins into the receptacle when summoning the fire brigade, ambulance, or militia.

"Are you comfortable?"

We say strange things, when not knowing what to say.

"Yes. And filled with remorse, and gratitude."

Been rehearsing it. "Tanya," I said, "what did you tell the militia? As briefly as you can, just the essentials."

She went straight into it, had been briefed by Ferris. "They asked me why I had come to Novosibirsk, and I told them it was to see my brother, as I always did when I had leave. I knew they would telephone Moscow to ask about me, and would find I had a brother here. I said I met General Vilechko by chance on the *Rossiya*, and he proposed an assignation when we arrived in the city. He seemed quite a gentleman, and said he would like to please me by 'arranging' early promotion for my brother."

She was surprising me, Tanya Rusakova. It would have taken courage, in that interrogation cell at Militia Headquarters, to admit that she'd made plans to meet a man who was later shot dead against a wall. But she'd had no choice: she couldn't have explained, otherwise, why she'd checked in at the Hotel Vladekino and then left there soon afterward, under the eyes of the concierge.

"I told them that when I met General Vilechko at the appointed place, I was shocked and horrified to see a man force him from his car and shoot him down. I ran away, terrified, but the man caught up with me and threw me into another car, where I was blindfolded. He took me to a house, and kept me there. Of course I realized he was protecting himself—I'd seen what he had done and could recognize him again."

I was listening with much attention. She'd taken things right to the brink, because she'd known she'd have to. She'd invented the simplest way to explain her *known* movements on that night.

"Are you still there?"

"Yes," I said, "go on."

"I told them that the man had kept me tied to a bed all night, but the next morning when he was away from the house I managed to escape. And then, when I was safe again in the street, I was stopped by a militiaman, and arrested because of my papers."

There was silence on the line, so I said, "And they asked you to give a description of the assassin."

"Of course. I said he was short, but very strong, with graying hair and a scar underneath his left ear. He spoke with an Estonian accent."

"And they tried to break your story."

"Oh, yes. They tried very hard."

And hadn't succeeded, because for a few days it would have remained unbreakable, until they'd taken their investigations to the point where they could destroy it, word for word, and get to the truth. *Did you bear any kind of grudge against General Gennadi Vilechko? Were you aware that he was the head of the regional state security office in Krasnogvardeiskaya at the time when your father, Boris Vladimir Rusakov, was rumored to have been executed without formality? Didn't you in fact request five days' immediate leave on medical grounds due to prolonged menstrual cramps at the time when General Vilechko was about to visit Novosibirsk?*

I didn't know what exact questions would have been asked, but that would have been their tenor, and she wouldn't have had any answers that would have kept her out of the penal-servitude camps for life on a charge of being an accessory to premeditated murder.

"You did well, Tanya," I said.

"I wanted very much to keep your name out of it all."

"I'm indebted to you."

"No. But perhaps it made up a little."

Made up for her leaving the safe house and getting herself arrested.

"Of course. Tanya, stay near the phone for twenty minutes."

The door of the bar swung open and crashed back against the wall and a man came out with his hands covering his head, two others after him and catching him up, landing a kick and sending him sprawling, setting on him as he lay on the ground, *"Fucking Jew . . . You come here again and you'll finish up in the river, cock-sucking Jew-boy . . ."*

The *Pamyat* brigade. Good-bye Stalin, hello Hitler, *le plus ça change,* so forth.

"When shall I see you again?" Tanya asked me.

"I don't really know," I said. She'd turned over sometimes, during the morning at the safe house, and had lain with her face against me, not moving away, moving closer. She didn't wear perfume, but I remembered her scent. "As soon as I can manage," I told her. "Put our friend back on the line, would you?"

The two men were crunching across the snow toward the bar, one of them with blood on his wrist.

When Ferris came on the line I just told him that if Rusakov was in the bar I'd call back in twenty minutes and let him talk to his sister for a moment. "I've got to have his trust, and her voice will give him proof that I've got her into safe hands."

"We'll stand by for you," Ferris said, and then—"I've been doing a bit of research, by the way, on your rogue agent. There was a man in the Ministry of Defense called Talyzin who spoke out rather too loudly against some of the die-hard generals, and they put him into a psychiatric ward when no one was looking. After six months he escaped, and from raw intelligence data going into London he might be your agent."

"Why?"

"Three reasons. It's believed he came out of the psychiatric ward with some of his marbles gone; two of the generals who put him in there were Kovalenko and Chudin; and he'd served in Afghanistan as a mine-sweeping engineer."

"Knows explosives."

"Yes."

"Another case of revenge, then, if he blew that train up. Attempted revenge."

"We've had reports of hundreds like that, following the coup. Old scores to be settled. They're still working on it for me in London, and if I get anything more I'll pass it on."

"That name again—Talyzin?"

"Yes." He spelled it for me. Then—"Control has also been in signals with me, asking for a progress report."

Bloody Croder. "So what did you give him?"

There was *nothing*. There was *nothing* to give Control.

"I just said that progress is being made."

It's the stock diplomatic answer the director in the field sometimes uses when London asks what's happening and there's nothing positive to offer. The shadow can be crawling on his stomach out of a wrecked support car with his clothes on fire and the host country's security forces moving in on him with war-trained Dobermans and if Control wants a report he'll be told that progress is being made, if only by the fact that the poor bloody ferret has managed to crawl another six inches with his smashed leg as the heat of the flames reaches his skull and his brain begins going into short circuit as a prelude to the big good-bye, I don't mean to dramatize, but that is exactly what happened to Siddons when he'd bought it in Beirut, while his DIF was reporting progress to that bastard Loman in London.

Compared with which of course my situation was decidedly cushy, I was only holed up in a phone booth in Siberia watching that poor bugger out there struggling to get up before he froze to death, but all the same I didn't take kindly to Croder, Chief of bloody Signals, asking for a progress report from a director in the field who was notorious for refusing to call up London when there was nothing to tell them, believing it quite rightly to be a waste of time.

"May he get the pox," I told Ferris and shut down the signal and dialed the ambulance service and told them there was a man outside the Harbor Light bar on the west bank of the Ob needing attention. Then I forced open the door of the booth against the rust on the hinges and went across to the Jew and helped him onto his feet and told him there was an ambulance coming, with any luck.

Pulled open the door of the place and got hit by the reek of black tobacco smoke and straight spirits and human sweat, the air hot against my face after the freezing temperature outside. When my eyes adjusted to the smoke haze I saw a man sitting alone in a corner on the far side of the room from the bar, a pair of gloves on the table, different shades of brown. He saw me come in but I looked past him and went over to the end of the long teakwood counter and ordered a Smirnov straight up, pulling out a stool and settling down to check everybody in the place, one by one.

I took fifteen minutes, not hurrying, because I didn't know Captain Vadim Rusakov any better than he knew me and even though he'd shot that general down he could still be working undercover for the *Podpolia* or for *Pamyat*, the extreme nationalist right, and could have brought people in here to look me over. Or he could have picked up ticks in the army barracks and brought them here without knowing it, and I just wanted to talk to him alone, wasn't in the mood for a party.

Bloody London.

Rusakov was the *only* hope I'd got of putting *Meridian* back on track and bringing it home. But he might know nothing, nothing at all.

Six or seven tarts, two of them Chinese, they brought them here regularly from Beijing and Vladivostok on the *Rossiya*, one of the taxi drivers had told me. The other women were jealous of them, of their slight and flawless looks, blowing smoke at them from their lipstick-reddened cigarettes, to loud laughter from the men.

A huddle of Russian naval officers round an illegal crap game, three sailors drinking themselves under a table near the door, one of them with a trouser leg soaked. A lone militiaman in uniform, too far gone to be on duty unless someone had slipped him a mickey for a giggle. Two dogs, one of them with a broken leg, snuffling and tearing at something unholy under one of the tables.

I poured the shot of vodka down the leg of the bar stool and put the glass back on the counter and left the change and made my way close to the walls until I came up to the table where the odd gloves were lying and pulled out the chair opposite Captain Rusakov and sat down and saw the chalk moving across the board for *Meridian* in the basement in Whitehall, *Executive reports possible breakthrough, is now in contact with valuable informer.*

Not really. There's just a chance, that's all, the last we've got. But remember, we're making progress.

Chapter 20

Vadim

"I saw you come in," Rusakov said, "sometime ago. Why didn't you come straight over here?"

"You get served quicker at the bar."

He gave a slow blink, perhaps of patience, then went on watching me with a gaze as steady as a beam of light. He had green eyes, like his sister, but you didn't notice their color so much as the concentration in them. He'd be good at interrogation, Rusakov, may have done a bit of that.

"Where is Tanya?" he asked me.

"Want to talk to her?"

His eyes lit. *"Yes."*

I took him outside and along to the phone booth and with my back to Rusakov dialed the number for the Hotel Karasevo and got Ferris on the line and asked for Tanya. Then I waited outside the booth, watching the lights of the ambulance dimming in the distance through the river fog.

Ferris allowed them a minute or not much more; he would have briefed her not to tell her brother where she was, since it was the nerve center for *Meridian*, and the longer she spoke to him the more easily she might let something slip.

When he came out of the booth Rusakov stood in front of me with his feet together, advanced one pace, gave me a bear hug, retreated one pace, and stood at ease.

"You gave her freedom," he said. "I cannot express my gratitude."

He'd put on seaman's clothes, as I'd asked him to, but

233

there was no disguising Captain Vadim Rusakov of the Russian Army.

"She'll be all right," I said. "She's in good hands." We walked back to the bar.

"She wouldn't tell me where she is."

"No, that wouldn't be a good thing. The line could have been bugged, you see."

"Then you will tell me."

"I'd rather you didn't ask. She's safe there, that's all you need to know, and it shouldn't be all that long before you can see her." I gave it a beat. "It depends on how much you're willing to help me."

He pulled open the door of the bar and stood back, boots neatly together. "As much as I am able, of course." But there was a note of wariness in it. He didn't like my not trusting him with his sister's location, didn't like to think she was in a place where the lines might be bugged.

Back at the table we ordered bowls of soup and some bread, and I listened to Rusakov until the food arrived, because I wanted as much of his background as I could get without asking questions, and his attitude toward the present-day regime in Russia. But first he had to unload some of his guilt.

"I should never have involved her in such a thing. She alerted me that he was coming to Novosibirsk, fine, I should have taken the matter from there, and told her to remain in Moscow."

"It wouldn't have been easy," I said, "to get that man to an appointed place without Tanya's help, and to have him identified on the spot."

"I should have thought of another way."

One of the dogs let out a yelp, been kicked, I suppose. "She wanted to be there, Vadim. She had a lot of rage in her."

He leveled his gaze at me for a moment. "I didn't think of that."

"They're not meant to have any rage, are they, it might frighten the males of the species. But it's there all right."

He talked about his father, showed me the photograph of a man in a black badly fitting suit, some kind of decoration in the lapel, the same penetrating gaze aimed at the camera, no smile. "He was an individualist, so they shot him. I am an individualist, but no one will be shooting me because I now live in the society for whose ideals he gave his life."

It wasn't the first time he'd said that. He'd rehearsed it until he'd got it right, perhaps because he knew his father would have approved of the formality. There was more room for pride now in Vadim Rusakov's heart, since he'd spent his rage in the rattle of shot last night when General Gennadi Vilechko had slid onto the snow with his back leaving streaks of blood on the wall behind him.

"This new society," I asked Rusakov when the food arrived, "is it going smoothly, here in Novosibirsk?"

He looked surprised, then said, "Of course, you only arrived here yesterday. Yes, the new society is going smoothly, on the surface. A few growls here and there, a few complaints, but no food riots, no looting of shops, no angry mobs yelling outside the government offices." He lined up the yellow plastic saltcellar with the bottle of sauce, doing it carefully. "But under the surface there is a great deal of tension, you know, among the people."

"And among the soldiers?"

"Among the soldiers the tension is deeper, since soldiers are not allowed to think. But it is there." His eyes suddenly on mine—"There have been cases of unexplained deaths. I have investigated some of them. The dead were all devoted democrats, *rabid*, one could say, sick and fed up with the way the army has gone down and down under the Communists, until drugs, drunkenness, and desertions have become the order of the day, reflecting the awareness of the military that they've lost the respect of the people in the streets." Spreading one hand—"Of course, the new democracy has brought new problems. The army is now forced to grow its own vegetables and milk its own goats, since food is scarce."

"These deaths," I said. "Who's doing the killing?"

"You cannot guess?"

"The *Podpolia?*"

"But of course the *Podpolia.*" He lowered his voice. "There are two factions at my barracks, just as there are in the streets—those who are ready to tighten their belts and support Yeltsin and his program, and the core of die-hard Communists who want the old order back."

"How strong are they?"

"They are not strong in numbers, but they are there, working in secrecy."

I'd got enough background, and broke some bread and started on the soup. It was still hot, salty, and had a flavor I didn't recognize, didn't particularly like. Dogs were at a premium this winter in Novosibirsk, if they had any flesh on them; I avoided the lumps of meat. "Vadim," I said, "your sister told the militia only that she came to Novosibirsk to see you, as she always does when she gets leave. They can't ask her any more questions now, but they'll be pushing on with their inquiries, especially in Moscow. They hadn't known, when she was at their headquarters, that her father— and your father—was ordered shot by General Vilechko four years ago, or they certainly wouldn't have released her at my request. As soon as—"

"At your request . . ." he said slowly, his eyes boring into me. "You have the power to 'request' such a thing from the militia?"

I broke more bread, leaving the soup. "I haven't the power to request anything of anyone, but I wanted your sister out of there, so I had to devise the means. My next concern is yourself. As soon as they dig up the information that you and Tanya bore a grudge against General Vilechko, they'll ask the army to arrest you and hand you over to them.

This could happen when you go back to your unit; the military police may well be waiting for you outside your quarters."

His eyes deepened, hardened. "I see." Then he said, "And Tanya?" I liked him for that.

"She's in the safest possible hands, don't let it worry you."

I assumed I could say that, for the moment. But someone had killed Roach, the support man, and Roach might have gone too close to the Hotel Karasevo, nerve center for *Meridian*, and at any given time Ferris himself, its director in the field, could need a safe house, and urgently. It might have happened before in the annals of the Bureau, that the DIF of some mission had got blown, but it's never happened when I've been in the field. The DIF is sacrosanct, untouchable, he has to be. He holds the lifeline for his executive.

"You are in," Rusakov was saying, "some kind of"—he spread his hand—"intelligence branch? The MPS?"

"Not the MPS. I operate pretty well on my own, and you should know that. If you find yourself in trouble, I've no authority of any kind to pull you out of it." I looked across at the door of the bar as a man came in. "You should also know, Vadim, that at this moment I'm the subject of an intense manhunt by the militia, the police, and the KGB— or the MPS, as we're now meant to call them."

His eyes deepened again; I'd seen the same thing in Tanya.

"So," he said with a brief nod.

The man looked all right, merchant seaman's rig and cap, bundling across to the bar, freezing, desperate for a rum grog. I looked at Rusakov again. "I think I told you, didn't I, that I saw your action of last night as a matter of summary justice, when Tanya told me what Vilechko had done to you both?" I was kneading a small piece of the dark, heavy bread, molding it in to a disk with a point on each side, like a spinning top. "Your quarrel," I said, "was with General Vilechko, and not—can I assume?—with the other two, Generals Chudin and Kovalenko. But do you happen to know if they're still here in Novosibirsk?"

I felt time slowing down.

How long have we got? I'd asked Ferris in that rat-infested shed where we'd made our rendezvous. *Have I got any kind of a deadline?*

He'd thought it out, taken his time. *Yes, we have a deadline. It's zero.*

The generals had been Zymyanin's target for information. That was what he'd told me before he was killed. They'd arrived in Novosibirsk and gone to ground and we had to find them, pick up from where Zymyanin had left off. That was still the focus of *Meridian*: Zymyanin had believed that the generals had information of a kind that would trigger alarm bells throughout the intelligence organizations of both hemispheres. We needed that information.

We don't know—Ferris—*that they might not have already finished what they came here to do. They could be leaving Novosibirsk tomorrow morning. Or tonight.*

They might have gone by now, and I waited to hear Rusakov say precisely that. He didn't.

"General Chudin and General Kovalenko are at present the guests of my commanding officer."

I spun my little top, and watched *Meridian* start running again.

"Oh really," I said. "The official guests?"

"No. Not official."

"But it's known to all ranks that they're in the camp?"

"It would be difficult to conceal it. Rumors are the lifeblood of the barracks. But nothing official has been posted in Daily Routine Orders or anywhere else."

"You've seen them? The generals?"

"Only once, and at a distance, crossing from a staff car to their quarters."

I picked up the little top again and spun it. "Have you any plans to wipe those two out as well, Vadim?"

His head came up in surprise. "Why should I?"

"I wondered if they were party to Vilechko's orders to have your father shot."

"No. It was Vilechko's personal order. I know the facts."

Had been rooting for those facts for four years, perhaps, until he was sure. Then he'd asked Tanya to keep watch on Vilechko as best she could, in Moscow. "Do you know," I asked him, "why those two generals are visiting your CO?"

"He himself is in the *Podpolia*."

"Has he got any power?"

With surprise—"He is the commanding officer."

"Put it this way: if he tried to bring the whole battalion into the *Podpolia*, what would happen?"

"There would be mutiny. He is known to belong to the hard-line Communists, but he doesn't dare come out into the open. That is why the visit of the two generals is not being publicized."

"There's a security guard round their quarters?"

"Yes. We doubled it, after a man was seen watching the area with field glasses from a car outside the camp."

"When was this?"

"Soon after the generals arrived. The observer drove away before he could be challenged."

Did he really, now.

I put some money on the table. "Vadim, I've got to make a telephone call. You want to wait here?"

"I will leave with you."

We pushed our chairs back and Rusakov said, "Thank you for the . . ." He gestured toward the table. For the dog soup.

"My pleasure."

He was at the door first, holding it open for me, and the black freezing air hit us in a wave as we went outside.

"Where's your car, Vadim?"

"Over there, the army Jeep. I will wait for you."

I felt a lift of relief when Ferris picked up the phone at his end, which wasn't reassuring: if there's one thing the executive in the field has to count on it's that his director is always at the other end of the telephone, inviolate. But the Roach thing had changed that.

"Bit of debriefing," I told him.

"Good." He didn't give it a cheerful tone, nothing hearty, I'd have killed him for that and he knew it. He wasn't expecting any kind of breakthrough at this stage of the mission: there was too much stacked up against us, with the executive on the run and a wreck on the river for a safe house.

But at least there was this: "The two remaining generals," I said, "are still in Novosibirsk. They're guests of the CO of the Russian Army unit, unofficially and under special protection." I filled him in with the details.

"This is quite good," Ferris said when I'd finished.

In point of fact yes, we'd caught up with the objective for *Meridian*, which was the information buried in the heads of those two men. The problem was that they were behind the wire fence and sentries of a fully manned and equipped army battalion, no real case for dancing in the streets when London received Ferris's signal.

"Rusakov," I said, "is now an ally."

"I would think so."

"I'm going to get him to keep the generals under observation while they're in camp. He's got men he can trust. So I'll need you to move your best support man into the immediate field, as close as you can to the safe house."

I could see Rusakov through the grime of the glass panels, sitting at the wheel of his jeep. He could be useful to us, useful in the extreme, but he was a stranger, not of the Bureau, untrained and unpredictable. I was quite sure he'd do very nearly anything I asked him to do, because of Tanya, but simple gratitude doesn't have the high-tensile strength that underlies our neurotic devotion to the Sacred Bull, and the more reliance I put on Captain Vadim Rusakov the more dangerous it would be.

"How far can we trust your captain?" I heard Ferris

asking. It wasn't telepathy; we both knew the risk of using strangers.

"I don't know him well enough to answer that. All I can do is be careful. How close can you get your support man to the safe house?"

"Five kilometers," Ferris said. He had the map in front of him.

"With a secure telephone?"

"Yes." He gave me the number.

"All right, and I'll need a mobile radio link."

"Noted."

"And a map showing the location of the army camp. When he approaches, he should whistle the Fifth." Then I asked Ferris—hadn't meant to—"How are things your end?"

"You worry too much."

Right, you do *not* ask your director in the field how things are with him; he must be seen at all times to be as secure in his sanctum as is the oracle in Delphi.

I wouldn't have asked him, perhaps, if Tanya weren't also there. He would know that. Ferris knows everything.

We shut down the signal and I forced back the door of the booth and went across to the jeep and got in. "Vadim, would you be able to keep the generals under covert observation while they're in camp? Use some of your men?"

"That would be quite easy. Their quarters are in a separate building from the barracks."

"Then I want you to do that. Look, we need to write things down. Is there—"

"Here." He reached across the seat and got a clipboard from the rear of the car and pulled the pencil out of its slot.

I gave him the phone number I'd got from Ferris and told him to write it down. "Vadim, that number is *classified*. Understand that."

He looked at me in the glow of light from the dashboard. "I understand. You may trust me. Do you know that?" He waited.

"Of course. It's just that if you found yourself forced at some time to answer questions, it might be difficult—"

"You may trust me in *any* circumstances." His eyes held mine.

"Fair enough. So look, if you find anything to report to me on the generals, phone that number and give your name. He'll be our liaison. Your name is also classified, so don't worry. I want to know whenever those people make a move. When they leave camp I want to know where they go. Can you have them tracked?"

Rusakov thought about that, stroking a circle on the lined yellow clipboard sheet with his finger. *Muster all ranks, B Platoon, 18:00 hrs., for kit inspection* had been written across the top, then crossed out. "It might be difficult," he said at last, "to send out a vehicle at short notice. I'd have to submit an order for it beforehand, and give the destination and purpose—except in an emergency, of course. But it would be difficult, again, to claim an emergency at a time when the generals were initiating transit."

"Yes, blow the whole thing. Then see what information you can get hold of before they leave camp. See if you can get their destination from the transport section."

"That would be easier, yes."

Two men came out of the Harbor Light, slamming the door behind them, one of them bent over laughing, the other one taking a leak against the wall, steam clouding up in the lamplight. "All right," I said to Rusakov, "I'll leave it to you. Anything you can do to get me information will be a blow against the *Podpolia*. But you'll have to keep in mind the fact that sooner or later the militia's going to ask the army to arrest you." I looked at him in the glow of the dashboard. "Have you any kind of bolt-hole you can go to in the town?"

He thought about that too. "Yes."

"Where?"

He looked down. "The house of a friend."

"She'd be ready to shelter you? Keep you hidden?" He

was silent. "I've got to know," I told him, "because I want to keep in contact."

He looked up again. "She would help me, yes." He wrote on the pad and tore off a strip of it and gave it to me. "Her name is Raisa."

The two men were lurching across the snow to a pickup truck with a mast lying across the rear, a furled sail round it; the domed glass of the lamp at its head caught the light from the bar, a ruby eye in the fog creeping from the river.

I put the strip of paper away. "Is there a fellow officer," I asked Rusakov, "or one of the men under you, who has your absolute trust?"

"Yes." This time he hadn't had to think about it. "A master sergeant."

"All right. If you can't avoid arrest, can he take your place? Make contact with me?"

In a moment, "I will ask him."

"You're not sure he'll—"

"I will ask him as a formality. But he will do it."

"Name?"

"Bakatin."

"Master Sergeant Bakatin. Then—"

"But I must tell you," Rusakov said, his eyes suddenly on mine, "I shall resist arrest. I shall resist very strongly."

"Of course. You put an *apparatchik* thug out of the way, no earthly reason to suffer for it." I took off my glove and offered my hand. "Keep in touch, then."

I put the Ford Escort in the same place as before, under the cover of the fallen roof of the shed, and walked the half mile to the river, taking time to check the environment and going aboard the hulk just after eleven o'clock, with the moon floating above the dark skeletonic arm of a grain elevator downriver.

The starboard bow of the *Natasha* had been stove in when she'd been wrecked, and I spent an hour shifting loose timber, stacking it against the bulkheads to form a tunnel that ran aft from the entrance to the cabin below deck and led to the smashed hatchway at the stern. Rats ran in the beam of the flashlight; they couldn't get at the provisions but they'd scented them and moved in to reconnoiter.

When the tunnel was finished I tested it out, checking for loose boards that might make a noise, leaving the flashlight in the cabin and feeling my way through the dark toward the hatch at the stern. I didn't think I'd need an escape route to deck level because Ferris would have tightened the whole support network after Roach had been blown, but these were confined quarters and if anyone came down here with a gun I wouldn't have any answer except to get out before he could use it.

It's just a touch of the usual paranoia, that's all.

Get out of my bloody life.

I went through the escape tunnel half a dozen times in the dark to get used to it, the feel of the timbers and the lie of the ground, the smell of rope in the chain locker and the crack of light between the boards just below the deck where a lamp on the shore made a gleam, establishing my bearings, making the journey twice as fast and in more silence the last time through.

Heating some water and washing, I tried to feel that *Meridian* had got back on track tonight: the generals were still in Novosibirsk and I had their exact location and it looked as if we could rely on Rusakov at least to signal a warning when they made a move, and that was about as good as I could expect at this stage of the mission.

I don't know if I'd managed to convince myself about this but it didn't really matter because it was less than an hour later when I heard the first four notes of Beethoven's Fifth Symphony come whistling softly through the dark and the support man came below deck with the radio for me and said he couldn't raise Ferris anymore on the telephone, the night porter at the Hotel Karasevo said his room was empty now.

Chapter 21

Rogue

He stood there watching me—Frome, he'd said his name was—the wavering light of the candle moving the shadows across his face, its reflection in his eyes, two pale flames, his breath clouding on the air.

Floating ice, colliding with the stern of the hulk, rang in the silence.

"And the woman?" I asked him. "Rusakova?"

"She's gone too."

He watched me, hands in bus driver's gauntlets hanging at his sides, moisture glistening on his fur hat where he'd caught it, I suppose, when he'd ducked down through the hole in the timbers up there, bringing away snow.

"And all measures are being taken," I said, a statement, not a question, something to say while I thought things out; of course all measures were being taken to find the DIF, at least find his tracks.

I felt like an astronaut—this is the nearest I can get to the idea of what it's like—losing one end of his lifeline when he's out on a space walk, floating away.

"Did he leave anything in his room?" I asked Frome.

"I don't know."

"What about her—did she leave anything?"

"I don't know," he said again.

"Then what the bloody hell *do* you know?"

Ice clinked out there on the river.

He watched me, Frome, the two pale flames in his eyes.

"Sorry," I said.

"That's okay. I mean, there's not much to know, see. I tried phoning him several times and the switchboard said he couldn't be in his room, so I went round there and checked, found his door unlocked and the room empty, same as hers on the same floor."

"No signs."

"None I could see. I took a good—"

"Toilet things?"

"Still there. So were—"

"Scrambler gone?"

"Yes. And the bug sniffer."

It didn't mean much. If anyone had got in there and managed to take Ferris they'd have taken those things as well, they weren't cheap and you'd never find any more like that in Russia.

"Bitch, isn't it?" I heard Frome say.

"What? Yes." He was still standing there. "You want to sit down?"

"No. I don't like leaving the car out there too long, bit of a giveaway. Try the walkie?"

I picked up the unit and switched it on and moved the dial off the squelch and pressed CALL and said *"Meridian"* a couple of times and got a response from support base.

"Executive," I said. "Two numbers for you." Rusakov's at the camp, and his woman friend's in the town. "If Rusakov can't signal, a man named Bakatin might come through, replacing him. Any news?"

Of Ferris. He'd know that.

"No. I'll raise you if he calls. The minute he calls." Remembering to hope, scratching around for straws, they all were, Frome was, I was, any straw of comfort we could find.

All right, yes, that's putting it a fraction too dramatically, about the astronaut thing, I mean that poor bastard's going to finish up somewhere on the far side of Pluto one day with his supertrained athletic body shriveled inside its metal-alloy shell and his wife remarried and his kids middle-aged, and when one of us poor bloody ferrets loses his DIF he loses his lifeline in a way, but it's not *that* bad, we can go on foraging for ourselves, get home with our heads still on if we're lucky, it's just that when the mission's running hot we tend to get a bit edgy and the last thing we want to hear is that we're cut off from our director and hence from London Control.

Make a note, we should perhaps make a note here, should we not, my good friend, to get it put into the training manuals at Norfolk: Do *not* learn to regard the director in the field as your bloody *mother*.

"I'll need your radio manned," I said into the unit, "round the clock."

"Yes, sir, understood."

I shut down the signal and looked at Frome. "Mind your head when you go back up there."

I should have got used to the broken bells by now, but as the dark body of the river moved under its scales of ice the sound kept sleep away for a time, and then I lay drifting at last, the current turning me and turning me back as I kept the fur of the dead cat close against my face, using it as camouflage to deceive the men who were waiting there along the bank with their guns swinging as they moved, watching for the target, for me, on the surface of the river, but that must be a dream, perhaps of an earlier mission, I'm always having them, they never leave us, I've talked about it to others in the Caff, and now the feeling of movement across the scalp, the delicate exploratory scratching and then the first nibble, with the small sharp teeth rooting more boldly among the hair—*Oh, Jesus Christ*—and I swung up an arm and felt the soft warm body before it vanished into the shadows, not a dream this time, no, and I got up and found a length of timber and lay down again with one end of it under my hand, waiting but drifting down again after a while, down into the lulling silence of the delta waves before I felt it again, this time on my foot and I hit out with the bit of timber and felt a splashing across my cheek and hit out again

and then sat up and saw it lying there, big as a boot, its
blood pooling across the boards in the candlelight, some of
it on my face.

It was gone four o'clock in the morning when I woke
next time, swathed in extra blankets with a hole for breathing
through. I hadn't felt them again; perhaps they'd recognized
the scream for what it was, had heard death in it and kept
their distance. I impressed future time on the subconscious
and it woke me accurately at seven, an hour before first light.
For my breakfast, turtle soup from one of the self-heating
cans, with two hard-boiled eggs and a slice of that Christmas
cake, 'twas the season, if not to be jolly, to indulge the ap-
petite, on the sound and ingrained principle that I didn't
know when I would eat again.

Then I opened the map Frome had brought me and
spread it out in the candlelight, walking my fingers round
the wooded area where the army camp took up three quarters
of a square kilometer. It was served by two minor roads that
joined and made a fork three kilometers from the main gates
of the camp. Then I folded the map and picked up the radio
unit and left the hulk and put *Meridian* into extreme and
imminent hazard, because I had no choice.

The crackle of gunfire came again, and the rooks took
off from the poplars that laced the east horizon, wheeling
and cawing. The rifle range was out of sight from here, below
a fold in the ground, and the sound of the guns was muffled,
echoing from the long corrugated iron huts that formed most
of the camp.

The new day was frozen, as the days before had been,
the earth invisible under the snow, the bare trees standing
in a black iron frieze across the hill to the south. The air was
motionless, its cold clamped to my face as I studied the landscape from beside the car.

Gunfire again, its echoes mimicking.

He could have been anyone, the man they'd seen watching the camp from his car, but I thought I knew who he was,

and if he'd been there yesterday he would be there today; he'd driven away before he could be challenged, but he would have come back, must have come back, standing off at a greater distance now, finding cover in the trees. They'd nothing to fear from him, the soldiers in the camp; they were an armed battalion. They wouldn't have sent out scouts to hunt for him; they'd been curious, that was all.

It could have been anyone, but I thought it was the rogue agent in the field—Talyzin, if Ferris was right.

There was a man in the Ministry of Defense called Talyzin who spoke out rather too loudly against the generals. . . . From raw intelligence data going into London, he might be your agent.

I'd sensed his presence in the environment ever since the *Rossiya* had been blown up, had thought I'd seen him once, getting clear of the militia blocks at the scene of the wreck, as I had. I didn't think he'd had anything to do with the death of Roach: he'd had no motive; and I didn't think he'd had anything to do with the surveillance on the Ford Escort that had brought that man Yermakov on my track, may he rest in peace. But I thought he might have set that bomb, the rogue agent, and if so, his motive would obviously have been to wipe out the three generals and their entourage, because it doesn't take high explosive to destroy the life force in a single human being—Vilechko, say—you can do it with one bullet, as Rusakov had done. So if it was the rogue agent who had set that bomb, then he would still be locked into his private—personal?—mission: the death of the two generals who were still pursuing their own operation in Novosibirsk, pursuing it just over there, in point of fact, behind the wire fence of the camp.

So I would expect him to be here, the agent, somewhere in the immediate environment, observing the generals, and perhaps it was that man on the hill between the trees, sitting in the car.

He'd been there before I arrived, or I would have seen him drive up; he would have had to use the furthermost road branching from the fork, and I could see its whole length, from the fork to the hill. The minor road didn't go up the hill, only round it, but he was nevertheless on higher ground, with a good view of the camp. He was also in rather good cover, buried among the trees, and I wouldn't have known he was there if I hadn't been looking for him, hadn't caught the glint on the windows of the car as the strengthening light of the day came creeping across the land from the east.

A crackle of gunfire, stitching the silence.

I'd etched the configuration of his car by now on the visual memory, and if it changed I would detect it at once— if, for instance, he opened one of its doors on this side. I would have put the distance between us at close to half a kilometer, but I could see that he was sitting in the front of the car, because his dark coat altered the reflective value of the window glass. The distance from his car to the nearest line of huts in the camp was more like a kilometer and a half, so that he'd have to be using at least a pair of 10 × 10's to pick up anything useful.

He could have been—*must* have been—there all night unless he had anyone in support, which I didn't believe: a rogue is a rogue, and works solo. They're a breed apart, often neurotic, occasionally psychopathological, you can't ever trust them. Even if you can persuade them into working with you, with your cell or your network, you can't turn your back on them, they'll slip a knife in if it suits them, sometimes for kicks, ask that bastard Loman, he'd been running Fairfax through *Tigerfish* in the South China Sea when that executive had been found floating in the offshore trash in Saigon harbor, and it hadn't taken the Bureau five minutes to find out that Fairfax had been using a rogue agent who knew the area, and that said rogue agent had decided to take one hundred percent of the credit for the successful completion of the mission and the only way to do that was by putting a bullet into the executive's brain and dropping him off a pier.

A glint came from the trees on the hill, this time in

motion, brightening and dimming out. I hadn't seen that before.

It was difficult at this distance to understand what that glint meant. It wasn't the degree-by-degree passage of the morning light reflected from the windows of the car up there: it was smaller, more focused—and I then I got it, because when it moved again I saw it had a twin.

I couldn't see his eyes, but I knew they were on me now, pressed to the 10 × 10's.

Crackle of gunfire and this time the nerves reacted a little, gooseflesh under the sleeves. The sudden contact that only the eyes can make at a distance between two creatures is intimate and dramatic. When that incredible girl looked up—remember?—from halfway across the crowded room and saw you watching her, there was a rush of hormones, wasn't there, as the glands kicked in; it was like swallowing all the perfumes of Araby in one gulp, I know the feeling, but that wasn't the feeling I had now as I sat in the car amid these alien snows and kept still, perfectly still, submitting to a hostile scrutiny I couldn't escape.

It wasn't unexpected. I'd known that if the man with the field glasses were watching the camp again today he would also make frequent checks on his environment, and my cover wasn't as good as his: there were no trees down here and all I'd been able to do was squeeze the Escort in between the ruined hulk of a barn and a drystone wall that ran past it—not even cover, call it camouflage.

It wasn't unexpected but there was engagement now; contact had been made at a distance between these two creatures out here under the early morning sky, and the scene had changed. He wouldn't just leave things like this, the agent up there among the trees. He wouldn't want to be watched. He would need to make a move, but it wouldn't be like yesterday's, because yesterday he would have had a whole battalion to contend with if he'd stayed his ground, and today there was only one man.

He would be a violent antagonist, if he chose to confront me. That would be his nature: he was a rogue. And he would be armed. Their lives in the field are short, but they'd be shorter still without the advantage of weapons. I'd known this when I'd left the *Natasha* an hour ago and put the mission into hazard, but I'd had no choice. I still didn't know whether I had any chance at all of monitoring the movements of the generals and infiltrating whatever operation they were running, but I knew that I'd never be able to do it if a rogue agent were in the field and moving ahead of me with the intention of finishing what he'd started on that train—of killing them off.

Listen, Zymyanin had said as the corridor of the train had rocked under our feet, *this is all I can tell you for now. The Bureau should do everything*—everything—*to keep those people under surveillance.*

That was why I was here this morning, with the ice caking the windows and the rasping of the digital clock on its worn bearings stressing the silence inside the car—to reach the objective for *Meridian* if I could, and get the information to London. I'd lost my director in the field but I'd set up a close support base with communications and liaison for Rusakov, but it would all be useless if I let that man on the hill take over the action.

I'd found him. Now I had to stop him, get him out of the picture.

He was here to follow the generals when they left camp, and in this we had the same purpose, but I believed it would end there. He had their death in mind, and when he'd followed them far enough from the camp to do the deed without bringing all hell on his head, then he would do it. Or it could be a suicide run he was here for, and the moment the generals left camp through those gates across there he'd move down from the hill to intercept and pump a volley of dum-dums into them as the alarm was sounded and the first of the armored cars was started up and sent in pursuit. He wouldn't get far and he would know that, but a suicide run would fit quite well into the thinking process of a typical rogue agent, and he could be one of the psychopaths, capable for instance of bombing a crowded train with no thought for women and children.

And if *that* was his plan, the hail of dum-dums would not only obliterate the generals. It would blow *Meridian* into Christendom.

He was still watching me. The field glasses hadn't moved since I'd seen them lock onto the image of the Ford Escort.

Gunfire, echoing from the huts. I kept still, watching the twin glints from among the trees, staring him down.

He would have plans for me, too, now that he'd seen me. It had been the major calculated risk I had to take. If he were here to wipe out the generals with a burst of fire he would do the same with me, immediately afterward, because I presented a threat: at least I would be a witness to his act of assassination and at most I might intercept him when he left the hill and block his run, setting him up for the armored cars. But perhaps he wouldn't wait for that. Perhaps he would deal with me first, soon, get me out of the way, as a spider moves onto the web and removes a foreign object that has fallen there and then goes back into cover to wait for the fly.

That was the risk, but it was calculated: it's the only kind I'll take.

And I had options. Perhaps, for instance, I could talk to him.

He was still watching me, so I started the engine. He hadn't swung the field glasses away, was still wondering who I was and what I was doing here. I wanted him to see me move off, so that he could follow me with the glasses, know that I was coming. I didn't want to surprise him: he might react, and lethally. I had to approach him overtly—he knew that I knew he was watching me; I wouldn't be some honest burgher out here to admire the view, because all the honest burghers in Novosibirsk were standing in line for a loaf of bread, poor buggers, be there all bloody day. He would know, that man on the hill, that I would be one of his kind, up to nothing innocent, and perhaps might sense a kindred spirit in the field.

A touch optimistic this morning, aren't we? A touch—
Shuddup.

The ice broke under the tires as I moved down to the fork in the road, and the bodywork creaked as we shimmied over the ruts. I had options, yes, but there weren't any others I could choose at this particular time. They were for later, if he proved a danger to *Meridian*, as I believed he was; then I would try to get past his weapons and contain him, bring him away from here, take him to the support base and tell them to look after him, get him medical attention if that were necessary, if he put up too much of a struggle and had to be subdued with some of the more extreme techniques.

I wished him no harm, be this noted. In looking for the death of those two generals he would, I was reasonably sure, be seeking to dispatch them to the same Elysian climes to which they would have dispatched others, perhaps hundreds, in the execution yards. The late Gennadi Vilechko, with at least a Rusakov's blood on his hands, had been their close confederate.

The ice crunched, the chains clinking now on the roadway, where military traffic had pounded the surface and reached the hardtop. I couldn't see from here whether the man was still watching me. I didn't need to see. He was watching me very carefully, I knew that, and a tingling sensation began in the exact center of my forehead. It was familiar, and didn't rate any attention: this wasn't the first time I'd moved deliberately into a potential line of fire and felt the phantom impact of a bullet, perhaps this time a dumdum, not my favorite, they blow the whole thing into a chrysanthemum, nothing left but the stalk.

I was halfway there now, a quarter of a kilometer from where I'd last seen him: a snowbank had blotted him out as I climbed the hill. He would use this, if he were trained, to change position and turn the car to face my direction so that he could see me through the windscreen when I appeared; or he might get out and stand there with the assault rifle ready to swing up into the aim as soon as he saw me. Then there'd be the delicate business of going closer to him under the gun, close enough to talk to him, and then, if the talk broke down and he told me to get out of this area on pain of instant death, close enough to get behind the weapon and effect a change in things. That would be the tricky bit.

I kept a steady pace in low gear, bumping over the ruts, watching for him among the higher trees.

I don't like this. You won't have a chance if he—

Oh, piss off.

Watching carefully now, trying to find the profile of his car or part of it, enough to know if he'd turned it round or had got out to wait for me.

Watch carefully.

The snow crunched under the wheels.

You won't have a chance if he—

I've told you before, *piss* off.

Crackle of gunfire and sweat broke instantly.

The rooks flew up from the camp.

Keeping a steady pace up the hill. Any change in the scene at this point—sudden acceleration, a burst of speed—could trigger his nerves and the gun.

There were widening columns of light now between the trees where I'd seen him last, but the configuration of his car wasn't there. He might have turned it so that its narrower front-end profile would be presented, but I thought I should see it even then: I'd marked his location at the outset, where the branch of a tree hung down at an angle, broken by a storm.

He'd moved the car. This was where he'd been, less than a hundred yards away—and then I saw him, moving in the distance along the hill road, and I gunned up and lost the rear end and steadied things and gunned up again more

carefully and started building up speed, saw him again as
the road straightened, saw that I was holding him now—at
a distance but holding him.

The observer drove away, Rusakov had told me, *before he
could be challenged.*

Skittish, then.

He was driving something European, not Soviet, possibly a SAAB but nothing fast like a Porsche. The speed factor
didn't come into things in any case: I'd simply have to gain
on him by playing with the gears to get as much traction as
possible on the snow, keep the Escort on the road, keep him
in sight until I could draw close enough to see where he was
going, to catch him if I could, yes, but in these conditions it
wouldn't be easy.

He was still the same distance ahead of me when the
road dropped from the hill and straightened out, and I was
trying to bring the speed up a degree when I saw he was
pulling away, not fast but gradually, taking me three kilometers, four, into the desolate open ground between the
military camp and the suburbs of the town, and it was here
that he slowed and then swung in a U-turn until he was
facing me and the first shots hit the front of the Escort low
down and began smashing their way upward in a raking
volley of fire as I dropped below the windscreen and it was
blown out and the shots began hammering into the metal
roof in a deafening percussion storm that blanked out
conscious thought, I was only aware of closeness to death,
could only see the snow and the sky revolving slowly as the
Escort rolled and churned among the drifts and hit rock and
bounced and rolled again, rearing now with the front end
going down and the whole thing swinging over, over
and down, crashing amid whiteness, whiteness and silence
and then a sunburst, sounds dying away.

Chapter 22

Zombie

It had happened before.

Fell forward. Forward and down, fell forward.

Lying with my face in the snow, freezing cold, cold iron mask on my face, get *up*.

Something was down there. Important?

Down in the snow.

I got up and the sky reeled and I sat with my back to the engine again. *Important.*

I reached down and dug around in the snow and found it, walkie-talkie unit, dropped it, I had dropped it, mustn't—must *not*—do that again.

The sky steadied. It had landed on its side, the Escort, and the hood had burst open, so I'd been sitting with my back to it, not very warm anymore, long—how long?

Thirty-two minutes. Patience, my good friend. Hurt anywhere?

A long icicle was hanging from the middle of the radiator where the fan had been driven into it by the impact; the engine bearers had sheared off. Yes, head hurting a bit.

Not skittish, then, no, he'd led me away from the camp, hadn't wanted anyone to hear the noise when he pumped that bloody toy, he tried to kill me, you know that?

Very cold out here, it was very cold. Yes, a violent man, the agent, didn't give anyone a chance, *kerboom* and *rat-tat-tat*, don't get in my way, not one of your more subtle espions, lacked reticence.

Car coming.

09:34.

But also cocky, like all violent men, they never doubt themselves or anything they do—he should have come back here and taken a look at me, made sure I was lying in the car with only the stalk left. Not, then, a professional.

Crunching over the dry brittle snow, the car, in the high pale light of the morning. It wasn't the agent. He would have come back here straightaway. This would be support. I'd signaled them.

But I watched carefully as the windscreen showed above the fold in the land, light flashing across the glass. It was a minute before I could see the whole vehicle, not a SAAB: the agent had been driving a SAAB.

I got onto my feet and the sky swung full circle and the snow came up and crashed against my face.

Sound of engines. *Two* cars.

"*Christ*, get him up."

I didn't want that, they could keep their bloody hands off.

"*Keep your bloody hands off.*"

"Anything broken?"

I got up by sliding my back against the roof of the Escort while they stood watching me, Frome and another man.

"Has the DIF signaled yet?" I asked Frome.

"Not yet."

"Has Rusakov signaled?"

"No."

"Jesus," the other man said, "what was he driving?" He was looking at the mess that gun had made all over the Escort. It's a bit of spook vernacular some of them affect, "He was driving an AK-47," that sort of thing. I asked him what his name was. "Oh, Dover, sir. You all right are you?" He stood staring at me, bland-faced. Where did they find *him*, for God's sake?

"Which car is mine?" I asked Frome. I'd signaled him for a replacement.

"Take your pick, but the Merc's more comfortable."

It was a four-door 280 SEL, too big, less easy to hide than the shitty-looking little Trabant.

Head was throbbing. The seatbelt had snapped when the car overturned. I asked Frome, "How serviceable is the Trab?"

"Oh, top line. She just looks like that."

"I'll take it."

Then I was face down on the snow again and they were helping me up and I didn't say anything this time, we'd got a mission running and if this was the only way we could run it then all right.

"We'll get you into the car," Frome said.

"I can walk. It's a head thing, that's all—"

"Bit of concussion."

"Yes." We picked our way over the snow toward the cars. "When the DIF comes through, tell him it was the rogue agent. I was trying to make contact with him and he didn't like it." Debriefing, not much to say and not a great deal to show for it except a bloody headache but that wasn't the problem: I couldn't monitor the agent anymore, he'd never let me get close.

Going down and I grabbed for the door handle of the Trabant but couldn't find it; snow came up again in a white wave.

"What time is it?"

"11:05," Frome said, his shadow huge on the wall, thrown by the lamplight. Ice rang against the beam of the hulk. I was facing the ceiling, flat on my back. "Been out a couple of hours. How d'you feel?"

"All right. Has he come through yet?" Ferris.

"Not yet."

"Rusakov?"

"No."

But I must tell you, I shall resist arrest. I shall resist very strongly.

Fine, but it would be a question of numbers when it

came; there wouldn't really be anything he could do.

"Call him?" Frome asked.

"No." I sat up and swung my legs over the edge of the bunk and stayed like that, waiting for things to steady. I didn't want to call Rusakov; he'd think we weren't sure of him.

"Make some tea for you?" Frome asked.

"What? No. Get back to base."

He didn't move, was watching me. "I think you need a doctor."

The whole bunk was shifting, but I'd got control of things now: I could shift them back if I kept still enough.

"I'm through it," I told Frome.

He let out an impatient breath, clouding the air in the lamplight. "You go flat on your face again in here, you hit the wall or the floor and you'll bash your head again, that what you want?"

"Look," I said and stood up, and the lamp circled slowly, finally stopped. "I'm through it now, so get moving. I want you back at base." The lamp had started circling again, but I found that if I moved my head with it I could get it to stop. Frome was watching me do it.

"Shit," he said, "if the DIF ever finds out I left you here looking like a zombie he'll have my balls."

"I'll put in a good word for you," I told him, and he turned and went out, clumping up the companionway.

I woke three times before dark and finally felt hungry and heated some soup.

This was at 5:07 in the evening.

"*Meridian*," I said.

"Hear you." Frome.

"Any signal?"

From Ferris, from Rusakov. There must have been, after all this time.

"No. You all right now?"

"Yes." Then I said, "You'd better tell London."

There was a brief silence before he said, "Will do."

I shut down the radio and saw them in the signals room, their heads turning as they heard Frome's voice coming over the amplifier: *DIF went missing 11:15 hours today, no signal since.*

Strictly no dancing in the streets.

The floes rang and rattled against the beam of the *Natasha*, and I went up the companionway and stood on the deck, leaning against the mast for cover. The air was calm, and the stars clung to the haze over the city like fireflies trapped on a web. There was still traffic on the river, a motor barge pushing its way through the white crust of the ice, smoke from its funnel lying in a dark rope across the water. I could hear a woman laughing somewhere, perhaps on board the wreck of the sailing boat farther along the quay, where a light was showing below deck. It was a wonderful sound, coming softly through the night, through this of all nights when joy was hard to come by. It came again, and I sipped courage from it, feeling release and renewal, not surprisingly, I suppose, given the natural grace of womankind to succor the needy.

I stayed for minutes there, clamped by the cold but letting the energy gather, not wanting to go short while I had the chance. Then I went below again, and before I'd reached the cabin the radio started beeping and I opened it up.

"Executive."

"Support. I've got a signal from Captain Rusakov. You want to write it down?"

"I don't think so."

Head had started throbbing again, I suppose because the pulse was faster: this could be a breakthrough.

"The two generals are going to be leaving the army camp at 17:30 hours. Armored transports have been ordered for that time."

Five-thirty: in nine minutes from now. *Armored* transports: that should take care of any suicide run by the rogue agent.

"Does Rusakov know the destination?"

"Yes. There's a building on the road east from the town, Kievskaya ulica. It's a mansion, used to be the residence of the state governor. The generals are going to have some kind of meeting there."

I opened the map with one hand and spread it on the table. "Did he give you a reference for the location?"

"It's set back in a park, a kilometer west of the power station. I've got it, have you?"

"Yes." There was silence while we both worked on our maps. "Twenty kilometers from the camp, twenty-five from here."

"Right."

I wouldn't be able to reach the camp before the generals left, but I could reach the mansion before they did, if the road wasn't snowed in.

"How soon can you get here?" I asked Frome.

"Gimme ten minutes."

"Bring the Mercedes." The little Trabant out there didn't have enough ground clearance.

"Got it."

I checked the time. "Listen, we're cutting it *very* fine— I want you to do a running drop and put me outside that building *before* the generals arrive."

"Oh Jesus," he said, "I better move it."

Chapter 23

Voices

The dark pressed down across the snows from horizon to horizon, and our headlights cut a dazzling swath through the landscape, the back glare painful against the eyes.

I had asked Frome to drive. He knew the car and I was still slipping focus now and then. There was a certain amount of discomfort hanging around: the seatbelt in the Escort had snapped while we were going through the final crunch, and the impact had opened the thigh wound and left sundry bruises. But the pain was a help, keeping the organism aware of itself during the time when consciousness wavered.

"Have you done a running drop before?" I asked Frome.

"Seen a couple."

The front end of the Mercedes hit a transverse rut where tracks crossed the road, and we slid at an angle until Frome got it worked out. I didn't say anything. He already knew we were running things critically close and that if we lost even five minutes having to dig ourselves out of a drift we'd be too late and blow the drop.

The generals' transport column would be somewhere to the south according to the map, and heading for the mansion in the park along a road more or less parallel to ours, and it shouldn't be long before we picked up their lights in the distance. The meeting would obviously be policed by the military contingent on board the transports, and once they were deployed in a ring round the building I wouldn't have a chance of getting inside. There could be security guards there now, and that was why I'd decided to do a running drop.

"We'd better go through it," I told Frome. "First, if it doesn't look as if I've got a reasonable hope of making it, don't do it at all, just back off and get clear. Second, when you give me the signal, keep running straight for at least five seconds, given a speed of ten or twelve miles an hour—*don't* turn earlier than that." The top of the windscreen began coming down across my eyes, and I realized my head was tilting backward against the padded rest as the sound of the car faded. Sat up straight and got in focus again. "Third, whatever happens, don't go *back* if there's any opposition around—leave me to make my own way out. Let's run through it again."

"Don't do it," Frome said parrot-fashion, "if it looks dicey, don't turn for five seconds, don't go back if there's a crowd. Got it."

I checked the time at 5:49 and twisted in my seat to watch the south. The lights of the city slashed the dark along the west horizon; the rest of the world was a snowfield, ghostly pale under the stars.

"*Shit*," Frome said and played with the wheel as the Merc drifted, the winter trunks of a copse of trees swinging across the windscreen, the lights throwing their shadows in a moving frieze against the snow.

I picked up the convoy to the south two minutes later, a thin chain of lights lying across the steppe.

"We're well ahead of them," I told Frome.

Another minute and we reached the east–west road out of the city, and the trees of the park lifted from the landscape, silver-gray, snow-covered, not far from the two chimneys of the power station to the east.

"Anywhere here," I told Frome and he pulled up on the churned surface of a truck exit to minimize wheelspin later.

I got a tire lever out of the trunk and dropped it onto the passenger's seat and stood for a moment watching the string of lights to the south. The convoy was near enough to show movement now: the transports had met the east–west road and were turning toward the park.

"Is it a go?" Frome asked me.

"Yes. Stand off somewhere outside the park. If I need you later I'll use the walkie."

I got down onto the snow and slid under the Mercedes, feeling for handholds good enough to use with gloves on, staying aft of the gearbox and to the driver's side of the drive shaft away from the exhaust silencer, finding a crossbar with enough space above it for my hands and swinging my feet up, getting one of them lodged above the chassis and kicking with the other one until my boot found purchase on the back-axle casing.

Light began flooding the road to the west and I could hear the rumbling of the military column, the faint ringing of the snow chains on the smaller vehicles, the drumming of diesels. My right foot had slipped off the rounded axle casing and I shifted backward, swinging my boot up again, but everything was blacking out and the sound of the transports died to silence, and in the silence I heard Frome's voice, a long way off.

"You all right?"

My shoulders were on the snow and the nape of my neck was freezing, but I couldn't move: the intention was there but the muscles were numbed. The light from the leading vehicle of the column was creeping under the Mercedes.

"You all right, are you?"

Said yes, but it didn't make any sound.

Cold against the neck, freezing cold, and my left foot coming away from the chassis and dropping onto the snow. The light crept closer, brighter now.

We needed to be inside the mansion over there. That was the objective for the mission, for *Meridian*: to get the information that was in the generals' heads, send it to London. But I was lying on the ground with the awareness floating insubstantially, awareness of the creeping light and the rumbling of heavy vehicles and the man's voice.

"You got a problem?"

I sensed him near me, Frome, caught a glimpse of his face as he peered under the car, felt the known world coming back into focus, the strength moving into the muscles, my fingers tightening inside the heavy gloves, my lungs expanding against the rib cage.

"Look, we're leaving it too—"

"Minute," I said. "Give me a minute." Reached for the crossbar and got a grip on it with one hand, both hands, the headlights flooding the snow and the drumming of the diesels filling the night as I got my left boot lodged again and kicked upward, finding the rear axle, shouting to Frome—

"*Get going.*"

His face vanished and the door of the car slammed above me and the engine gunned up and the rear chains cut into the snow as the wheels spun and then got a grip and the tension came into my hands and I locked my fingers and closed my eyes, *we stay like this,* felt a drop of oil against my face as Frome made the turn through the gates of the park, *we stay exactly like this with the fingers locked, this is all we have to do,* someone shouting somewhere, perhaps a guard at the gates, is he armed and do we wait for a shot, *no, we stay like this and think of nothing else, nothing at all,* the gears banging as the military column slowed outside the park, the transmission shunting, the light brightening again as the leading vehicle turned, then dimming out as Frome took the Mercedes in a curve alongside the building, *we stay like this until the time is right and he signals, exactly like this,* the clinking of the Mercedes' snow chains echoing from a wall now, from stone or brickwork, my body swinging as the car straightened and I hung on, *if it doesn't look as if I've got a reasonable hope of making it, don't do it at all, just back off and get clear,* the tension in the fingers burning now and my shoulders brushing the snow and the light of the convoy spreading again and then going out as the double knock from the tire lever sounded against the floorboards above my head and I let go and dropped.

Smell of furniture polish, leather, ancient fabric, woodsmoke.

The first three doors I'd tried had been locked; the fourth

had taken me into a boiler room, and this short passage had led from it to a huge rotunda.

Two galleries circled it on the first and second floors, the higher one set back from the lower by its own width, their beams and pilasters a deep red mahogany. The windows of the rotunda were mullioned, its doors gilded like the ornate balustrades of the galleries above. The lower walls were silk-panneled, and boxed silk canopies overhung the doors. Logs burned in a huge open hearth.

In the center of the rotunda, at a ring of tables below three brilliant crystal chandeliers, sat a group of Chinese military officers, most of them wearing the epaulets of high rank, and when the main doors of the building were banged open they got to their feet. As the two Russian generals came down the steps with their aides and bodyguards, a Chinese officer, gray-haired and with a general's flashes on his lapels, left the group at the tables and went to greet the Russians, who returned his salute. An interpreter from each party came forward and stood waiting.

Slamming of metal doors and thudding of boots as the rearguard of the generals' convoy halted outside. Shouts: orders to deploy.

In the center of the rotunda, introductions were being managed with the aid of the interpreters: much formality, punctilious bows. I recognized the aides and the bodyguards who had been with the generals on board the *Rossiya*.

I was aware of the short passage behind me, the one that had led me here. I was aware of the shadows above the two galleries that circled the dome. I listened for sounds, for soft, alien sounds—not to the voices of the international delegates in the center of the rotunda, the clicking of boots and the scrape of chairs—for sounds nearer than that, closer to where I watched.

Because he was here in the building too, the rogue agent. Talyzin—was that his name?

There was a man in the Ministry of Defense called Talyzin,

Ferris had told me. *From raw intelligence data going into London, he could be your agent.*

The SAAB had been outside, buried among the trees, when I'd rounded the building trying the doors. I had looked for it, or I wouldn't have noticed it. It had arrived here only minutes before I did, it must have. Talyzin hadn't been waiting there on the hill road to launch an attack on the generals. He hadn't been waiting to follow them here—or wherever they might have gone. All he'd wanted to know was *when* they would leave the camp, and the moment he'd seen the transports gathering and the figures of the two generals framed in his field glasses he had left the hill road and driven here first, ahead of them.

He'd known when they left the camp that they'd be coming here.

And so I was aware of the passage behind me, and listened for alien sounds.

" . . . Marshal Jia Chongwu . . . Major General Yang Zhen . . . Lieutenant General Zou Xinxiong . . . "

More introductions: salutes, bows, and handshakes, no smiles—the atmosphere was heavy with significance. These people weren't here to exchange courtesies; they were here to work.

"Colonel Rui Zhong . . . Colonel Wang Yongchang . . . "

Their voices carried clearly under the immense dome of the rotunda, and the scraping of chairs as they sat down would have pushed the needle of an audiometer into the high sector. I would have to listen very carefully to pick up any sounds the rogue agent might make.

Security guards had taken up station on the ground floor, all military, all of lower rank. Three men in plainclothes were moving along the walls, not going anywhere, just stirring their feet as they watched the assembly in the center. They would also be security, not civilian but MPS, former KGB officers, or possibly GRU.

The tables in the center were not uniform, had been pulled out of the rooms and offices leading off from the rotunda. As a courtesy the most ornate pigeonhole desk had been offered the leader of the Chinese delegation, and he was sitting behind it now, flanked by an aide and an interpreter. The desk was mahogany like the walls, and overlaid with gold scrollwork at the corners. It was massive, an important piece.

Preliminaries were still going on, and I went back along the passage and took the corridor that followed the curve of the rotunda. Doors were set in the wall at intervals, some of them open to reveal offices; I took care when I passed them, but he wouldn't be in any of these rooms, Talyzin: he would be watching the assembly in the rotunda, and watching it from one of the galleries, remote from the security guards below. I believed he would have the assault rifle with him, the one he'd used against the Ford I'd been driving. But even if he'd left the rifle in the SAAB outside he would still be armed.

The staircase I'd been looking for was simple, with a thin iron banister, curving upward behind the main wall of the rotunda; it was presumably used for cleaners and maintenance crews. I'd seen the main staircase to the galleries when I'd arrived here: an ornate affair leading directly from the well of the main chamber. Talyzin wouldn't have used that one; he would have used this.

I tested every stair as I climbed, putting my feet on one end, against the wall. Voices came from below, fainter now but still intelligible.

"... We have just learned that Marshal Trushin should be arriving very soon—his plane was delayed by bad weather. He is replacing General Vilechko, and will receive a transcript of the preamble as soon as he reaches here."

I tested another stair.

"I am asked by my colleagues"—first in Mandarin, then translated—"to offer our sincere condolences on the loss of the late General Vilechko in such tragic circumstances. We feel personally bereft of a valiant comrade-in-arms."

I thought that was interesting, because it was in line with the show of formality I'd seen before, the salutes and the bows and the handshakes. Despite the military uniforms, these were the studied courtesies of statecraft. It told me

something. It told me a very great deal more than I wanted
to think about at this particular moment.

A stair creaked under my weight and I froze. I didn't
think the sound could have carried as far as the gallery above,
but I was moving into that deadly zone where a slight in-
discretion, a lapse in attention to even the smallest degree,
could be terminal. This was the final phase of *Meridian* and
I'd gone into it before I'd realized, and if I could send anything useful to London I'd be doing it within the next few
hours: that, or lacking discretion, lacking attention, I could
go down without feeling anything much, just the instant
inferno as the bullet hit the brain and blew the circuits and
brought down the dark.

The nerves edgy, that was all, because those bloody
things had come intimately close as they'd smashed the
windscreen and ripped into the car.

"Your sympathies are appreciated, gentlemen." The
voice of the Chinese interpreter, full of throaty aspirates, took
it up as soon as he got the drift. "But fortunately, we are certain that Marshal Trushin—a Hero of the Soviet Union—will
be able to help us further our cause with a degree of courage,
energy, and foresight equal to that of our late comrade."

Our cause . . . Yes indeed, our cause . . . I would have
given a great many rubles, a great many yen, for a tape
recorder here with me now. I could of course raise Frome
on the radio and give him a short, urgent debriefing for
onward transmission to the signals board in London through
the support base in Novosibirsk: *Russian and Chinese—repeat
Chinese—military talks taking place Novosibirsk, subject a joint
cause.* But I'd have to go down the stairs again and into one
of the rooms below to do that, and it was vital that I found
Talyzin first and in some way got him compromised, made
safe, so that I could concentrate on taking in the information
I was here to get.

The Bureau should do everything *to keep those people under
surveillance.* Zymyanin. Had he known there was to be a
clandestine meeting in Novosibirsk, of great significance?

Talyzin had known. He'd known the generals were coming here.

He'd been here before.

I reached the fourth stair from the top, my eyes level with the floor of the first gallery, the scalp tightening. The gallery was in deep shadow, thrown by the chandeliers below; I could make out the shapes of tables here and there, of chairs; above them, catching the light, leather-bound volumes lined the walls. If Talyzin were here he would be here to watch the assembly down there, and to watch it he would have to sit or stand near the balustrade, where his face would also catch the light.

I couldn't see him.

It was necessary then to move higher, to climb the last three stairs, expose my head, shoulders, the heart area, moving slowly, watching for him, tracing the curve of the gallery full circle.

" . . . And it is our conviction that the opportunity for us to assume joint command of all those territories hitherto known as the Soviet Union is immediately available to us, and that such an opportunity is not likely to occur again within the foreseeable future. The people of Russia and the so-called independent states are in a mood of imminent rebellion, thanks to the catastrophic breakdown in the economy. It is therefore the first step in our overall enterprise to oust the present government in Russia and the so-called independent states by inciting rebellion in Moscow and the major cities and demonstrating to the people that we alone have the power to put bread into their cupboards and shoes on their feet, to reinstate peace and stability and usher in a secure and promising future for their children—and their grandchildren. Our troops and our tanks will act demonstrably as the allies and the saviors of the people, thus ensuring their loyal support as we gather the reins of power."

The two voices, Russian and Chinese, echoed among the shadowed reaches of the dome. I could see the complete circle of the lower gallery now, and if Talyzin were there he must be well back from the balustrade, watching perhaps through its polished redwood uprights.

Crawl. Crawl, then, to the next curve of the staircase, crawl in the shadow, silent and dark-garbed, moving a centimeter at a time past the ornate archway, a thing unseen, a creature of the shades, crepuscular, a night crawler of harm to none, yet with the hairs lifted at the nape of its neck and its arms goosefleshed, its ears alert for the bang of the gun and the whine of the homing shot.

Crawl.

" . . . We consider our opportunity propitious in the extreme. The belated attempts of the government of the United States to buy the allegiance of our peoples at a time when they find themselves in need of the very basics of human life have brought the capitalistic empire-mongers to their knees economically, and their naïve decision to reduce arms production in the imagined light of global rapprochement makes the way ahead for us the easier. . . . "

Faint light slanted across the next four or five stairs, and I crawled up them with the deliberation of a sloth, getting to my feet in the higher shadows. I lost some of the general's preamble between the first and second galleries but it came in again as I neared the top of the staircase.

"We fully understand the uneasiness of our Chinese neighbors in view of the possibility that Russia and her satellites might one day embrace capitalism and as a result cede their nationhoods to the West, leaving China as the last bastion of communism on the globe, isolated and beleaguered, outvoiced and outnumbered in the halls of international debate, an island of a thousand million people in a hostile sea . . . "

Then their voices began coming out of silence, and I moved my head, trying to lift it off the stair, nerve light flashing, an awareness of time passing, the pain of a splinter driven into my hand when I'd slumped, losing focus again.

" . . . And that together, as one ideologically homogenous federation, we would claim no less than one fifth of the earth's total territory and comprise no less than one fourth of its population, a potential workforce of one thousand three hundred million people dedicated to the Socialist cause . . ."

I got to my feet, the flat of my hands against the wall, stood there for a minute or two, feeling my way back to full consciousness before I began climbing again.

" . . . in the future. On the one hand the Russians will enjoy free and unencumbered access to the whole of the eastern seaboard of China from Korea to Vietnam, bringing Hong Kong and the Philippines within closer reach, while on the other hand the Chinese will enjoy direct access to the borders of Western Europe—including Germany, Austria, Switzerland, and Italy, once the independent states and Yugoslavia have been brought into the protection of the Federation. The opening up of new channels for international trade and the physical presence of the forces of the Federation in areas at present under the control of the West will be on a scale of unprecedented global significance. . . ."

I reached the higher gallery, sighting along it through half its circle as the voices echoed from the dome of the rotunda. I still couldn't concentrate on this preamble of theirs but it occurred to me that this wasn't normally the language of military men, however high their ranking: they were delivering this ground-breaking address of aims and intentions with a phraseology sufficiently rounded and structured to bear repetition through those generations of children and grandchildren, to be handed down through history with the weight and solemnity of the Magna Carta and the American Constitution.

Easy to see it as an expression of mass megalomania, but in the still-recent affairs of man the scions of a dozen nations had amicably established the most powerful union of states on earth. Nothing in the flux and turmoil of human enterprise could ever be termed inconceivable.

Not mine, thank God, to ponder. This was for London, if I could manage to get it through, for the presidents and their ambassadors and their ministers of defense.

If I could get it through.

There was nothing here on the half-circle of the gallery I could observe, and when I moved, with infinite caution, to the point where I could see the whole of it, there was still nothing that I could make out as a face and shoulders, a sloped barrel, nothing.

I hadn't expected him to be here. I'd expected him to be on the lower gallery, and when I'd checked that one I'd had to check this, in case I'd been wrong. But he was nowhere.

Nowhere in the entire building, perhaps.

The nerves caught this thought in a closed loop, reacting even before I'd had enough time to assess the conclusion— the pulse was accelerating and the blood leaving the surface as the survival mechanism tripped in.

Given the possibility that it had been Talyzin who had bombed the *Rossiya*, I might expect him to go for the two generals surviving Vilechko in the same way and by the same method. He'd known where they were going when they left the camp: they were coming here. He'd been here before, then, and if that were the case then he wouldn't be here now, inside the building, he'd be somewhere outside, wouldn't he, concealed in the SAAB, waiting with his hand on the remote control as the generals and their aides and interpreters sat together in the well of the rotunda around the ornate redwood desk with the gold scrollwork at the corners.

Talyzin is a bomber.

That is his way.

Everything slowing down.

He is waiting out there *now*. With a remote control in his hand.

A detonator.

General Kovalenko is sitting at the ornate redwood desk, turning a sheet of paper. I can see him through the bars of the balustrade.

What will I see first, floating upward into the great dome of the rotunda? His head?

No. Their heads. All their heads, as the initial percussion

at the core of the charge expands, billowing outward over the milliseconds, its force thrusting its way hugely into the immediate environs, finding the panels of the redwood drawer and sending a million splinters into the air an instant before they are consumed in the white and orange fire, finding the live bodies of the men gathered there and blowing them into nothing more substantial than a fountaining of blood, a flowering of crimson tissue and cartilage and skin, the whiteness of bared bones.

A spark crackles in the hearth below and deafens me, sending a shock wave through the nerves.

And then the whole building, the galleries and the walls and the dome, blowing outward like a drum, bellowing, radiant with apocalyptic fire.

And the body of this hapless ferret, too, blown out of all proportion, joke.

"... Later"—and a voice woke me from nightmare— "we shall go into the details for you, gentlemen"—the Chinese interpreter rendering the last word as "honorable comrades"—"and specify the target cities where we shall incite simultaneous rebellion by the populace. We shall present to you the blueprint—if you will—of our entire operation, in order that you shall understand that for our part we are committed to an undertaking of heroic and historic proportions, comparable with the equally heroic and historic decision of the Chinese military authority not only to bury past disagreements but to submit their present format of socialistic ideology to the radical changes necessary to meld it with that of our own, thus ensuring the unification of purpose essential to the creation of a federal world power of greater strength, of greater resolve and of greater military capacity than has ever been seen before."

The echoes of their voices died within the hollows of the dome.

But then, honorable comrades, you are not aware, are you, that if such a grandiose enterprise should come to pass, you will not be there to pluck its fruits.

Tell them then—go down there and push the armed guards back as they close in on you, address the honorable comrades: *There's a bomb in that desk there and if you don't get out of this place as fast as you can run you'll go through the bloody roof.*

Or words approximately to that effect but they wouldn't believe me because the generals' aides would recognize me as the man on the train they'd framed for the killing of Zymyanin and they'd have me under armed escort in five seconds flat— *All right then, look in the bloody desk, see for yourselves*—but that might not do anything useful either because there could be nothing there, the whole idea could be a product of my imagination—

But you don't think it is—

I can make a mistake, you know, like anyone—

We've got to get out of here before it goes off, we—

Oh for Christ's sake *shuddup*, the sweat crawling on me because yes I thought it was true, I thought there was a bomb down there and I hadn't got a great deal of time to think, say two seconds, you name it, three, not long enough, so *go down those stairs* and out through the boiler room and work your way round that bloody *SAAB* 540 and get him before he can press the tit, wouldn't be terribly easy would it, getting past the military guards out there, they were surrounding the whole place, so I can't get out of the building and I can't warn those people down there and I can't stay here and wait for the time to run out to the big *kerboom*, so what action *can* I take?

Survive.

Go down the stairs and through the boiler room and tell those gallant soldiers out there that they can take me in charge, blow *Meridian* off the signals board and survive, but tell one of them they really ought to pop in there and tell the grand architects of the new world order that if they don't watch it they'll go through that bloody roof.

I started moving toward the staircase, might be time, there might be time, the scalp tight and a lightness in the chest, everything still slowing down, and then I saw him.

Chapter 24

Curtain Call

He was in shadow, on the gallery below.

I'd expected him to be there but still I'd missed him, earlier, perhaps because of the angle of view. I was watching him between two uprights of the balustrade.

Sound of vehicles outside.

He was sitting at one of the little tables near some book-shelves, watching the delegates below. Not waiting, then, in the SAAB. Waiting in here.

The vehicles were nearing the building, snow chains clinking, voices, orders shouted, the slamming of doors.

We have just learned that Marshal Trushin should be arriving very soon—his plane was delayed by bad weather.

The thudding of boots on the marble outside, a door banging open.

I used the background noise to move quite fast along the gallery until I was immediately above Talyzin, the bomber. There was light on my face but no one was looking upward; they were watching Marshal Trushin and his aides making their entrance.

He was sitting at his ease, Talyzin, and on the little table beside him was the detonator.

The time gap narrowed with a slam and I knew precisely when he would reach out and press the button. It would be when Marshal Trushin sat down with the others. But it couldn't be a suicide run—there was no need for that. Talyzin could go outside if he wanted to, the way he'd come in, and make a run through the guards and press that thing before they could take him. They wouldn't know what he'd got in his hand; they'd go for him because he was running, that was all; but he'd use the remote and they'd be too busy watching the building go up to feel like running after him.

But he wasn't going to do that. He was comfortable here. The electric-shock treatment and the sensory-deprivation chambers and the other tricks they'd used on him inside the psychiatric hospital had left him just a teeny bit skewed in his skull, still cunning enough but skewed, and now that he'd got all these old friends of his together he was ready to give them the message: they shouldn't have done what they did to him, it wasn't fair.

And he wanted to see it happen.

Boots banging again down there, snow dropping off them and glistening on the parquet floor, chairs scraping back, people getting up.

"Marshal Trushin, let me present Marshal Jia Chongwu of the Chinese Red Army...."

He wanted to be there when it happened. He wanted to watch it all for those few milliseconds as the big ornate desk blew apart and the men around it began jerking backward in a reflex action before the edge of the blast wave reached them and their uniforms began wrinkling, he wanted to watch everything he could before he could see no more.

And since time has a way of slowing down when our attention is locked in with reality he might be given quite a show, two or three minutes even, as each minuscule stage of the explosion followed the last, an hour, long enough to start a miniseries.

"... Major General Yang Zhen ..."

Salutes, bows, handshakes, while Talyzin watched them from above, a puppetmaster with their last curtain call in his hands.

He hadn't moved the detonator, or reached for it yet. He would wait for them to sit down. He wanted them to be comfortable too.

"... Lieutenant General Zou Xinxiong ..."

The voice of General Kovalenko drifted upward into the great dome of the rotunda, left echoes rippling.

"...Colonel Rui Zhong...Colonel Wang Yong-chang..."

Then they were moving toward the chairs, ushering gestures the order of the day as the senior ranks were given precedence and Marshal Trushin was invited to sit at the ornate redwood desk in the place of the Chinese.

I cleared the balustrade and dropped.

Talyzin had been directly below me on the lower gallery but I went down in a slight arc because of the balustrade and caught his shoulder, spinning him round on the chair as his hand went out for the detonator. He reacted with great strength, empowered by shock, rage, dementia, and smashed his knee into my rib cage as we went down together, the breath coming out of me in a soft explosion as I twisted over and felt for a target, not in the killing area because I didn't think it would be necessary, just in the nerve centers to incapacitate.

Heard shouts from below, boots on the staircase, Talyzin's hand on my throat and squeezing strongly, triggering reflex and freeing my arm for an elbow strike that reached the side of his head and he lurched and went down and I thought it was over but he came up suddenly like a diver surfacing and went for the table *and got his hand on the detonator* and I couldn't reach it, went for the throat, for the kill, the fastest way, the only way to get the strength out of his arm, out of his fingers as his weight dropped and the table crashed over and the detonator hit the floor *and he reached for it again* but his arm was exposed and I doubled it backward at the elbow and heard it snap, dropped him against the bookshelves and picked up the detonator and backed off as the first two guards reached the top of the stairs and aimed their rifles, shouting.

Talyzin didn't move.

"One of you look after this man," I told the guards.

"He's injured but watch him. I want the other one to follow me down the stairs—now *move!*"

There were more of them waiting for me in the well of the chamber but I told them to get back, called out to the generals: "You know what this is?" Held the thing up.

It seemed to fox them, understandably. Here they were planning the creation of the new world order and suddenly there was a disheveled-looking clown standing in front of them holding up a remote control for their TV set.

No one said anything, didn't matter, I'd spell it out for them. "Marshal Trushin, this is a remote-control detonator for the bomb installed in the desk you're sitting at now." I gave it a couple of beats to let him think about it, and they woke up, all of them, I could hear the body movements going on, the rustle of uniforms as they shifted on their chairs, reacting. "I am not going to detonate that bomb if you agree to follow my instructions. Do you agree to follow my instructions, Marshal Trushin?"

In a moment he asked in a flat voice, "Who are you?"

"*Do you agree?*"

Trying to get my breath back under control, I think he broke a rib up there, Talyzin, with that elbow strike, the lung didn't feel as if it had much room on that side.

I waited.

If the marshal didn't agree, I was done for. I couldn't detonate that bloody thing anyway, I wasn't tired of life and we'd still got a mission running, I wanted *information* out of these people, the information that Kovalenko had told the Chinese delegates he'd give them later.

But all he would need to say, Trushin, was "*Take that man,*" and there'd be nothing I could do.

Behind me I heard the guard coming down the staircase, his boots thudding laboriously under a weight: Talyzin. I didn't know if the killing strike I'd made had gone right through to the larynx; he'd moved a little after I'd made it, tried to reach the detonator. I took four paces back to bring him into sight; he was hanging across the guard's shoulder, the broken arm dangling.

From the center of the rotunda Marshal Trushin was staring at me, stone-faced, jowls of a bulldog, black eyes locked on mine as he listened to one of the generals' aides, the one who had framed me on board the *Rossiya* for the death of Zymyanin. His voice was unintelligible at this distance because he was speaking softly, urgently, saying—I very much hoped—*Marshal, this man was on board the* Rossiya *two days ago, and could well have set that bomb. Perhaps we should listen to him. . . .*

A log tumbled in the hearth and I heard a man catch his breath.

I went on waiting.

Marshal Trushin was still watching me. The aide was silent now.

"I agree to follow your instructions."

Et voilà.

"Very good. If anyone in this chamber leaves his chair, I shall detonate. Is that clear?"

Silence.

"Is that clear?"

"It is clear," Marshal Trushin said.

I turned round so fast that the guard flinched, his eyes on the detonator. "Make him as comfortable as you can," I told him. "Tell him there's a medical officer coming." Those bastards over there had wrecked Talyzin's brain and I didn't thank them.

There was a telephone in the first office I came to and I picked it up, watching the well of the chamber through the doorway as I dialed.

"Military Barracks," the woman at the switchboard said.

I asked for Ordnance Unit 3.

Took an age, stood listening to the static on the line.

I shall resist arrest. I shall resist very strongly.

But it wouldn't do any good. He'd be outnumbered, and—

"Captain Rusakov."

"Vadim," I said, "this is Viktor Shokin, and I'm with the generals. You know where they are?"

"Yes." A lot of energy in his voice, a lot of questions I didn't have time to answer.

"I need you here. We've got to contain the generals' military escort—their orders are to protect the generals and they're not going to listen to me. Do you trust them, Vadim?"

In a moment, "Not necessarily."

"How many *trusted* men can you muster for an emergency sortie?"

"Two hundred, under my own command."

"Tanks?"

"One squadron."

"All right, I need you to surround this building and take the generals out and put them into detention. At the moment they're under my control. And bring a medical officer, will you? We've got a man with a broken elbow. We also need a bomb-disposal unit. How soon can you get here?"

"Allow forty minutes."

"I can handle that. Any questions, Vadim, even from your CO, tell the officer commanding the military police to put him under arrest—this is a national emergency."

"I understand."

I put the phone down and opened up the radio.

"Frome?"

"Hear you."

"Where are you?"

"Half a mile from the building, south edge of the park, but listen, the DIF got through to base an hour ago, wants you to signal."

I asked Frome for the number.

"All right," I said and shut down the radio and walked as far as the archway, the detonator in my hand, took a look, saw that no one had moved, they were policing themselves, had to, if anyone thought of trying to get out of this place before it went up they'd shove him back in his chair.

I turned and went into the office and picked up the phone again and dialed.

"Yes?" Ferris.

"Executive."

"I'm sorry," Ferris said. "They were getting a bit too close, so I thought we'd better move. I told the support base as soon as I could. They said you're very active."

I gave him the picture.

Ferris is not easy to shake, but it was a couple of beats before he answered: "I'll report to London." Then—"What's your condition?"

He'd caught my breathing rhythm. "Lingering concussion, broken rib."

"Frome is still in support?"

"He's standing by but I don't need him. Look, they'll know what to do in London but from this end I'd say they should get this to the Russian president on the hot line and suggest he grill these people without wasting any time, because they've set up this rebellion nationwide and it could be hard to stop."

"Noted." Then I think he said something else, but sounds were fading and the floor was coming up, so I got a grip on the desk and steadied things and put the detonator down on the flat solid surface, took my hand off it, we didn't want, did we, didn't want the whole thing to go *kerboom* by accident, wouldn't even be good for a giggle, sounds coming in again, that poor bastard Talyzin moaning out there, something Ferris was saying.

"What?" I asked him.

"London will be pleased."

"Oh. Those buggers." Then I said: "Listen, those Rusakovs—get them out from under, will you? Tell London to talk to Moscow right away, do it at high level. Give or take a bit of circumlocution, they've been instrumental in putting down this coup by wiping out Vilechko. Tell London they're my friends, and I've earned this much, all right?"

Promptly and soberly—"I'll treat it as fully urgent."

Couldn't say more than that: fully urgent means *everyone* stops what they're doing and listens, right up to the prime minister.

I think I'd been silent for a bit, because he asked me, "Are you all right?"

"What? Yes. Need to rest up a little."

"As soon as I can get the heat off you locally through London and Moscow we can find somewhere better for you."

"Don't worry," I said, "I'm going to place myself under Captain Rusakov's protection until then."

"All right. I can reach you at the barracks?"

"Yes, through him. But get the heat off him too, soon as you can."

"Understood," Ferris said, and we shut down.

They came soon after that, Rusakov's troops, their lights flooding across the snows, the night full of noise as the tanks rumbled through the trees of the park.

I thought I'd better reassure Frome, got him on the walkie-talkie: "Don't worry, these are ours."

"Jesus, we got an army now?"

Rusakov jumped down from the leading armored vehicle before it had stopped, his gun out of its holster.

"Who is the officer in charge?"

No one answered. No one moved. The men watched Rusakov.

"Lay down your arms and stand-to!"

They began looking at one another, and then a sergeant brought his rifle up and Rusakov saw it and used a head shot, dropping him, watching for other movement as one of the tanks rolled its turret and swung the machine gun up a degree, firing a burst as a group of men brought their assault rifles to aim at Rusakov.

"Lay down your arms!"

Weapons began dropping as the smoke cleared, and the men moved toward the tanks with their hands in the air. Hydraulics hissed as the turret rolled again, the gunner watching for targets.

"*All right, stretcher-bearers!*" Then Rusakov saw me and came over.

"Where is the bomb?"

I told him, and he waved a vehicle in, black with the yellow insignia of a bomb-disposal unit on the side.

I opened up the remote-control detonator and pulled out the batteries and threw them a long way into the snow.

"Vadim," I called out to him, "we need to get the generals out of there first, under your arrest."

He swung back to look at me.

"On whose authority?"

It was a reflex question out of the military code book, that was all—I could have told him on the pope's authority, or Tootsie's, and he would have accepted it—those generals in there had been the confederates of Vilechko. Rusakov also knew that I'd been able to "request" his sister's release from Militia Headquarters and he knew I'd been able to seize control of the generals here together with their entire armed guard, so he wasn't going to quibble.

"On my authority," I told him. "The president of Russia is being informed of the situation and I can guarantee his approval of any action we take. Meanwhile I assume total responsibility."

He turned away even before I'd finished, shouting orders to his lieutenant and two sergeants and bringing a rifle platoon to the entrance of the building.

"All right," he told them, "we're taking prisoners. Block all exits when you get inside and hold your fire unless I order you to shoot."

He led them in at the double and by the time I got there he'd drawn up his troops in straight extended order to avoid cross fire. The generals and their aides were already on their feet, some of the chairs overturned on the parquet behind them.

Boots clattered to silence in the echoing rotunda.

Rusakov took three steps forward, came to attention, and saluted.

"Gentlemen, I have orders for your arrest. Please surrender your arms."

Marshal Trushin also took a few steps and the two Russian generals followed, flanking him.

"There is a mistake, Captain." Trushin was a bull of a man, six feet six in his black polished boots, battle ribbons ablaze on his uniform. "I shall hold you responsible for this intrusion, and will inform your commanding officer that—"

Rusakov swung his head a degree. *"Take aim!"*

A phalanx of assault rifles swung up and steadied.

"Captain, you are exceeding—"

"Sergeant Bakatin and two men forward—take their weapons!"

Trushin knocked the first man's hand away but the sergeant brought the muzzle of his rifle to rest against the marshal's stomach while the soldier snapped open the polished holster and drew the revolver. The Hero of the Soviet Union's heavy face was white as the surrender began. Most of them were in a state of shock as Rusakov's men worked their way among the prisoners, taking their weapons.

Vadim Rusakov stood watching, a hand on the gun at his belt.

I was losing focus again, and straightened up, hearing the echoes in the great dome of the rotunda... *Our troops and our tanks will act demonstrably as the allies and the saviors of the people... thus ensuring their loyal support as we gather the reins of power....*

Another gun came out of its holster.

"Have your weapons ready, gentlemen! Smarten up!"

And another.

The opening up of new channels for international trade and the physical presence of the forces of the Federation in areas at present under the control of the West will be on a scale of unprecedented global significance.

Another gun was surrendered, and then one of the Chinese, a general, drew his revolver and raised it to his temple and the shot blew his head sideways and he fell slowly, the others too shocked to catch him before he crashed across a chair, breaking one of its legs as he went down.

"Leave him there," Rusakov ordered. "Secure his gun."

His men moved among the prisoners as blood crept in rivulets across the parquet floor and the smell of cordite sharpened the air.

Thus ensuring the unification of purpose essential to the creation of a federal world power of greater strength, of greater resolve, and of greater military capacity than has ever been seen before. . . .

The last weapon was held butt-forward in surrender by a Russian colonel, and as the prisoners were escorted outside to the vehicles I picked up the walkie-talkie and signaled Ferris through the support base, told him we were finished here.